I0561242

INTO
THE
SUNRISE

*A Woman of Heart,
Courage, and Integrity*

KATHRYN JANE

INTO THE SUNRISE: A Woman of Heart, Courage,
and Integrity
By: Kathryn Jane
Cover by The Killion Group
ISBN: 978-1-988790-04-6

Copyright © 2017 Kathryn Jane
All Rights Reserved
This book is a work of fiction. Names, characters,
places, and incidents are either products of the author's
imagination or are *used in a fictitious manner.*
Any resemblance to actual events or locales or persons,
living or dead, is entirely coincidental. No part of this
book may be used or reproduced in any manner
whatsoever without written permission except in the
case of brief quotations embodied in critical articles and
reviews.
kathrynjane.com

Books by Kathryn Jane

CATS Volume 1
CATS Volume 2
CATS Volume 3

INTO THE SUNRISE

INTREPID WOMEN SERIES
Book 1 – Do Not Tell Me No
Book 2 – Touch Me
Book 3 – Daring To Love
Book 4 – Voices
Book 5 – Lies
Book 6 – All She Wanted
Book 7 – Dance With Me

ACKNOWLEDGMENTS

Without the Killion Group designing my covers,
Demon for Details doing a fabulous job of editing,
Judicious Revisions proofreading and both L. J.
Charles and Barb lending their talents as critiquers,
this book wouldn't look or sound
anything like it does today.
Ladies, I thank you all profusely!.

For William, the son of my heart.

KATHRYN JANE

PART ONE

Awakening

ONE

Lexington Kentucky, Winter 2001

CN Dark Angels was an unusual name for a racehorse, but this was not your average thoroughbred.

Sure, she looked innocent enough standing in a bright, airy stall, nibbling from a pile of alfalfa, but Chase witnessed her performance earlier, and yeah, wing-nut was putting it mildly.

Angel approached the door and sniffed at his hands as though looking for treats. He huffed a breath toward her and was pleased when she blew back, with her ears forward and her eyes without a hint of aggression. But then she jerked her head up high to stare past him.

Turning slowly, he wasn't surprised to find a stranger assessing him from the doorway of the fancy Kentucky barn. Probably making assumptions based on appearance because Chase stood out like a painted pony among blue bloods. His ancestors had blessed him with a wiry frame, skin more copper than brown, and straight black hair.

Closing the distance between them, the man wore a polite and almost welcoming smile, oozing the kind of confidence one was born with.

"Richard Selby, COO." Would Chief Operating Officer be the fancy name for farm manager?

"Chase Mathews." He shook the man's hand, noting the lack of calluses or roughness.

"How can I help you?"

Tilting his head toward the filly, Chase said, "Nice horse. Too bad about her mind."

"Are you interested in buying her?"

Okay, so they weren't going to exchange pleasantries. That was good. He preferred straight talk. "I don't have the kind of money you're asking, but I'd sure love a chance to work with her."

Selby shook his head. "You must have missed her performance in the round pen."

"I was there." He reached up to stroke the filly's face.

"You think you can break her, even though the best in the business couldn't?"

Chase turned his back on the horse and met the man's look square on. "I think it would be a damn shame to give up now and never see her on a racetrack."

"You'd rather she hurt a few people or beat herself to death first?"

"Of course not. But she's at least worth the time it would take to bring her around."

"Well, you're the only person here today with

that opinion." There'd been a big crowd for the showing. Lots of money and experience gathered on the platform above the round pen, watching her go berserk.

"How many were here?"

"Forty-nine signed in at the gate."

Chase stifled a grin. "Fifty to one odds. I've always been a sucker for a long shot."

Selby looked him right in the eye. "Mind if I ask you a personal question or two?"

Chase's mouth twitched. Might as well make it easy for the guy. "I'm Canadian, got a job mucking stalls when I was about fourteen, worked my way up to race riding, which ended when I grew into my boot size. These days, I rehab problem horses, break a few for other people, and run my own small operation in Canada, called Buck Hill Ranch."

With a glimmer of a smile, Selby nodded. "Ever encountered anything as crazy as she is?"

He shook his head. "Nope." Then shrugged. "Well, maybe a black-tail doe with a broken leg. She didn't think much of humans either."

With a nod toward the filly, Selby said, "Twice we've had to scratch this one from sales because she threw wrecks in the van and required extensive vet work to put her back together."

Chase rubbed the filly's forehead. It was as though they already had an invisible connection and her spirit was reaching out to him. "Would you be interested in leasing her?"

"I'd have to speak to her owner. What kind of terms?"

Chase was adept at negotiating this kind of

thing. "Ninety-ten split for two years, renegotiable after one if she's made over a hundred grand."

Selby pinned him with a serious look. "You're absolutely certain you want to take her on?"

"Very." Should he have played it cool? Probably, but he didn't want to miss this opportunity. "But I'd like to work with her here for a few days before I move her."

"We'll see." Selby walked the full length of the long barn while he made the call, and was looking pleased when he returned.

"Here's the bottom line. Mr. Sanderson, the filly's owner will give you an eighty-twenty split for twelve months. She's your financial and legal responsibility from today until this day next year. The paperwork will be drawn up and here for you to sign at this time tomorrow."

Chase barely managed to resist a fist pump and completely failed to squelch the unprofessional grin. He stuck out his hand. "Deal."

Selby's smile was wry. "I wish you luck, young pleased when she blew back, with her ears forward and her eyes staying soft, without a hint of aggression. But then she jerked her head up high to stare past him.man. She *is* bred to be something very special but her mind... Well, like I said, good luck with that."

"I believe Angel is capable of great things. But for now, I'll focus on getting her home in one piece."

"You have your own rig?"

"Yup. I'll bring it back with me in the morning."

"I hope you have good insurance. She doesn't like closed spaces. Tends to want to move walls and partitions, and she's not dainty about it. As a yearling, she managed to gut a trailer in less than ninety seconds."

TWO

Ranch Country, British Columbia,
Early Spring 2001

Unbecoming behavior for an adult, but Dusty didn't care. She sprinted down the hall anyway, around the corner, and slid to a stop, but her father's housekeeper beat her to the phone.

"I'm sorry, he's not in," she was telling someone while smoothing a hand down the front of her long black apron.

Dusty waved her arms. "He's in his office. I'll get him." She shot out a side exit to what looked like a detached garage and knocked on the heavy wooden door, yelling, "Dad."

There was no response. Probably asleep in his easy chair. She grabbed the knob but the door didn't budge. She heard an odd sound. A groan? Was something wrong? She pounded on the door. *"Dad."*

"What the hell do you want?"

"Are you okay? You sound funny. Open the door."

"Go away, girl."

The familiar words were like a slap, and she sagged against the doorjamb. "There's a phone call for you."

"I don't take calls when I'm working. The damn housekeeper knows that." His voice grew stronger, or louder at least.

"I'm sorry, I didn't know." How could she? It had been more than ten years since she fled the isolated ranch where she grew up. *What made me think anything had changed?*

"Never mind, I'll take it. Go away."

She wanted to bang her forehead on the hard wood, but instead did what she'd always done. Headed for the barns.

***

Annoyed by the distraction, John tore his gaze away from the computer screen, rubbed damp palms on his thighs, then groped for the phone.

"Hello."

"I'm sorry, John, did I wake you?" asked Chase.

He cleared his throat. "Of course not. What do you want?"

"I was hoping to borrow your training gate for a couple of weeks. If it's not inconvenient. I mean, as long as you're not using it."

John allowed his fingertips to stroke the mouse.

Scrolled down, had to squeeze his eyes shut against the images making his blood pound. "Tomorrow, first thing. I'll bring it over." He hung up, glanced toward the door. The deadbolt was definitely locked.

***

Doing everything possible to ensure Angel would have a good first experience, Chase removed a section of rails so they could back the starting gate into a long, narrow paddock, essentially creating two smaller pens.

The low rumble of a diesel engine grew louder in the quiet morning air, and John's big, black one-ton came over the rise with the training gate in tow—a four-stall replica of what was used at most tracks.

Before the truck came to a full stop the passenger door flew open, and a tiny two-legged dynamo raced toward him, launched herself, and, catching her, Chase swung her high off the ground. By the time he put her down they were both laughing.

Dusty stuffed her hands in her back pockets and grinned at him. "Hey, cowboy."

It hit him like a brick how much he'd missed that smile, and her cheeky attitude. "You've grown up some."

She rolled her eyes. "Ya think? It's been more than ten years."

She had curves now, and long, silky hair. Racing photos of her perched over a horse's back hadn't done her justice.

"She's just passing through." John's voice had a sharp edge.

"Not staying to visit?" Chase asked.

Instead of answering John asked, "Where's your hired man?"

Chase hated that term, especially in the demeaning way John used it. Murray deserved better, but there was no point arguing with a man like John. "He's on the road, moving horses."

"Guess you'll need my help, then. Where do you want this thing parked?"

Chase pointed to the paddock, and the three of them worked together to get the gate backed into position, then used portable panels to block the gap between it and the fence.

With the stall gates open, a horse could easily pass through to get from one side to the other.

"Might as well get some schooling done while you have the two of us to help," said John.

Chase would prefer to work alone and give Angel a day or two to get used to seeing the gate in the paddock, but he'd learned many years ago to pick his battles with John.

He headed to the barn with Dusty in his wake, like old times.

Pointing to the first stall, Chase said, "Grab Jake—retired racehorse and first-class babysitter— and lead the way. I'll follow with Angel."

"What's taken' so long?" shouted John.

Dusty's shoulders went up. "Nothing changes," she muttered while she slipped the halter on Jake and led him out into the sunshine.

9

Chase intended to have Dusty lead Jake into one of the gate's stalls, then wait for Angel to be loaded into the one beside them, but Angel had other ideas. She stood stock still, refusing to move.

"It's okay, mama." Chase rubbed a reassuring hand down her neck, and she lowered her head a bit, took a step closer.

"Change of plans," Chase told Dusty. "Edge out the fronts with Jake, just a step at a time, and I'll let her follow him through the same stall instead of going in one by herself."

"Ya don't need to do that. She'll go. Needs to learn," John may have opted to sit in the truck, but he wasn't about to leave them to do the job on their own.

"With this one, it's baby steps, John, and I always set her up to succeed." Chase winked at Dusty, and she urged Jake to take a step, then stop.

Angel's original stubbornness apparently forgotten, she was not only willing to follow the other horse, but started to get overeager, as though afraid Jake would get too far in front of her.

"Better keep your head up, girl," came John's caustic warning, and Chase winced. "That old horse will step on your toes if the filly crowds him."

Dusty's spine straightened and she muttered, "Like I'd ever let a horse step on me." She flicked a glance at Chase. "Not like I'm new at this, and Jake's obviously about as tame as they fuckin' come." She rubbed the horse's face and he leaned into her hand.

"Rest assured, John, I've put a ton of groundwork into this one, and you know I'd never

10

put Dusty in danger."

The old man made no comment, and the schooling continued, with Angel carefully following Jake until her flanks grazed inside of the gate and set something off inside her. Muscles bunched, nostrils widened, and ears swiveled as though searching for danger, but Chase spoke to her in a low voice, until she relaxed enough to continue with the forward progress.

After passing back and forth through the gate several times, Angel quit reacting to it, and Chase said, "That's good for today. Now we'll turn them loose and leave it open. Make going through their choice."

Once he tossed a flake of alfalfa on the ground at each end of the paddock he leaned on the fence with Dusty to watch them dig in.

"Who sent you this one?" asked John.

Project horses were sent to Chase from all across Canada and the US. He had a good rep, and a knack with the crazies. He'd never met a horse, or any animal for that matter, who didn't—given enough time—respond to kindness and patience. "No one."

"Don't bullshit me. How many has she hurt?"

"None. I'm the first person to get on her back." Okay, that was an evasion of sorts, but Chase was trying not to be disrespectful.

John crossed his arms. "How many others tried?"

"None."

"Son, this filly's way outta your league. Got class comin' out her ears. I'd bet she's worth more than this place of yours—not that it's anything special, but land is land. No way you could come up with the asking price for the likes of her."

Dusty's visible flinch had Chase jumping in before she could defend him—as she often tried to do when she was a kid and John was being verbally abusive. Oddly enough, John usually shut up back then. But these days, Chase had a voice of his own.

"I picked her up when I was in Kentucky. She'd had a couple of van wrecks, appeared to be a confirmed freezer, and they were looking to unload her as a broodmare prospect."

John's mouth twisted. "Still outta your league. Bet you made 'em a deal." He shook his head. "When you gonna learn not to be so stupid, boy?"

"Dad."

Chase laughed. "I took her on a legitimate one-year lease. Whole thing's on paper and notarized. She's insured for a million dollars."

Dusty gaped at him. "Holy f— cow, she must be royally bred." She turned to stare at the filly. "She didn't freeze today."

"She trusts me, and I know when not to push her. She's claustrophobic, probably from the shipping accident when she was a weanling."

"Does she flip?"

A good question. About half the freezers he'd known would flip over backwards rather than go forward. "Nope. Locks up solid and unresponsive to normal urging, but when she's forced out of it, she lunges forward. Skyrockets until exhaustion sets in."

John was studying the horse across the fence.

"You know, even with her back end to you, she's been keeping one ear cocked, listening to your voice. I think you've made a good connection. Earned her trust."

No kidding. And wow, praise from John. "I've spent months doing what takes weeks with any other horse. There's not a single step forward until the previous lesson is solidly established, and company is my secret weapon. I started by leasing Stumpy, another two-year-old filly, to ship home with Angel, and they made the trip without incident. Now Jake is her security blanket. Anytime I try something new with her, she waits for Jake's reaction before she decides whether or not to go along with the lesson."

He thought about the first time he'd ridden Jake in the pen with her. She kept staring up at Chase, then nuzzling Jake, as if asking him if he was okay with such nonsense.

Dusty was frowning, an expression he'd seen more and more often before she took off—quit school at sixteen—and headed for the racetrack. "How do you know for sure if she's ready to start her next lesson?"

"When she gets bored, we move on."

"Will you give me the mount when she's ready to run?"

"She's months away from running, hasn't even breezed yet." Once she was fit enough, he'd have to ship her to a recognized racetrack to get recorded times on her. "She won't be needing a jockey for weeks, maybe months. Besides, I'm not planning to run her in Alberta."

"Well, that works. I'm done with the prairies. I'll be hanging my tack in Vancouver this year." She hesitated a beat. "*Will* you give me the mount when she's ready?"

He tipped his chin toward the horse. "That'll be up to her."

Dusty muttered in response, "Just as well. She's probably smarter than you." And with that, she approached the filly, talking to her in a soft, rhythmic voice.

Chase watched Angel run her velvety nose over Dusty from the toes of her Ropers to the hair she'd tied in a knot on the top of her head.

"Dusty hasn't lost her touch," Chase said to John, while keeping his attention firmly fixed on the scene in the paddock. "How come she's home?"

"Man trouble." John nearly spat the words.

"Ouch." There'd been plenty of racetrack gossip when the "Torino kid" landed a big fish. Seemed like she'd been with him a while, too.

"She'll be better off without him."

"Nobody's good enough for your little girl."

"Damn straight." The tone of John's voice took Chase back a gazillion years.

He'd been pinned up against a wall, suspended by the fistful of shirt his new boss—the man currently snarling at him—was hanging onto.

John's face was nearly purple and spit flew with his words. "Don't you ever. EV-ER. Think about touching her. You hear me? You lay a hand on my daughter, and I'll cut your nuts off. Then slit your throat for good measure.

Unable to form words, Chase had nodded.

Barely managed to squeak out, "Yes, sir."

Not like he was interested in a kid he thought was a boy until ten minutes ago.

***

Over the next few days, Dusty spent hours doing groundwork with Angel to gain her trust, and on the last afternoon before leaving for Vancouver, Chase legged her up on the filly. He climbed aboard Jake, and they headed for the track he'd built not far from the barn.

For one full lap they galloped side by side. Then, easing up, he let her go on alone, but Angel's head went up, ears swiveling. Had he allowed her to become too dependent on Jake?

Chase was pleased to see Dusty sit back a bit further and urge the filly to keep moving forward. Satisfied she had the filly's attention, he watched them round the top end of the track and head toward him at a nice, solid pace. They looked good together, the horse moving effortlessly, and the rider perfectly balanced on the balls of her feet.

"Another lap?" she hollered.

"Yup," he shouted back.

In that instant, Angel's front legs went straight like a couple of two-by-fours, bringing her to a dead stop, and sending Dusty sailing over her head like a freaking lawn dart. Chase bailed off Jake and ran, but before he could reach the crumpled heap, she somehow managed to scramble to her feet.

"Son of a…" She swiped a hand across her mouth and spit dirt.

While he held onto her shoulder and brushed debris from her clothes, she made a lame attempt at batting away his hand. Dust swirled around them.

"Never gonna outgrow your handle at this rate," he said with a grin, and she shoved him away. He'd nicknamed her Dusty when, time and again, he found himself dusting her off after getting bucked from the back of the cranky pony she loved. John had declared it a great nickname for a future jockey, and later Chase found her in the tack room, carefully printing the letters on the back of her chaps with a felt pen. He liked to think she adopted the name as a symbol of her determination.

"Go catch your horses and leave me be," she said.

But Angel and Jake were happily standing just a few feet away. "They're not going anywhere. Be still," he said, and released the chinstrap of her helmet so he could get a good look at her eyes, then used his thumb to stroke away a bit of sand at the edge of her bottom lip.

She sucked in a startled breath, and he thought he saw a question in her big, green eyes, a tiny crack in the toughness she wore like armor. Cupping her cheek, he lowered his head, barely skimmed her mouth with his own.

She wrenched away from his steadying hand. "What the hell was that for?"

"Didn't you see the mistletoe?" He winked, giving her an out he hoped she wouldn't take. One Christmas, years ago, she hung a bunch of mistletoe in the barn doorways and he'd been hard-pressed to avoid her teenage games. She was bound and determined to get a kiss, and he'd been equally determined to steer clear of trouble.

She marched toward Angel, but glanced back at him. "She was going great until you spooked her."

"I didn't spook her."

"You did so."

"All I did was answer *your* damned question. It was your own loss of concentration that earned you a piece of real estate."

Her face reddened and she turned away, gathered the reins and a bunch of mane in her left hand, and swung up on the filly. She stuffed her feet in the stirrups and set them well in front of her center of gravity, then chirped to get Angel to move away from Jake.

Instead of going right back to a gallop, Dusty went through the basics with Angel, stops and turns, changes of direction, small circles, then big. Overall, it was a gentle workout, but an intensely connected one, and once they finished two laps at a nice, controlled gallop, Chase was certain Angel both trusted and respected the quietly determined woman on her back.

Such a talented and accomplished horsewoman, yet when it came to her personal life? According to rumors, she was a train wreck.

As a little girl, she always seemed starved for attention, and he'd bet she was still hungry for someone to love her.

None of his business.

They rode back to the barn and went through the motions of putting the horses away with the same kind of rhythm they had back when he was working with her dad's horses. They knew each other's moves, and it was comfortable in spite of the lack of conversation.

"When do you leave for the coast?" he asked, when they were strolling toward her bright blue jeep.

"I could go tonight, or first thing tomorrow. I'm meeting my new agent at noon."

Three hours to Vancouver and she'd be a world away. How long until she forgot about the simple life here?

He stared out across the fields and paddocks full of horses. It would never be quite the same. He was sure to see her everywhere he turned, and her voice would be in his head. Funny, that hadn't been the case when his wife left him. He'd simply found peace in her wake.

"Stay one more night, then get up early, and you can get in a ride before you hit the highway. No better way to start the day." Did he sound pathetic?

"Not if I get dropped again." She sighed "You won't tell my dad, will you?"

"Naw, your flying dismount is safe with me. How about stopping for coffee now, before you go?"

"Got anything stronger?"

"Seriously?"

She shook her head. "Coffee's fine." She stayed silent until they were in his kitchen, then, out of the blue, asked, "Do you remember your first year working for my dad?"

Hell of a segue. He looked up from the coffee pot he was filling at the sink. "Of course. Why?"

"Did you think I was a pest?"

"Yep."

"Why?" Her head was tipped like a curious pup, reminding him of the child she'd been when they met.

"Well, first off, I didn't pay you much mind because I thought you were a boy."

"What?"

He'd be willing to bet she didn't even realize she'd stuck her chest out. "Everybody called you Mel—and kiddo, in dirty jeans and chaps, with the short hair and freckles, you looked like a boy."

"You eventually figured out otherwise."

"Not until your dad said something about his daughter hanging out in the barn. Believe me, it took a minute for it to sink in."

"I don't understand why I wasn't a pest until you found out I was a girl."

He measured coffee into the filter, set cups out on the counter. "Some stray kid in the barn is way different than the boss's daughter tagging around after me." And the boss threatening his manhood. He put a spoon beside the sugar container already in the middle of the table.

"So you had to be nice to me or piss off my dad." She gave him a dramatic eye-roll, and he laughed.

"I would have been nice to you anyway."

"Why?"

Well, this could be tricky. Best go with the truth. "I dunno, maybe I felt sorry for you."

She frowned. "I had the run of a big, fancy horse ranch, and lots of stock to ride whenever I wanted. What was there to feel sorry about? You were the homeless kid living in a tack room."

All of which was true. And he hated that he'd made her defensive, but he was nothing if not honest. "You were lonely." He ached to touch her with a comforting hand, but was afraid she'd slap it away.

"So you put up with me for years because you felt sorry for me. Thanks." She headed for the door.

Oh, hell. He dropped a hand on her shoulder. "I liked you, Dusty. I enjoyed teaching you how to read horses, and I thought you were an okay kid for the most part."

Her bright green gaze met his. "But I was still a pest."

He shook his head. Odds were, his honesty would earn him a slap, but he couldn't help who he was. "You were."

"I don't get it."

He raised his eyebrows. "Mistletoe?"

Her face went pink, she opened her mouth to reply, but snapped it shut instead.

"Cat got your tongue?"

"I was just a kid, for crying out loud." She huffed out a breath. "And it wasn't really my fault. Before Christmas break, all the girls at school were plotting to get kissed under the mistletoe. It was a big deal. And I only had you or my dad to choose from."

"What about everyone else? Seems to me the bunkhouse was full back then."

"But they mostly stayed away from me, which left you as my only real option. Besides, they were old." She shrugged, and he let his hand slide down her arm.

"Ouch. And here I thought you had a crush on me."

"In your dreams, cowboy."

The way she tipped her chin up at him made it damn near impossible not to lean over and kiss her cheeky mouth. "Well, forgive me for thinking mistletoe mysteriously moving around the barn to new locations, and you appearing with your lips stuck up in the air underneath it, meant anything special."

"I was twelve."

"You were fourteen." *And thank God you didn't look like this then.*

"Is that coffee ready yet?"

"Ya know, when you blush, I can still see a couple of those freckles." He ran his thumb across the bridge of her nose, let his fingertips linger on the soft skin beneath her ear, and very slowly, without breaking eye contact, he mentally brushed his mouth over hers.

Holy shit. Cannot go there. He spun on his heel and made for the coffee pot.

THREE

Stunned by the power of what hadn't happened, Dusty leaned on the door and tried to unscramble her brain cells. He'd almost kissed her, and her body was still on edge, ready to press against taut muscle and go wherever he led.

"Coming?" he called out from the kitchen.

Dusty swallowed hard and mentally slapped herself. A few months of doing without was starting to make her a little bit crazy, and she needed to get a grip.

Took a couple of big, deep, breaths, and made her way to the kitchen. Half of her glad Chase was acting as though nothing happened—which was, of course, true—the other half miffed because he wasn't as stirred up as she was.

But she shook it off, and they spent the afternoon talking horses and racing, until Dusty asked the question niggling since she'd first seen Angel, "Do you think she's your breakthrough horse?"

"Breakthrough?" His frown was telling.

"Your ticket to the big time." Because Dusty's own dreams included the Kentucky Derby and at least three Breeder's Cup mounts, she expected him to have similar goals as a trainer.

"I'm not chasing dreams anymore."

"Why not?" Dreams were goals, and without them, she'd have trouble dragging herself out of bed at three or four in the morning, to work horses seven days a week.

"Don't know for sure. I guess I'm comfortable where I am. I have the ranch, and new foals every spring to keep me busy." He shrugged.

Dusty shook her head at him in disbelief. He used to be focused, determined to make it to the top as a jockey. She'd assumed when his height eventually made him hang it up, he'd switch his dreams to training the best horses, running them in the premier races. "No Kentucky Oaks or Breeders' Cup plans for Angel?"

"Nope. I'll give her one start here in the interior... Then—"

"You can't run a horse like her at a B-Circuit track. She's star quality. Royalty, for crying out loud."

He had that indulgent, talk to the kid on her level, look on his face. "Just one start, with me on her back to teach her about the crowding, and the confusion that comes with racing."

"Let me ride her instead. You saw her with me today." *I'll win by the length of the stretch.*

"I saw you sailing into next week when she dug

her toes in."

"I meant after that, you idiot. We bonded, Chase. She trusts me." She waited a beat for effect. "Why won't you?"

"It's her I don't trust, because one day, a few short months ago, I saw blind panic in her eyes, and watched her almost kill herself trying to leap over the walls of a round pen. Trust might not be enough to keep her from reacting as if her life is threatened."

He shook his head. "She has a loose screw somewhere, I know exactly what I want to do with her, and I'm not about to try and explain it to you…or anyone else, for that matter."

Dusty raised an eyebrow at his tone. "Fine, do it yourself."

"You can ride her for her second start—her first win."

"Her second win. Even packing you, B-circuit horses will never outrun her."

He met her look head-on. "Oh yes, they will." He was dead serious, and there was no mistaking the message.

Infuriated, she fought to keep her temper in check. "Let me get this straight. You haven't ridden a race in—what? Six or seven years?—and you're gonna simply waltz out of retirement and *throw* a race? I don't like your chances. She's way too much horse to hold back without the entire world seeing you do it. You'll get suspended for at least a year, and break her heart in the process. It's a stupid fucking idea."

Chase was shaking his head. "All I'm going to

do is educate my filly in a race. After the break, I'll take her back behind the pack to make sure she gets dirt in her face. Then she'll learn how to weave her way between horses until she gets to the front, after that, we'll be past the wire and I'll ride her away from the field."

"Don't underestimate the racing officials just because it's a bush track. You *will* get suspended."

"You think I have to let her win."

"Earth to Chase." She wanted to knock him upside the head, and was almost shouting. Needed to dial back. Took a breath. "There is no other option."

He frowned and opened his mouth to say something, but she cut him off.

"If you want to practice rating techniques, do it in the morning. Stage some mock races with your buddies, but don't try to pull that crap in the afternoon. Trust me on this one." What the hell was he thinking? Hadn't he drilled into her that honesty and integrity were the most important rules to live by? Oh, and he always threw in the old "respect your elders" thing, too. What the hell had happened over the years to change him so much?

"I have no intention of trying to throw a race."

"Then why not make her first start in Vancouver?"

"Because they don't have quarter horse races, and I can't ride there at a hundred and twenty pounds."

Her eyes raked over him, moving from throat to boots and back up again, assessing his body—as though she hadn't been doing just that for the last

25

few days. Five ten and perfectly proportioned. A soft T-shirt and snug jeans encased the perfect combination of strength, muscle, and a darn fine ass.

"Cowboy, you're a long way from one-twenty."

His mouth twitched. "I still remember how to pull weight."

"And do you also remember that's why you gave up riding?" She'd kept track of his career, almost as obsessively as the silly girls hanging over the rail between races, trying to pick up riders.

"Pulling weight was making me sick."

"Exactly." Shedding pounds quickly, and often using questionable methods, took a terrible toll on riders. "And I heard you were a *very* unpleasant person to be around when you were reducing."

"Ouch." Now he was actually laughing at her while he pretended to pull a dagger from his heart. "I forgot how damned honest you are."

"For your own good, cowboy. You'd need to shed about thirty pounds of muscle to get to one-twenty. Not impossible, but guaranteed to make you sick as a dog—a mean-as-a-snake, hungry dog."

The ringing of Chase's phone was a welcome diversion, and they grinned at each other before he answered. Dusty glanced at her watch.

Shit. She bolted for the door.

John was leaving for the South Seas tonight, and she'd planned to be home early to visit with him. He was already annoyed at how much time she was spending with Chase and Angel instead of him. Not that he ever came out of his office while she was there, so what could it matter?

26

Yet again, she'd screwed up, and she could count on her father to start in on her the moment she got home. She threw herself into the Jeep and booted it down the long driveway, leaving an impolite cloud of dust in her wake.

***

At six-thirty Chase's phone rang again.
"Hello?"

Dusty sounded businesslike. "Do you have plans for supper?"

"Hadn't thought about it. Why?"

"Dad's gone, my car's packed, Teresa—his housekeeper—is gone, and I don't feel like sitting here alone until morning. It's either have dinner with you or hit the road now."

As a kid, she used to wander down to the bunkhouse whenever John was off on a trip because she hated being alone at night. They'd let her play cards with them. Damn fine poker player they made of her too.

"I've got steaks in the freezer."

"I'll bring potatoes." She hung up, and he stared at the phone for a minute before putting it down, his mind going several directions before he shut down the thoughts and headed for the freezer.

Twenty minutes later she arrived and slid a pink cloth bag onto the counter. She seemed upset, maybe a little sulky. He thought about asking her what was wrong, but figured she'd tell him when she was ready.

"Potatoes?" he asked.

She pulled out two big bakers and handed them to him. "They need a scrub. Want me to do it?"

"Nope, I've got it." He angled his chin toward the bag. "What else you got in there?" Dessert, maybe?

With a flourish, she produced a bottle of tequila, then half a dozen limes.

He raised an eyebrow in question.

She shrugged and parked her butt on a tall stool alongside the island. She plunked her elbows on the wide counter, rested her chin in her hands, and stared back at him. Neither said a word.

Chase dropped the steaks in a bowl of water to thaw, scrubbed the potatoes, stabbed them with a fork, and tossed them in the oven. Then he opened the fridge and surveyed the contents of the crisper drawer.

"You want a salad?"

"Not," she snapped.

"You don't have to bite my head off."

"Sorry." She didn't sound it. "When I'm riding, I live on salads. Hate them. Therefore, when I'm on holiday, not so much as one lousy lettuce leaf will pass my lips, not even on a drive-thru burger."

"You, reduce? Give me a break. You're a natural featherweight." Chase walked around the counter, pulled her off the stool, looked her up and down, turned her sideways to check out her ass, then grinned. "And put together real nice, I might add."

She rolled her eyes, and he caught a glimmer of a smirk edging her mouth. "I'm one-ten stripped. But I get a lot more mounts when I can tack eight, and I hate the sweatbox more than I hate leafy green vegetables."

Chase had horrible memories of keeping his body at an unnatural hundred and twelve. Reducing had nearly killed him. He used every trick available, from sauna and diuretics, to five-mile runs wearing a plastic rain suit. What he was no good at was flipping—eating whatever he wanted, then puking—a weight control method used by at least half the jockeys he rode with.

He shook off the memories and focused on Dusty. "You ride at a hundred and eight pounds?"

"I can get down to five if I hit the sweatbox, too."

"That's nuts. You have talent. You don't need to be a flyweight to get mounts." Didn't she realize giving up extra weight meant giving up strength? And who wanted a weak, dehydrated jockey piloting their horse?

"According to Mitchell, I needed the added advantage."

"Who the hell is Mitchell, and what the hell does he know?"

"He *was* my agent. You know, the guy responsible for getting me mounts while taking home thirty percent of my earnings? I was living with him for the past few months too."

"Oh. I thought you were with someone else. An owner."

"I was. But I left him and moved in with Mitchell."

Chase opened a jar of pickles and set them on the counter with a fork. "Vegetables," he said, and she snickered.

"Why'd you leave the rich guy for the agent?"

She sobered. "He was nice to me."

"You shack up with a guy just because *he's nice to you?*"

She met his stare and didn't back down. "Sometimes it's the right thing to do for survival."

"What the hell does that mean?"

She shook her head. "None of your damn business."

The hell it's not. He wanted to shake some sense into her. Instead he checked the steaks and said, "What else do you want besides steak, potatoes, and dills?"

She stayed silent until he turned back to look at her, then said, "Tequila," and flashed an impish grin he couldn't resist.

Laughing, he put shot glasses, a saltshaker, and the limes in front of her. "I haven't done this in years."

"Shame on you." Dusty reached for the bottle but he grabbed it and held it out of reach.

"One condition."

"What?"

"Give me your keys."

"Why? I don't plan on getting drunk."

"Me neither, but I want your keys anyway." *I'm not taking any chances.*

"Why?"

Chase's jaw clenched. "This is not negotiable, Dusty. I want your keys, or we don't open the bottle."

"Does that mean I get to spend the night with

you, cowboy?" She made a comical attempt to bat her lashes at him.

His serious gaze never even flickered. "Yes. The spare room is ready and waiting."

She groaned, reached into her pocket, tossed him the keys. "You're no fun at all."

After that, the atmosphere lightened again, while they bantered and joked their way through dinner, and about half of the tequila. It was late when they settled onto the big leather sofa with half a bottle of brandy and two glasses on the wooden table in front of them.

Dusty snuggled into the cushions. "I haven't felt this good in months."

"Good? Or drunk?"

She bristled a little, but kept a smile pasted on her face. "I'm not drunk. I haven't even had a brandy yet."

"There was tequila..." He held up both hands, palms out, to stop her response. He'd had several shots of the Mexican fire himself, but Dusty threw them back like she was on a mission. He hadn't commented, only watched and wondered why. "Okay, if you're not drunk, why do you feel so good?"

"I dunno. Maybe 'cause I'm about to start a new chapter in my career, or my personal life, or...I dunno." She giggled, looking instantly self-conscious. "Maybe you're right, and it is the tequila."

And maybe he should prod a little, find out what was going on with her. "You just up and walked away from your life in Alberta, your career?"

"Yup. Well, except I drove...because I bought the jeep...with my own money, too, so it was okay, and everything I needed fit. I'm free now. Or at least I think I am."

Chase closed his eyes for a moment, rubbed a hand over his face, couldn't believe he was opening this door. "Of the man?"

"Of everything. The men, myself, whoever, whatever—all of it, I guess. I was tired and lost, and then found, and then I wasn't sure about anything." She shook her head as though to clear away cobwebs. "I know I needed to be free, and I am. I can start over."

His lips twitched. "You don't think your past will follow you wherever you go?"

Color drained from her face. "Oh, hell, I hope not." She reached for the brandy, poured a generous splash in each glass.

"You were a brilliant apprentice, and as a journeyman you were gaining the respect of the Alberta horsemen. That's what you need to carry with you to the track in Vancouver."

She nodded. "It's how I got a good agent to pick me up—take my book."

The color started to come back, but his curiosity got the better of him. "What was so awful that you want to pretend it isn't a part of who you are? A piece of what makes you unique?" He hoped she would focus on the career aspects and not the men in her past.

"Who I was with him."

Shit. Well, suck it up, pal. This just ain't gonna

get any easier. "Mitchell?" The name almost stuck in his throat.

"No, he was…" She shuddered and shook her head. "Peter was the bastard before him."

Her eyes darkened with pain and sadness while he waited for her to elaborate. She blinked, and a single tear tracked down her cheek. He gently wiped it away, and she leaned into his hand for a moment and sighed.

"How come some stuff never goes away?"

"What stuff, Dusty?" He shifted, turned so he could watch her face but not touch her. He was guessing she needed to do this on her own.

"Do broken hearts ever mend?"

"Yeah, but it takes a while. Did Peter break your heart?"

"No."

"Who broke your heart, baby?"

Unshed tears made her eyes a glossy forest green. Her voice was soft, almost childlike. "I did." She sniffed. "I broke my own heart."

"Then you will have to find forgiveness for yourself."

She downed a big gulp of brandy, squeezed her eyes shut, and blew out a long, slow breath. Looked over at him. "I'm a bad person."

"You are not. You wouldn't harm a fly." And he believed that.

"But I did."

"You hurt a fly?" He wished he could take her pain away. Knew he couldn't.

She looked at him like he was a complete idiot, grimaced, and said, "Oh it's such a long story, and I

33

don't know if I can... If I should... It's bad enough that..."

"You used to trust me with everything."

"I...used to be an innocent kid, too." She stared at her hands. "You're the only real friend I have. The one person who doesn't want something from me, who doesn't judge me. Peter wanted everything, but nothing, and all I ever wanted was to belong to someone, but then he..."

Chase kept his voice quiet and gentle, yet, stern. "Stop babbling. Whatever it is, all you gotta do is spit it out, one sentence at a time. You have to know nothing you say will ever go beyond these walls." Her eyes darted to the brandy glass. "And no amount of booze will help you, so why not just get on with it?"

She stared at him as though she was about to tell him to go to hell.

"Come on, Dusty. One sentence about your man Peter. Did you love him?"

"I don't think I did."

"Why were you with him?" *Oh, hell, bite off my tongue. Now she'll probably go on about the great sex.*

She hesitated. "He was at a club I went to after the races one night, with a bunch of girls from the track. Tall and good-looking, with a beautiful body and a great tan. I'm a sucker for dark skin. I suppose that's because I'm half Italian." She shrugged.

"Everyone flirted with him, but he asked *me* to dance, and I was the envy of everyone. I was gonna get— Hmm. Well. I was the one going home with the guy they all wanted."

Chase leaned back in order to watch her face while she continued.

She snuggled into the deep sofa. "We partied for about a month before he asked me to live with him, and I jumped in with both feet. He bought me sexy clothes, and took me to the clubs to show me off, and it was great fun. I was suddenly someone special, and it felt fucking awesome." She shrugged. "I know, shallow and pathetic, right?"

How many times had he heard stories and assumed people were exaggerating, jealous, misjudging her? And worse, how many times had he talked himself out of picking up the phone and checking on her? *Sonofabitch.*

"I convinced myself it was okay, because—hey, Dusty Torino was now more than a country bumpkin who could ride a little...and put out." She swallowed hard. "I was Peter's girl. No more one-night stands, no more sweaty guys with bad breath and body odor. No more tack rooms or back seats." She met his gaze with a defiant look.

"No more dirty jeans and shit stuck to my boots. I looked and acted like a real lady. Designer clothing, and had everything that went with 'the good life.' Manicures, pedicures, massages, spa vacations, fast cars, wild shopping sprees, quick trips to Vegas and New York. It was *such* fun."

She'd been an idiot. Sold herself out. He didn't dare think about the sweaty dates. He took a calming breath. "You were happy."

"I was having a ball. I'd never known the kind of excitement that could spread over weeks, months even."

He studied her face, stayed in the moment. "What happened? Why is he a bastard now?"

Staring across at the night-darkened window on the other side of the room, she shrugged. "I don't know."

He was firm. "Truth, Dusty."

She swallowed hard. Her voice was low, the fire and excitement gone as though it had never been there.

"Something happened." She pressed her fingertips together until they went white. "Something bad."

Every muscle in his body went on full alert. He forced himself to stay in place, not lean forward and take her hands, reassure her. "Did he hit you?"

"No. He was never violent, physically."

Well. That, at least, was a relief. He wouldn't have to track the guy down and kill him.

"But his reaction when—" She hesitated, appeared to regroup. "I was stunned to discover he had no feelings for me at all. I was truly nothing more than an item in his life, with no more importance than one of his fancy cars or trucks or boats or whatever. With sickening clarity, I remembered laughing when he traded in a car because somebody keyed it. And I," her eyes widened as though she still couldn't believe what had happened, "*I,* was no different than any of his other possessions. I was replaceable. Not worth any measure of inconvenience."

While Chase maintained his silence, Dusty stared at the bottle on the table in front her. "He was proud of me, and treated me like a princess while it suited him, but once he decided I no longer suited his lifestyle, he dumped me like worthless trash."

Her voice dropped to a whisper. "When I got down on my knees and begged, all he gave me was an ultimatum. Threw my plane ticket on the bed and told me I could join him in Barbados on his terms, or be gone before he got back."

What Peter had done to her, what he'd reduced her to *was* horrible, but wasn't she better off away from someone who obviously didn't care about her?

"So I went..." She darted a glance at Chase. "I went out for a while. I had an appointment."

What was it she decided not to tell him?

"When I got home, I sat on the bed for what might have been hours, looking at the ticket. Then I took a shower and wandered around the house for a few more hours."

Dusty hadn't intended to tell him the whole story. Or had she? Chase was always there for her when she was a kid. Maybe she needed him that way again.

"I remember standing in the doorway of my closet, looking at the beautiful clothes, and walking through the elegant house, touching things, and thinking to myself, everything is window dressing and pointless. I looked in the mirror, saw the country bumpkin Peter had dressed up and made glamorous, and I got it. Beauty really is only skin deep, because underneath the fancy clothes, *I* was no different, and under the skin I," her voice cracked, "I was even less."

She reached for her drink, swallowed a burning

mouthful, savored the pain of its descent.

"It took a couple of days to pull myself together. To decide I wanted no reminders of the plastic life I'd been living. Got in a cab with nothing but the clothes on my back." She actually considered walking out naked, but she'd already experienced more than her share of humiliation.

"You dug yourself out of a bad situation," said Chase. "That's a *good* thing, Dusty."

Her jaw dropped. Good? "It's not *good* to have no idea where to go. What to do next."

The emotions she'd refused to deal with back then swamped her, threatening to overwhelm. She needed air. Shoved off the couch and marched to the door. Opened it and stood there, taking deep, calming breaths until the shaking eased. "I was so fucking scared and alone. Lost. Frozen in time, with nowhere to go, no one to talk to. Isolated in a city I barely recognized." She sat back down, but stayed on the edge of the couch, with her hands gripped together in her lap.

"I had no real friends left, because I snubbed them while socializing with Peter's crowd. I couldn't call my dad, because…well, because I couldn't." She sighed. "I borrowed the cab driver's cell phone and called my agent. He took me in."

"That would be Mitchell, the *nice* guy you shacked up with."

His tone made it clear what he thought, and he was right, so why not come clean? "He didn't ask questions. Looked after me and helped me figure out what to do next. It was simple, really. Peter insisted on paying for everything when we were together, and set me up with his money man. Every cent of my earnings at the track were, as he put it, wisely invested. I cashed in everything, bought the Jeep and some clothes, but even though I could afford a hotel, I stayed at Mitchell's place. And yeah, I let him... I had sex with him."

Chase's expression never changed, but her gut clenched.

"It was just sex. You know, like dates, pickups. A little fun, a little sweat, I get what I need, he gets what he needs, no big deal." Bile crept up her throat. "Besides, Mitchell had been there for me, what else could I do?"

His mouth had been wet, and his tongue nearly gagged her. She'd used her hands to stop the foreplay, brought him into her, thrown her head back and faked an orgasm. Her nails raked his fleshy back, urging him on, desperate for him to be finished.

She could still hear his belly slapping against her in time with his steady ugh, ugh, ugh, until that final uuuggghhh, when he came. And collapsed. Her nostrils filled with the sharp smell of his sweat, and the cloying scent of aftershave when he kissed her before sliding off. As he lay there, basking in his own afterglow, he had no idea, no clue she felt like a freshly salted slug, shriveling up and dying a slow death in a trail of her own slime.

She shook free of the memory.

"When he fell asleep, I drove straight to the track, to the Jocks' Room, hit the shower and stood under boiling hot water, scrubbing my skin nearly raw, but I still didn't feel any cleaner. Then I drove back to his place, parked around the corner, and waited until I saw him leave. I went in, got my stuff, and bolted."

She looked down at her empty glass, and Chase, without saying a word, pushed the brandy bottle out of her reach. She got the message, made no comment, did without the blast of amber fire she longed to feel in her throat.

"I took a room in a residential hotel. Lived alone—something I hadn't done in years. I hated it, but I made myself stay. I deserved the punishment."

"How long?"

"A month."

"Then what?"

She shuddered. "I wanted to go to the track. See the people. Face Mitchell and my shame." Her voice cracked, and she fought past the lump in her throat.

"I couldn't do it. Knowing I was nobody was easy when I was alone. But the thought of people actually ignoring me like before, and looking through me as if I wasn't there… It was easier to slink away and *be* invisible." A sob escaped while she wrestled for control.

"I turned out to be trash, exactly like my dad said I would." Her chin quivered.

"Stop it." The sharpness in his voice startled her.

Oh, God, she couldn't lose him, too. "I'm sorry, please don't hate me." Control slipped and the sobs racked her.

"Don't talk stupid." He took her hand. "Come here." He pulled her into his lap and held her close, stroking her hair. "I think you need to stop feeling sorry for yourself and look at what you have to be grateful for."

She sniffed. "Like what?" Even to herself she sounded like a ten-year-old, but this closeness was stirring up a much more adult response.

"Your exceptional talent and work ethic have given you a great career, your father adores you, and I'm here for you to blubber on."

"You still love me?"

"Amazing as it seems, I suppose I do." He set his chin on the top of her head, and she snuggled against him, just like when they'd been a couple of lonely, motherless kids on a ranch in the middle of nowhere, and she'd pretended he was her big brother. Worshipped the ground he walked on. And he looked out for her. Almost abandoned his own dream of becoming a jockey because he was worried about leaving her alone.

But she'd worked hard to convince him she could more than handle herself. Pushed and shoved him away, insisting she had other, more important friends at her new school. Didn't need him anymore. And she cried every weekend when he went off to the races.

She yawned.

"Hey, don't be nodding off. There's a nice, comfy bed ready for you in the spare room."

"Carry me?"

"Not a chance."

Dusty leaned back to study the serious look on his face, pushed herself off his lap. "Tuck me in like old times?"

He shook his head with an amused expression. "Against my better judgement. I'll be in shortly. Second door past the bathroom."

There was a tiny nightlight glowing on the far side of the bed, and the covers were turned down. She peeled off her clothes, crawled in, and instantly wished the room would stop spinning.

The side of the bed dipped under his weight.

"Chase—"

"Did you say your prayers?"

"I'm not a kid anymore."

He leaned over and braced a hand on either side of her. "No? Then why am I babysitting?"

His warmth spread over her, seeped under her skin. She stared into stormy gray eyes and imagined how they would change, heat up with desire.

And she couldn't help herself. Wanting to taste him, she twisted her hand into the front of his shirt and pulled him down toward her. "I'm all grown up now, cowboy, and…"

He didn't resist, and when she'd drawn him down until his lips were only a breath away from touching hers, she continued, "…and I don't need mistletoe."

Her other hand slid around his neck, and he made no attempt to pull away while she kissed him until she was wishing she could crawl inside his skin. Reality slapped at her, and she abruptly let him go.

"If you were sober, and I wasn't babysitting right now, you'd have hell to pay for that." His voice was low, sexy.

"Talk's cheap," she taunted.

He held her challenging gaze for what seemed like forever, and then his mouth was grazing her forehead, her cheekbone, sliding down to her throat. Then stopped.

When she opened her eyes to meet his serious stare, she saw something she didn't recognize. Slowly, ever so slowly, his lips teased hers until a groan escaped her, and he took possession of her mouth, ignited a fire between them that caught her by surprise. She wound her arms around his neck and gloried in the feel of his hands on her bare flesh.

She slid her fingertips under his T-shirt, touched his heated skin, and he wrenched away. Kept moving until he was out the door and out of sight.

She heard a door slam, and imagined him out on the porch, gulping clean night air while she battled conflicting emotions.

Joy fought with guilt, and there was no clear winner before sleep claimed her.

FOUR

Even the slightest movement sent pain ricocheting around in Dusty's head, and she was certain her tongue grew fur sometime during the night. She wanted nothing more than to go back to sleep, but the rich smell of coffee was relentless. As were the niggling flashes of memory from the night before.

She started putting together the bits and pieces, but, as usual, there were gaping holes. She'd grown used to the blackouts, and didn't much worry about them, because Peter had always looked after her.

Sure, the doctor said she shouldn't drink, and she hadn't since leaving Peter, but last night she'd needed the false courage so she could tell Chase her story.

Had she told him everything? Unlikely, but she couldn't be sure. What she did remember, very clearly, was his mouth on hers, the touch of his hands. She was fairly certain they hadn't had sex, but something had happened, had changed her deep inside.

Warm breath tickled her ear, and her heart stuttered. She concentrated on keeping her breathing even and her muscles lax, while she sifted more carefully through flickering memories, but could find nothing past the kiss. She swallowed hard, rolled over, and opened her eyes.

First there was a painful stab of light to jack up the throbbing headache, and when she managed to focus, what she saw was a big, black nose about six inches from her face. Dark amber eyes stared into hers, and a muted whine came from his throat.

"Duncan's been dying to meet you," Chase said from somewhere behind the dog. "Okay, Dunc, get her up."

The huge German shepherd's front paws landed on the bed, and he set to licking her face with great enthusiasm. Laughing, she pushed and shoved, but he wouldn't stop.

"Call him off," she managed to gasp the words out.

"Duncan." The dog immediately hopped off the bed and waited for a command. "Outside."

"You too. Out," Dusty ordered while yanking the covers up under her chin.

"Yes, ma'am." He touched his brow in a kind of mock salute. "You need anything? Your suitcase or something?"

"Sure, whatever, just close the door!"

"Bashful all of a sudden, Dusty?"

Oh, so that's how he wanted to play it? "Not in the least." She swung her legs over the side of the

45

bed and sat up, allowing the sheet fall and expose her nakedness while she reached to retrieve her clothes.

Laughing, he turned on his heel and left.

Dusty eyed the puffy pillow on the far side of the bed. Did she dare hope it meant she had, indeed, spent the night alone, and her foolishness hadn't gone beyond a kiss? *I may have to quit tequila for good if it's going to keep getting me into this kind of trouble.*

When she emerged from the bedroom, she found Chase at the stove.

"Mmmm. Smells delightful." She leaned past him to have a look at the pans stacked with bacon, eggs, and potatoes.

"Quite the breakfast."

"You need a good meal in your belly before you hit the road."

She wandered to the window and spotted the truck and trailer parked beside the barn. "I see Murray's back."

"Which explains where Duncan came from." He was leaning against the counter, and there was something about the intensity of his stare that made her ridiculously self-conscious.

"When did they get in?"

"A little after midnight."

She stuffed her hands in her back pockets. "Long haul from southern Alberta. Everybody ship okay?"

"All bright-eyed when they stepped off the rig."

Dusty wished she'd been awake when they came in. She loved a barn in the wee hours of morning, the contented munching of hay, shuffling of bedding. "I guess Murray was pretty tired if he drove straight through."

"He says his body understands the drill, and Duncan keeps him awake."

Chase's half-smile took her right back to this morning, when she thought it was him breathing on her, about to kiss her. She was stumped for words. "Duncan?"

"The dog."

His smile was full-on now, and it made her stomach flutter. She needed to get out of here before she did something stupid. "I have to hit the road soon myself."

"Come on, let's get you fed first."

Conversation was nonexistent while they dished up and ate, and afterwards, while Chase washed the dishes and Dusty dried, the silence grew strained.

Stayed that way until she gathered her belongings, set her suitcase on the porch, and went to say good-bye to Angel.

Chase watched until she was out of sight, then waited for a few minutes before following. She was gazing through the fence at the new arrivals when he caught up with her.

"Angel is very curious about these fellows," she said. "Trying to pick up their scent."

Chase looked over his shoulder at the big filly several paddocks away. She was watching with an all-too-familiar wide-eyed stare, with her ears flickering and nostrils flared.

"She doesn't miss much."

Dusty muttered, "Most girls don't."

47

Whatever that was supposed to mean went over Chase's head. He pretended not to hear her, and pointed at the colt closest to them.

"What do you think of him?"

"He looks strong. And I like the determination in his eye."

"Goes along with his pedigree. I've already turned down twenty thousand for him." And with the cost of running the ranch, that had been a hard thing to do.

"Twenty thousand for a foal still with his mother? Are you nuts?"

"Nope, the stud fee alone was twenty, and I'm hoping to get over a hundred for him when he's a yearling."

"If he's that special, and you're willing to gamble on waiting a year, why not go for broke and train him yourself?"

"Nope." He watched the baby butting his head up against his mother's belly, as though the milk wasn't coming fast enough.

"You said the other day you were ready to give up training, but I didn't think you were serious."

"I am."

"Why?" She stared as though he'd made some kind of rash statement.

"I'm sick and tired of the rat race. When Angel goes back to Kentucky in January, I will be more than happy to hang up my trainer's license." He'd live here then, year 'round, at peace with the land. With his heritage.

She shook her head. "When will you take her to Vancouver?"

"When she's ready."

Dusty rolled her eyes. "And when will that be?"

"I don't know." Which was true, but he was also trying to get a rise out of her.

"Oh, for crying out loud, give it a guess."

He laughed. "You of all people know how it goes with two-year-olds. How many of your dad's horses ever got to run at two? Half, maybe? Even if you can get them ready to run, they get a sore shin, or the snots, or something else, and then it's back to the farm and start over again in a month." He held his hands out, palms up. "If the world was perfect, I'd run her in Kamloops late May, then be in Vancouver by mid-June. But chances are I'll be lucky to get her started by August."

"Will you call if you need me? Seriously, Chase. I can gate school her, or ride a company horse, or whatever. I really want to be there for her, and I'm just a phone call and a three-hour drive away."

"I promise I'll call." *What the hell, the can of worms is open now, why not see where this is headed?*

"I wish I could stay and work with her."

"You have a career to look after. And a new agent to meet with in—" He checked his watch. "Four hours."

"Are you trying to get rid of me?"

"Of course not. But if you're hoping for a successful go in Vancouver, you'd be smart to start it off on a good note and not be late for your meeting. It's not easy changing tracks. New people, no loyalties…"

Dusty didn't want to hear it. Turned on her heel and marched toward the house. She was tired of lectures. John had delivered a final one before he left on his trip last night.

That on top of three weeks of living with her father's massive ego was more than enough to remind her why she left home the day after her sixteenth birthday. She'd watched him alienate people her entire life, and not once had *he* been the one to change.

He'd gone through a dozen different racehorse trainers before giving up the thoroughbred business altogether and turning his ranch back into a cattle operation. His latest passion was trying to convince the world he'd developed a line of cattle resistant to mad cow disease. Next he'd be working on cloning them. Too bad he couldn't clone himself. Then the world would be perfect. She gave her head a shake. Why the hell was she thinking about John?

Chase caught up and draped an arm across her shoulders. "Have you got a place to live yet?"

"Nope. I'm staying at a hotel until I find something."

"Do you still like cats?"

Well there was a subject change. "Sure, why?"

"The boathouse I've stayed in down there for the past few seasons might still be available."

"Boathouse?"

"Used to be. But it's been converted into a nice cottage. Right on the water, and far enough from the main house to be quite private."

"And it comes with cats?"

"And my friends, Linda and Rick. They love to

go sailing for a week at a time in the summer, but they have cats, and depend on whoever rents the boathouse to be their cat sitter."

"Sounds reasonable."

"You'd love them, I'm sure."

"The people or the cats?"

"Both. Linda and Rick are fortysomething, she's a psychologist, and he's an attorney.

"Will she try to shrink me?"

"What?"

"She's a shrink. Will she try to fix me?"

"I doubt it. She's never messed with my head. Do you want their number or not?"

"Sure, I'll call when I get to town." Maybe.

Once they reached the house, Chase gave her the phone number, then followed her out to the jeep.

"Thanks for breakfast, not to mention supper. And," heat rose up her neck, "the place to crash."

Chase smiled. "I'm gonna miss you, kid."

Dusty glanced up as he moved closer. "I'm not a kid anymore, Chase." *This is a grown-up libido you're messing with.*

His hands rested on her shoulders. "You give'm hell down there, lady, ride the hair off those horses, and don't let the big city jocks intimidate you. Remember, you can always outwit them."

"Yes, sir."

His grip tightened and his voice lowered. "And don't you *ever* forget to call me if you need me." He gave her the faintest of shakes. "Don't you dare drive around wondering where to go or what to do, *ever again*. You call me."

She stared at the ground, blinking away the

burn of tears. "I will, I promise."

He put a knuckle under her chin and forced her to look up at him. Then he hesitated, shook his head, and muttered, "Never mind." His arms went around her, and he held on for a few too many heartbeats while Dusty wondered what it was he hadn't said.

He planted a firm, warm kiss on her forehead, then opened the door and steered her into the Jeep. She started the engine and slid the window down to wave as she slowly drove away.

"Hey, Dusty."

She braked and leaned out the window, her heart pounding way too hard. "What?"

He grinned. "Stay out of the tequila."

She laughed, pressed her foot on the accelerator, and spewed gravel all the way down the driveway, leaving one of her dreams behind.

FIVE

Kamloops Racetrack, British Columbia,
Early Summer 2001

Chase looked like an extension of the horse. Crouched low over Angel's back at a full gallop, his weight was perfectly balanced on thin aluminum stirrups, and his back flat as they approached the five-eighths pole. Picking up the pace with each stride, the filly was in full flight at the half-mile marker.

Dusty felt like she was out there with them, and almost forgot to press the button on the stopwatch in her pocket. Seconds ticked by in hundredths. Split times froze when she tapped the left side, but her attention never wavered from the pair rounding the turn and flying down the lane toward her with powerful strides eating up ground.

With a flash of color they blew past her and were nearly out the other side of the clubhouse turn before they slowed to a comfortable lope. By the end of the backstretch Chase brought Angel to a full stop, turned her around, and headed back to the off gap.

Dusty met them there, and when Chase spotted her, a sexy smile spread over his face. "Wow, if that doesn't make a great morning perfect."

"Hey, what gives? Thought I was supposed to work her."

"Sorry, the track guys came through the barns and told us we had twenty minutes to finish up because the trucks had arrived early with the new surface material. If I hadn't worked her right away, I'd be stuck until tomorrow."

Dusty shrugged. "Oh, well, it was almost as much fun watching you breeze her."

"Yeah? How'd I look?"

"Big." *But freaking brilliant and amazingly talented.*

"Jesus, I'm down to one-thirty-five."

"Stop there, okay? I happen to prefer you with meat on your bones."

Chase raised an eyebrow and opened his mouth, but she cut off whatever comment he was about to make by taking hold of the lines and saying, "Get down off that horse, dammit. She needs to be cooled out properly."

"Yes, ma'am." His grin was back before he landed. "Bath water's ready for her at the barn."

Once Angel was bathed and cooled out, they did her up in standing bandages, let her graze a little between the barns, then tucked her into the stall beside Jake's.

"You owe me lunch," Dusty said when they were done.

"Why?"

"Because I drove all the way up here to work her, and you not only cheated me out of it, but I had to cool her out instead. Seems to me I should at least get fed before I have to drive home." She didn't want to go back to the coast. She wanted to spend time with Chase.

"How long did it take you to get here?"

"Three hours." As if he didn't know.

"Yup, lunch seems fair." He grabbed her hand. "Come on." Her Jeep was parked beside his truck, and when they reached it he asked, "Where do you want to eat?"

"I don't care. You pick."

"We'll take both vehicles. Follow me, okay?"

When they pulled onto the highway she knew, and when she parked beside him in front of his house, she hopped out and asked, "Is this lunch, or are you going to put me to work again?"

"Lunch. Thought it would be nicer to hang out where we can relax for a while. Okay?"

More than. This was way better than some noisy restaurant.

Chase built fat roast beef sandwiches, made iced coffee, and even came up with fresh berries for dessert. They sat on the porch watching the horses in the paddocks while they ate, then lingered for a while.

"God, I miss this quiet," Dusty murmured.

"City getting to ya, kid?"

"Sometimes. I love the boathouse, the ocean,

the people, but once in a while I long for the air here, and the silence I grew up with. I don't sleep as well down there." She had sunk deep in the old sofa, relaxed, muscles limp.

"Looks like you could use a nap right now. Why don't you close your eyes for a while?"

She tucked her legs up. "I need to be on the road by six."

"You will be." He touched her shoulder. "Go to sleep. I'll be back in a bit."

Chase carried their dishes to the kitchen and put them in the sink. Took his time washing up, and when he peeked out, she was fast asleep. He couldn't resist. Poured himself another iced coffee, and settled in to watch over her.

It was well past six when he started tickling her toes. She wriggled for a minute, then sighed and went still when he began massaging her foot. "Dusty you need to wake up."

"Hmmmm?"

He took a deep breath. If she didn't wake up soon, he was gonna have to kiss her. No choice. Couldn't help himself if she kept resisting him like this. He let go of her foot and edged over. "Dusty," he whispered near her ear.

His heartbeat quickened when she stretched like a contented cat. And when he touched her face, she turned to slide her mouth across the inside of his wrist.

"I was having the nicest dream." Opening deadly sexy eyes, she hooked her fingers in the collar of his shirt. Tugged ever so gently, and it never occurred to him to resist. "In my dream, you wanted to kiss me."

His lips grazed hers, and when she gave back tenfold, he was lost. Her hands slid under his shirt, spread, skimmed over his back, and heat pulsed between them, but somehow an odd sound penetrated. An engine. Diesel. Idling. Reversing?

Chase pushed himself away and looked around. Hot air filtered the dust settling over the driveway. Who had been there? Why?

Dusty glanced at her watch. "Shit."

"What?"

"I have to leave. It's past seven. I thought you promised to wake me at six?"

"I tried, but it took a while." He went for a poker face but failed miserably and she leaned over and gave him a quick kiss.

"Sorry. I've always been tough to wake up."

"My pleasure." His smile spread.

Dusty shook her head, stood and stretched, exposing a sexy little strip of skin where her T-shirt and jeans parted company.

Blood was leaving his brain, heading south. "Don't do that."

"Do what?"

"Stretch." He pointed at the edge of the T-shirt. "Makes me want to do things." Taste...

Dusty laughed. "What kinda things?"

Chase quickly put space between them, distance that was more than air. His voice was low. "Not tonight. You're already late, and some things shouldn't be rushed."

While Dusty walked to her jeep, she wondered if he'd change his mind, if he'd touch her again.

But he kept his distance until she was inside and rolled down the window. Then he leaned in and planted a hot kiss on her before saying in a soft voice, "Drive safe, baby."

She had him by the collar, tugged him back toward her and whispered, "Okay, cowboy." Kissed him quick, pushed him away, and sped off in a cloud of dust.

Once over the hill and out of sight, with her heart still refusing to calm, and mind in a turmoil she pulled over. *What the hell was I thinking? Why did I leave? Should I go back? Is he waiting for me? I don't have to be in Vancouver until morning.*

She ran her fingers through her hair, gripped them together at the back of her neck and swore out loud, but kept toying with the images. His skin hot against hers, his mouth, his needs, hers, the deep ache. Fast, hot sex... *If I go back now, will he be able to send me away?*

She slammed the jeep into gear and accelerated, gravel spitting out behind her as she pulled onto the road and continued the drive to the coast.

Chase stalked toward the barn, but veered off, heading for the training track instead, because he wasn't in any shape to work with sensitive thoroughbreds. A couple of laps on foot should smooth him out.

Conscience scraped like a branch against a window.

How could he want her this way? This much? Someone he'd protected like a kid sister? Someone he'd teased and tormented, as a brother should, and loved, respected, and cherished as a friend.

Sure, they were both adults, and she wanted him as much as he wanted her, but did that negate his promise never to touch her?

He marched back to the house to make a phone call, and the next day he spent hours in a sweat lodge with a friend. Someone he trusted, someone to help him search himself, and ask tough questions. Yes, he felt better by the time he left, but the answers to his questions remained elusive.

***

When two long weeks passed without a word from Chase, Dusty bit the bullet and called to see if he needed her to breeze Angel. He invited her to come up on Monday, but she could tell he wasn't comfortable when she arrived.

She worked hard to stay at arm's length, yet not push him any further away. And so it went. Every Monday morning, Dusty made the drive and worked the filly.

They even went trail riding twice. Loaded Angel and Jake in the trailer and took them into the mountains for a change of scenery. Chase deemed it a great way for Angel to get away from the daily training regimen. At first she was skittish and uncertain, but with Jake and Chase at her side and Dusty on her back, she eventually relaxed and grew more confident. Enjoyed the change of scenery.

Riding in the mountains also helped Chase and Dusty get past the sexual tension and back to an easy camaraderie. They worked well together, and found companionship even in silence. Dusty's heart ached for the loss of intimacy, but having his friendship was better than nothing.

On the first Sunday in August, Angel officially became a racehorse. With the permission of the racing officials, she entered the starting gate alongside quarter horses, to go four hundred and fifty yards with Chase on her back—at a hundred and thirty pounds.

Angel behaved like an old pro and, as expected, the other horses easily opened lengths on her while they hotfooted away from the gate. But after about three hundred yards, she began closing in on them, weaving her way through the pack, getting up for fifth money at the wire, and then easily blowing by the rest.

Sure, she only passed finished horses, but many people took note of her performance and jotted down the name, C N Dark Angels, for future reference, because she'd shown an amazing turn of foot. Speculation in the beer garden was she'd win at first asking against Thoroughbreds.

Chase hoped they were right. He called Dusty right after the race and told her not to come up on Monday. He'd be hauling the horses to Vancouver instead.

He had no way of knowing his plans were about to get nixed.

SIX

*Vancouver Racetrack, British Columbia,
Late Summer 2001*

Dusty was pulling into the horsemen's parking lot in the dark of pre-dawn when her cell phone buzzed, and she didn't bother with hello. "Who needs me, Marty?"

"Mary Dalton has a set of workers tacked and ready, but her rider's a no-show. Can you catch one for her?"

"Sure. Grabbing my gear as we speak, and I'll be there in five."

The phone went dead and Dusty did a mental happy dance. Marty was a man of few words, but a damn good agent. He'd done a great job for her this spring by convincing the local horsemen to give her a shot. Vancouver had what was called a tough room to break into. The riders were a tight-knit bunch, and not exactly warm and welcoming when a new jock tried to get established.

And the trainers not only had a reputation of sticking to the riders they knew, but apparently most didn't think female race-riders were as good as males. Marty managed to get a few of the smaller outfits to give her a break, and her own work ethic had opened even more doors. She was there seven mornings a week, just before the track opened at five-thirty, willing to work horses for anyone who asked. Even galloped a few.

Her mind wandered back to the day she met Marty.

She'd offered a hand to the serious-looking man sitting at the table closest to the back door of the coffee shop, and said, "Hi, I'm Dusty."

"Really," he said with a straight face, then tipped his head and smiled. "Sorry, I bet you get that a lot."

She grimaced. "Enough to consider using my real name instead, but I'm really not the Melanie type, ya know?"

"Dusty isn't a bad handle."

"Thanks," she replied then cocked her head slightly. "Martin Turin, I presume?"

"Marty will do, and if you'll sit down, we can get to the business at hand."

Dusty sat, and a waitress appeared, turned over the coffee cup in front of her, and filled it to the brim.

Marty got right to work. "What do you tack? I mean naturally."

"One twelve on three square meals a day. I can pull ten if I absolutely have to, but prefer to ride no lighter than eight. I don't like giving up strength for pounds, and nobody wants me hitting like a girl."

One corner of Marty's mouth twitched. "Okay. I've looked at your stats, and nothing stands out. Looks like you're equally effective on colts and fillies, going short or long, and you have a bit of a bias for coming off the pace, but still have good numbers on front-runners.

He took a swallow of his coffee. "Anything else I need to know? Any history to get in your way?"

"History?"

"Enemies? Reputation? Before you answer that, I realize everyone has something in their past. But at least if you warn me, I won't get any nasty surprises." He looked her square in the eye. "I hate surprises."

Dusty got where he was coming from. "I'm definitely not halo material, but I've got no enemies, no nasty secrets following me around. I'm a hard worker, and I don't scare easy."

"What about the owner you lived with in Alberta? You were the only rider he used, and I heard you turned down good mounts to ride for him."

"I did ride first call for him, but got plenty of other mounts in races he wasn't in. I lived with him for two years. We have no ties left."

Marty pinned her with a very serious look. "That brings up my rule number one. While I'm your agent you will *not*: live with, sleep with, or even screw around with, *any* owner or trainer on the grounds, period."

Dusty was taken aback. "Seriously?"

"And before you go getting all offended, let me tell you this rule applies to each and every one of my riders, male or female. I cannot do my job properly if my hands are tied by your outside... ah... loyalties. You wanna play, find somebody outside the gates."

Dusty thought about that for a minute, then said, "You'll have to make one exception to your rule or you can't be my agent." He opened his mouth to speak but she held up a hand. "Please listen first, it's important."

"Okay."

"Do you know Chase Mathews?"

"Yup, decent sort, Ind— First Nations kid. Great rider, but lost the weight battle, became a trainer. You doin' him?"

"No." She shook her head. "But I'm going to ride his horse. I've known Chase forever. He made me what I am on horseback. He has one horse, and I promised him I'd ride her when he brings her to Vancouver."

"What if you already have a mount in the race?"

"That will be up to you to figure out, because I'll be riding Angel, *no matter what*. You're welcome to fire me then if you want to."

"Angel, you say?"

"The finest piece of horseflesh I've ever thrown a leg over. Kentucky-bred daughter of a mare who's produced seven millionaires by four different stallions."

"Don't make sense her bein' here, then. There must be a hole in her."

Dusty laughed. "Oh, there is—was... She was unbreakable, but Chase figured her out."

"And you've been on her."

"Yup. Dropped me the first time, but we have an understanding now, so it won't happen again." When Marty's eyebrows went up, Dusty explained Angel in terms that made more sense to an agent. "I watched her gallop a two-minute mile, then breeze a half in forty-six flat—while packing Chase, not some lightweight rider. Never turned a hair."

"Sounds impressive."

"Years ago, when I was sale-prepping two-year-olds in Florida, I got on some amazing horses. Lots of them were seven-figure babies and went on to be superstars. Yet never once did I feel the kind of power this filly has."

"When will she be ready to run?"

"Sometime in the summer."

"Okay, Miss Dusty. I like your honesty and your enthusiasm. I hustle your book, you still ride the fancy filly."

She shook the hand he held out. "Deal."

Dusty was brought abruptly back to the present by Mary shooting out the bottom of her barn.

"Thanks a ton for bailing me out, Dusty. These two colts have been walking the shedrow for twenty minutes, and Shane still isn't here, damn his prima donna hide."

Zipping her flak jacket, Dusty said, "Do you have a pilot for the other one?"

"My gallop girl can ride the rabbit. I hope you don't mind taking the dirt."

Dusty smiled and ran the zipper of her jacket to

the top. "Of course not. What's the plan?"

"I need you to sit far enough back for your colt to get a good face full. Then you can hook up at the head of the lane and finish together."

"How far we going?"

"Seven furlongs, out the mile. And I have a pony to break you off. Otherwise he'll be too tough for you to get to the pole."

Dusty laughed. "So I'm gonna get dirt in my face, *and* get my ass pulled off?"

Mary grimaced. "I promise to make it up to you."

"You'll put me on a live one?" When a rider does a favor for a trainer, the anticipated reward is an opportunity to ride one of their horses in a race. And that means a live mount with a legitimate chance to win, not a fifty-to-one shot.

"You bet. Maybe even this colt, if I'm still pissed at Shane for not showing up today." Her voice dropped to a mutter, "Or yesterday. Rumor has it he's been partying hard, and he can't seem to get up in the morning."

Dusty hid a smirk. The real problem was that Shane could *only* get it up in the morning. He had a reputation for partying hard at night, taking home a jockey jumper, passing out as soon as he got there, and then banging her all morning. Might as well take advantage. It would be good to get her foot in this door while Shane was screwing up.

"Good morning," she said to the groom stopping in front of her with the chestnut. Dusty lowered a couple of sets of goggles from her helmet and settled them over her eyes, then adjusted the length of the stirrups before Mary legged her up.

Once on the track and jogging the backstretch, Rachel said, "I've never done a work like this before. I hope I don't screw it up."

"You don't have to do anything but sit chilly, work the horse you're on and ignore me."

"But I have to hook up and finish with you."

Determined to make the younger woman feel less stressed, Dusty explained, "*I* have to hook up with *you*. It's my job to get it right, not yours, and I promise, if you work your colt nice and even, chirp to him at the three eighths marker, and start riding your ass off at the quarter pole, I'll catch you at the top of the lane, and we'll finish together."

"You're sure?"

"Scout's honor. Leave the hard stuff to me, and you'll look like a magician."

Rachel laughed. "Okay, see you there." She urged her horse into a lope.

Dusty turned her attention to the pony-girl at her side, "I suppose this guy breaks off like a rocket ship?"

"Yup."

"Okay then, best hang on to us right to the pole."

Dusty switched her focus to the horse under her. Closed her eyes for a second to let her body sink into his rhythm, allowing her knees, like shock absorbers, to adjust to his stride.

She began to hum softly as they neared the seven-furlong pole, shortened the cross in her lines, and pushed her hands down against his neck. He picked up speed, and when they reached the marker, the pony-girl let go of one end of her lead strap and it slipped from the bit, giving Dusty full control.

He broke off hard and fast while Dusty's feet stayed, as they say, on the dashboard—shoved out in front of her, bracing against the stirrups to gain a measure of leverage—to combine with her steady grip on the reins and maintain control while she gauged the speed of the horse in front of her.

Rachel's mount was keeping a nice, steady pace, and Dusty was able to sit about three lengths back, taking all the racetrack they kicked up in her face. At first, her colt tried to avoid the onslaught, but gradually began to accept it. For about half a mile he endured the gritty kickback before Dusty asked him to pick up speed and actually run into the dirt. It hit harder, and he tugged against the left rein, trying to move out of the line of fire, but Dusty stayed firm, making him press on into it until they reached the three-eighths pole.

She loosened her hold, chirped, and, as he gathered speed, she quickly reached up and pulled down the outside set of dirt-caked goggles, exposing clean ones so she could see their target more clearly.

Rachel was only a length and a half in front of them when Dusty allowed her mount to alter course, close the gap and fly to the wire, side by side with his workmate.

They crossed the line as one, with Rachel on her belly riding and Dusty still sitting chilly. She had a ton of horse left, but because Mary wanted the colts to finish together, Dusty couldn't let her colt run on by, and he gradually relaxed while they galloped out the mile together.

It was a picture-perfect execution, and Rachel's excitement was palpable when she was riding off the track beside Dusty.

"Man, that was fun."

Dusty's grin was equally wide. "You did good. Any interest in becoming a jockey?"

"You think I could?"

"Probably. You've already got one of the most important skills."

"I do?"

"Yup. You followed instructions to the letter. Oh, and you're pretty good in the tack, too." Dusty remembered what it was like to come up through the ranks, and how much a word or two of praise meant.

"Dusty." Marty's shout came from somewhere to the left.

"Yep?"

"George has one ready for you."

Mary came up alongside her and clipped a leather shank to the colt's bridle, saying, "Go ahead and bail, girl. The work was great, and I thank you immensely."

Dusty jumped off the colt, gave him a pat, and said, "Anytime Mary, glad to help. And he needed it. Didn't like that shit in his face at first, but stopped fighting and ran into it willingly after the first bit of urging. Coulda passed the other one anytime. Tons of horse left."

Dusty turned and headed toward George's barn. She glanced at her watch. Chase should be here soon.

She worked three more horses before she was free to check to see if he'd arrived yet.

"Nope," answered the guard at the stable gate. "No ship-ins yet this morning."

Dusty began to worry. Chase said Angel's traveling woes were far behind her, but maybe not. Maybe she'd thrown a wreck in the trailer. She called his cell again, only to hear the annoying, anonymous voice inform her the customer was not available. She stuffed the phone back in her pocket and headed for the racing office. Maybe he called them.

Three hours later Dusty had exhausted every avenue.

According to Murray, Chase left the ranch around midnight with plans to load the horses, then gas up in Kamloops, and be on the highway by one-thirty.

The Kamloops racing office confirmed Chase's horses, truck, and trailer left the grounds sometime between midnight and six am.

Staff at the filling station said he was there shortly after one in the morning.

Dusty called a friend who worked at the highway tollbooth. Sue was on days off, but contacted the two people who'd been on shift, and neither recalled Chase's truck and trailer passing through.

That was enough for Dusty. She phoned Murray again, changed out of her riding clothes, and headed north. Murray would search the southbound route from the ranch, meeting Dusty somewhere in the middle.

She didn't like the sick feeling in her stomach.

It was just as well that she didn't know Murray was feeling it too.

SEVEN

Shortly after nine that night, Dusty arrived at Chase's ranch. Murray, who'd returned three hours earlier to feed and water the horses, was walking across the yard to greet her, with Duncan solemn at his side.

"Looks like you two haven't heard anything, either," she said, and he shook his head.

Dusty took a second to stretch her cramped legs. "I've been in every coffee shop, gas station, and truck stop from here to the toll booth. Talked to every trucker in the area, every waitress, rancher, and radio operator. Driven hundreds of miles of dirt road, and stopped at every bit of trash along the way, hoping for a clue. But there's nothing, Murray. It's as though he freaking fell off the earth—truck, trailer, horses, and all."

"They've found something."

She didn't like the look on his face. "What?"

"A couple of kids found his boots on the river

bank, near Spences Bridge. Cops think they could have been tossed from a northbound vehicle."

Dusty's stomach clenched, but she shoved dark thoughts away. "They can't be absolutely sure they're his and—"

"They're his. Had 'em made when he was in Texas last year. His name's stamped inside."

"Maybe Chase threw them, to give us a clue."

"That's possible." But his expression said improbable.

"We can't believe anything else, Murray. There has to be a logical explanation for his disappearance."

"Such as?"

"Maybe he ran into somebody with a breakdown and horses on board. He could have detoured to take them wherever they were headed. Or maybe he came across an injured critter and he took off to get help." She'd hang onto any idea she could.

Murray shrugged. "Knowing Chase, he could be off helping somebody. Maybe out of range for his cell. Probably on some back road. Stayed for the night to rest the horses." He was playing along, but didn't look like he believed what he was saying.

"I'm gonna yell at him for a week when he shows up."

He rubbed Duncan's head. "We'll search again in the morning."

"Spences Bridge is way west of where we've been looking," she said. "That opens up a whole new territory. If I leave here around three I can be there by daylight."

"And if I feed the stock at five, I can be on the road by five-thirty."

They spent the next half hour at Chase's kitchen table, poring over maps of highways and back roads, making plans for the morning. Dusty would start where the boots were found and work her way north. Murray would head west, then south.

He went to the counter to get one of the phones she hadn't noticed sitting in a double charger. Handed it to her. "It's satellite, and expensive as hell. Only use it as backup when you can't get a cell signal."

He pointed to a button. "Here's the speed dial. One's for the cops, two's for me. Check in every hour. I need to know where you are, and that you're okay."

"You don't need to worry about me. I'm used to looking out for myself."

He put a hand on her arm. "I didn't think I needed to worry about Chase either, so humor me, would you? Besides, I'll catch holy hell from him if you go missing too. And be sure you have both of my numbers on your own cell too, okay?"

Dusty almost laughed at his fussing, but the expression on his face stopped her. "I promise. Every couple of hours."

"At least." Murray stopped on his way out the door. "Law enforcement is going over footage from highway cams, truck stops, satellites, toll booths, park entrances, and private ranches. Every truck driver in two provinces and three states is looking for him." He started to leave, but turned back and pointed at the dog by her side. "Take him with you tomorrow."

She opened her mouth to argue, but Murray's next statement stopped her.

"His instincts are better than ours, and he may pick up something you miss."

Dusty nodded solemnly, and stood at the door watching until she saw the lights go on in his trailer.

She stroked a hand the length of Duncan's snout and over the top of his head. "Want some supper, pal?"

His tail swished gently.

"I bet Murray already fed you, but what the heck."

Dusty found dog food in the pantry and gave him a generous portion before absently opening the fridge, and was surprised to see a carton of orange juice, a jug of milk, eggs, bread, butter, and cheese.

Chase would have left the fridge empty, knowing he was leaving for at least three or four weeks, which meant Murray must have picked up provisions for her. Nearly undone by his simple kindness, she swallowed the lump in her throat, poured a big glass of juice, and went out to the veranda. Settled on the overstuffed sofa and let her head fall back against the cushions.

Her mind wouldn't let go of the image of Chase's boots flying out a truck window as it sped through the darkness. Why wasn't he wearing them? Who threw them? And why? Was it a clue, or a red herring?

Had there been an accident? Or would someone want to do him harm?

She stared out into the blackness and wondered

what he could see or hear. Was he inside or out? She closed her eyes and tried to imagine him somewhere.

Began talking to him in her mind, assuring him she would find him somehow, begging him to give her a clue, and promising to keep searching, no matter what.

***

Chase's heartbeat pounded inside his head, slammed into the backs of his eyes, and he couldn't see anything. His mouth was desert dry, and there was something powdery under his fingertips.

He had no idea where he was or why, but his instincts were screaming at him. He needed help and needed it now.

Dusty.

***

Dusty jerked awake. Chase was calling her. She stayed very still, straining to hear his voice again.

Nothing.

She must have been dreaming.

She pressed a tiny button on her watch and the face lit up. Midnight. Three more hours to kill.

She headed for the spare room, but thinking about her previous stay in that room wasn't conducive to sleep. Not only had she been kissed brainless and then left wanting, but earlier that evening she told Chase about having sex with Mitchell.

Was she an idiot? Yes. And she nearly told him about why Peter was so done with her. What the hell had she been thinking? Hah. Thinking had gone out the window after one too many shots of tequila.

But that was past—a place she tried not to go anymore. She was all about living in the present, and she wanted her present to include Chase.

She wandered into his room, and tortured herself by holding his pillow to her face so she could inhale his familiar scent. And again she was back to the night in the spare room, remembering the steely glint in his gray eyes before that first kiss. The shock on his face when he realized she was ready to make love with him then and there wasn't a good memory. Especially because that's when he bolted.

Dusty let the pillow fall to her lap, and unshed tears blurred her vision. "How dare you disappear on me like this? I'm not done making an ass of myself yet."

Duncan shoved his nose against her hand, and the concern on his face made her feel bad. "Sorry, pal." She stroked his head, smoothing back the soft ears. "You and I are going to find him tomorrow." She blinked hard to focus on the clock. "Today. Matter of fact, we're gonna get started early. No point sitting around here if I can't sleep."

She took a shower, brewed coffee, and was pulling away from the house with Duncan riding shotgun by one-thirty.

She watched her rearview mirror until the lights came on in Murray's trailer. "We're good," she told Duncan. "He knows we've left."

Continuing her one-sided conversation, Dusty said, "I think we should take exactly the same route Chase might have. Highway five to Merritt, then west to Spences Bridge. Then we'll go south a ways, because the cops could be wrong about the northbound vehicle."

Tapping her fingertips on the steering wheel she glanced sideways. "Once we get to the truck stop, we'll about-face. Whada'ya think, Duncan?"

The dog stared at her but said not a word. Thank heavens.

Dusty continued babbling while Duncan quietly observed until they reached the place where the boots were found, and she discovered the entire tiny town was asleep. She drove south to a truck stop with a twenty-four-hour diner.

The owner was certain no horse trailers had passed the night before, and he'd already given the police the footage from his security camera outside the front door.

Dusty climbed back in her jeep and pointed north.

Four hours later, she'd quizzed every human she could find on the canyon highway. Had stopped at each town and village, and took a break after striking out in Clinton.

She was giving Duncan a bit of a walk across from the hotel when the manager—a man she'd talked to about half an hour earlier—came out the front door and waved at her. As he approached, Duncan tugged hard at the leash, and Dusty had to grab him by the collar.

The man held out a blue and brown ball cap,

and the dog lunged at him, nearly pulling her arm out of its socket. She quickly began to apologize, "I'm sorry. He's usually very well-mannered but..." The words fizzled out as she stared at the cap with a Buck Hill Ranch symbol on it. "Where?"

"Jack, my janitor, said he found it under the front steps when he got here at six this morning. He put it in the lost and found bin, but saw no need to mention it until I told him about the guy you're looking for."

Dusty reached for the cap. "It's Chase's."

"You're sure?"

"Absolutely." She held it out to Duncan, who appeared to want to suck it in through his nostrils. "Not even a hair of doubt. Could I speak with him, your janitor?"

The hotel manager nodded, and Dusty followed as far as the door, then waited outside, looking around, and wondering if Chase had stood here, or merely glanced this way in passing. Or none of the above.

When the janitor emerged from the hotel, he politely answered Dusty's questions, simply nodded when she thanked him, and then disappeared quickly.

Dusty returned to the jeep and sat with Chase's cap—and Duncan's head—resting in her lap while she updated Murray.

"You're saying it was lying there, as though tossed or placed?"

"It sounds that way, Murray. If it had fallen, it shouldn't have been under the edge of the stairs."

"Okay then, what's your plan? Highway or

back roads?"

"Back roads. Something makes me want to try the Big Bar Lake area."

"Okay, you drive up there, and I'll cover the highway from here down to that cutoff."

"Deal."

"But before you take off, do me a favor, would you?"

"Sure, what?"

"There's a small grocery store right there on the main street. Go in and get some food and water."

"You're fussing."

"Humor me. You're gonna travel some desolate country today, and the dog needs to eat and drink, even if you don't."

Dusty laughed. "Okay, okay, I'll grab supplies."

"Call me sometime, too."

"Quit nagging."

"Wouldn't have to if you'd call."

"I called."

"Yeah, that's once today. You trying to give me an ulcer?"

"Sorry. I'll call."

Dusty left Duncan in the jeep with all the windows rolled down while she walked half a block to the grocery store. She didn't want food. Wasn't the least bit hungry, and was quickly on her way back with two six packs of water, a cello-wrapped roast beef sandwich, and a bag of trail mix.

Her heart skipped when she spotted a big white SUV sporting a roof bar and the bright RCMP symbol on its door. An officer was standing on the sidewalk beside her jeep.

"Are you looking for me?"

"Yes, ma'am, assuming you're Melanie, and this is your vehicle."

"Right on both."

"Good. Apparently you have some evidence pertaining to a missing person, and I would like to retrieve it from you."

Dusty was surprised. "Chase's ball cap?"

"It's evidence, ma'am."

Dusty didn't want to part with the only bit of Chase she had right now, but also didn't feel like an argument. She needed to get back on the road.

"Fine," she said, and opened the passenger door. The cap was gone from the front seat. Looking further, she almost laughed when she spotted Duncan sprawled across the back. She quickly stifled her amusement, then turned to the officer.

"Sir," she pointed, "that is Chase's dog, and I'm absolutely not brave enough to take the cap away from him. But you're welcome to try."

The policeman leaned in, but Duncan's low growl had him backing out quickly.

"It would appear the dog has already destroyed any trace evidence, so he might as well keep it."

With great effort, Dusty managed to keep a straight face while she held out her hand to the officer. "Thank you, sir."

He gave her a steady look. "I understand you're going to search in this area today." He waited for her nod, then continued, "Please be careful to watch your gas gauge, ma'am. There are no service stations between here and the Green Lake cutoff."

"Thanks, I'll keep that in mind."

Before long she was off the highway and cruising miles and miles of dirt road. Windows down—so she wouldn't miss anything like a shout or Duncan picking up a scent—meant no A/C, and to prevent kicking up too much dust she was going dead slow.

Between her and the dog, they consumed nearly a dozen bottles of spring water, and she fed Duncan the sandwich while she nibbled on the trail mix.

Murray called her several times. She scolded him about telling the cops about the ball cap, and he laughed when he heard how she managed to hang on to it.

***

Chase dragged himself up to lean against the rough logs of what looked like an old line shack. It was stinking hot, and his head still pounded, but he needed to get his shit together. He had a goose egg on the back of his head and a dull throb in his shoulder, but the rest of him was apparently uninjured.

Where the hell he was, and why he had only socks on his feet, was a mystery, but he didn't waste energy trying to come up with an answer.

Instead, he staggered to the doorway and took a good look around, hoping to see his boots, but instead found another bottle of water. Guzzled about half of it.

EIGHT

Disappointed, and with a sick feeling of dread eating at her stomach lining, Dusty cleared the Buck Hill gates shortly after dark. She was hot, dirty, and frustrated, but all was forgotten when she crested the last low hill. Her jaw dropped and her heart shot into her throat.

Light poured from the windows. Trucks and cars were parked everywhere. Was he home? It took only seconds to grind to a stop and leap out with Duncan at her heels as she vaulted onto the porch and burst through the back door.

And froze.

The kitchen was filled with men. Strangers. Silence hung in the air like an entity, and every chair at the table was occupied by someone she didn't know. Others stood behind them. Dusty searched for a familiar face and eventually spotted Murray in a corner but before she could say anything to him, her father stepped into view.

"Gentlemen, meet my daughter Melanie—better known as Dusty." He waited a beat for effect. "Which she truly appears to be at the moment."

There was a general chuckling among them.

She didn't laugh. It was an old joke, and she wasn't feeling amused. "What's going on?"

"We're setting up an air search for tomorrow. Got everything worked out. We can handle things from here on, and you can get back to your job on the coast."

"Really?" She frowned. "And who is *we*?" Chase had been missing for nearly two days, and out of the blue, her father was taking over, planning and organizing, and shoving her aside. His mouth twisted while he chewed the inside of his cheek, and she had to shake off the odd feeling suddenly dogging her.

"Mel, these are my friends, all of them pilots with their own planes, and they've offered to help. They know how much Chase means to me."

She cast another glance around the room while he continued. "We've broken the area down into a grid, each one of these men is taking a section and they'll be organizing volunteers from their local flying clubs. Planes will be in the air tomorrow from dawn until dusk, looking for Chase and his rig."

Well, that certainly couldn't hurt.

John pointed at the maps spread over the table, and continued. "We're planning to search an area covering up to eight hours of ground travel in every direction from where Chase was last seen. Each aircraft will have a pilot and at least one spotter, preferably two.

She stared blankly at the maps with her jaw clenched. He was shoving her aside as usual. He was smarter, had more friends, money, connections. She didn't count for anything. Because she wasn't a man. Her voice wavered a bit when she asked, "Who do I go up with?"

She waited for him to say there was no room. She couldn't go with them. But he surprised her.

"Anyone you like. Pick your area."

"North of where I drove today. Maybe around Hundred Mile."

John's hand moved just a hair, and the big, gray-haired man sitting in front of him spoke. "That would be my section." Dusty flicked a glance toward Murray. Yes, he'd seen it too.

"Dusty," said John, "Meet Patrick Aden, your pilot for tomorrow."

Dusty held out her hand as the man stood and leaned across the table toward her. "Ma'am. I'm staying at your father's place tonight, and my plane is at his strip. If you could meet me there before daybreak, we can be in the air at first light."

"I'll be there."

"Gentlemen," said John. "Time to get some shut-eye."

Chairs scraped back, and when the thudding of booted feet faded away, there was nothing left but an eerie emptiness.

Mechanically, Dusty went about setting the room in order, picking up and washing all the coffee mugs, leaving them on the drain board to dry. She wiped the counters and the table, then swept the dust-covered floor. That's when she found a sheet of paper stuck under a chair leg, and when she turned it over, her gut clenched.

There was a picture of Chase beside his truck and trailer, and in big, bold letters, the word MISSING was printed across the top. She didn't read the other words. Couldn't. Dropped the paper in the middle of the table and backed away until she bumped into the wall behind her.

With her glance shooting around the room, she was hyper-aware of every detail. Dirt she'd missed under the table, water droplets clinging to the cups, light from the stove reflecting off the refrigerator door, and even her own image in the window over the sink.

The images crystalized, then blurred, and she immediately swiped at the tears. Gave herself a mental shake.

She had to face reality, and quit treating this like Chase was somehow misplaced. She'd refused to acknowledge the word *evidence* whenever she heard it, choosing not to think of the possibility of a crime.

She'd gone doggedly forward, brushing the realities aside. But the darkness of dread caught up with her, slipped under her skin and made its way to her heart.

Chase was really missing. He might have been the victim of a crime. He could, in fact, be dead and she would never...

Her own voice cut into her thoughts. "Do not even consider wallowing. He's still out there somewhere, and tomorrow we're going to find him, so get a grip."

She left the kitchen. Went through the dim hallway to the bathroom. Turned on the shower, stripped off her clothes, and climbed over the edge of the tub.

She methodically scrubbed away the dust and grime while she worked at ridding her mind of dark thoughts. When she stepped out later, squeaky clean and tingling, Dusty had found new resolve.

She toweled off quickly, gathered up her filthy clothes, went to the laundry room, and put them in to wash. Then, still damp and naked, she went back to the bathroom to clean up, rinsing dirt from the bottom of the tub, drying the shower curtain, then wiping steam from the mirror.

When she was finished, she stared at her own reflection. Stuck her fingers in the hollows between her throat and collarbone, then ran them down the middle of her chest to settle on the points at either side of her concave stomach.

"You're a bone rack," she said out loud, and, turning on her heel, she marched into Chase's bedroom, opened a drawer, helped herself to a T-shirt to cover her skinny body, and proceeded to the kitchen.

Standing in front of the open refrigerator, she shook off her desire to close the door and walk away. She needed to eat, even if she didn't feel like it. Protein. She reached for the eggs, cracked two in a mug, beat them with a fork, set the microwave at two minutes, grabbed her cell phone off the counter, stuffed her bare feet into shoes, and scurried out to the jeep.

Digging the charger from her glove box, she plugged one end into her cell and the other into the cigarette lighter. Dusty strode back into the house, stuffed the satellite phone into the charger on the counter, and opened the microwave when it began to make that annoying beeping sound. She poured herself a glass of milk and used it to wash down the eggs.

When the washer stopped, she tossed her clothes into the dryer and glanced at her watch. It was only eleven-thirty. What the hell was she going to do for the rest of the night? The obvious answer was sleep, but she didn't feel the least bit tired. She was edgy. Full of pent-up energy. Like a horse who hasn't been allowed out of the barn in days.

She wandered around the house, looking at pictures and things, and it dawned on her that the place had been decorated by Chase's ex-wife. Although much of the decor at least *reflected* his tastes, there was way too much fancy stuff, like expensively framed photographs, paintings, and even collector plates. He didn't talk about his marriage much, and Dusty began to wonder if his ex-wife would care that he was missing.

Eventually beginning to wind down, she found herself sitting on the veranda again, listening to the sounds of night, wondering if Chase could hear them too. Or if he couldn't. She jumped to her feet, refusing to dwell on negative thoughts, headed into his room, lay down on the bed, wrapped herself in his comforter, and drank in his essence. Enveloped in his scent, she could almost feel the warmth of his body.

Dusty concentrated on a future with him at the center of it, and she willed him to live through whatever was keeping him from her..

NINE

The scorching sun was almost directly overhead, and with waist-high scrub providing no shade, it was a bad time to make a move, but night would be worse, with nocturnal hunters as likely to pick him off as not.

And if he waited any longer, Chase was afraid he would keep passing out until he died in the tiny shack. No one would find him here. The only way he was going to get help was by following the dusty cow path outside.

One foot in front of the other. He concentrated on counting his steps, to prevent other thoughts from crowding his mind, and he was careful to only take tiny sips of the water—he'd found another bottle hidden under the piece of burlap where he first regained consciousness.

He trudged on until there was a second path alongside the one he was following, and it took a minute before what he was looking at actually registered. Tire tracks worn into the ground had created faint ruts. He hoped it meant he was on his way to a real road, although it would likely be gravel, and much harder on his feet.

Sweat had stopped dripping into his eyes, and that wasn't a good thing. Meant he was becoming dehydrated. Keep walking. Must keep walking. No point dying here in the middle of nowhere. Scavengers would be dining on him before he was dead, and wasn't that a grim image?

When he came to a fence, gate, and cattle guard he would have shouted in celebration if his throat hadn't been so dry he could barely swallow the last of his water. He carefully picked his way across the metal pipes of the cattle guard, because he didn't have enough strength to open the barbed wire gate, but lost his balance and suddenly found himself on hands and knees at the side of a rough road. Dizzy. Damn sun was killing him.

He contemplated crawling into the only shade around, in the ditch under the guard, but rejected the idea out of fear that he'd be hidden. And maybe there was a search plane. Better to stay in the open.

He lay beside the hot metal, with one arm hanging down into the shade, and was slipping away again, barely conscious, when an odd smell niggled at him. Burning. Flesh burning. He dragged his shirt up to cover his head and the back of his neck.

"Ya need to wake up, mister." The voice was coming from a very long way away.

Chase's eyes were too dry to open, but, as though a wish had been answered, cool water drizzled over the side of his face and the back of his head.

"Ya need to hang on, pal. Help's right here. Just hang on, fer Chrissakes."

The roar of a helicopter's rotors drowned out the rest of what he said while helicopter downwash created a swirling storm of dust, gravel, and super-heated air.

When the machine shut down, there were more voices. Then water, oxygen, and a needle stuck in the back of his hand. He knew the drill. Had been there before. Gave himself over to the pros and drifted away again.

***

Dusty was sick to death of being trapped inside the tiny cockpit. But what was the alternative? Drive around? At least in the plane they could cover more remote areas. She stared at the side of the pilot's face. He'd been silent for hours, and with the radio headset firmly covering his ears, there was no point trying to talk to him.

The helplessness and despair she managed to keep at bay up until now was slowly rising up under her skin, into her mind, insidiously pushing aside her strength, her resolve.

What if they didn't find him? What if she never saw him again?

She couldn't imagine life without Chase, because even though she'd gone years without seeing him, he'd always been there in her mind, her heart. Like a talisman she knew she could reach for when she needed support. And simply knowing he was there meant she never needed to call on him. Knowing he was on the same planet with her used to be enough, but that had changed.

Trying to get a grip on her fears, she sucked in a deep breath and let it out slowly. Chase was all she had to fall back on, to hold onto—considering the non-relationship she had with her father. She had next to no family, no religious beliefs, nothing else to count on.

Alone in the world, several thousand feet above the earth, she wondered if there was a God. More than one? Who the hell was responsible for everything? People, animals, the earth, the sky, Chase's disappearance? Was there a God of the sun? The moon? A creator? A puppeteer? Who? What?

Perhaps this was like television, and there were people watching her saying, look over there, no you're in the wrong place, hurry, maybe left, look right. No. Don't turn your back. Look out.

Or was there a deity watching her make mistake after mistake in her life?

Should she be praying right now? Or was it pointless? What if Chase was already dead? Tingling began in her fingertips and moved up her arms, colors danced and sparkled before her eyes, and a great weight lay on her chest. She couldn't get air. Couldn't breathe. Needed to move.

A prickling sensation at the back of his neck had Patrick glancing over at Dusty, and then he continued to stare. She was sitting bolt upright with her feet squarely braced. Every muscle appeared to be clenched, and her anxiety was palpable. Her left hand was clenched tightly on the safety belt release, the right was fastened on the door latch, and bone shone white through her taut skin. Her eyes, though opened wide, were vacant and unseeing.

"Dusty." He spoke firmly. Nothing changed. She appeared to be lost inside herself. His concern ramped up. "Dusty," he said with more force. But the young woman only inches away from him was apparently deaf to his voice. He banked the plane to the left, altering course and making sure she couldn't get the door open, all at the same time.

He was going to get her on the ground as quickly as possible. He'd heard stories of people completely zoning out and stepping out of a plane in midair, as though oblivious to where they were. And he wasn't going to be one of the pilots with that story to tell.

Her father warned him she was unstable. That was why the plan was worked out before she arrived last night. No matter what location she wanted to search, Patrick would announce it was his area.

Sure, he owed John, but right now all bets were off. No way he was keeping her up here any longer in the state she was in. He wasn't taking any chances. Nobody was stepping out of his aircraft until it was on the damn ground. He reached over and squeezed her knee hard. "Chase has been found. He's alive, Dusty. He's okay."

She surfaced slowly. Her gaze moving to the hand still squeezing her knee. When she looked up into his face, he let go.

"What did you say?"

"He's been found." Patrick had known for more than an hour.

She turned to stare at him. "Where?"

"I don't know, exactly."

"What do you mean? Tell me what you do know." The crazed look in her eyes was enough for Patrick. Last thing he needed was her freaking out. He tapped the side of his headset.

"I just got word. He's been found, and is being airlifted to Kamloops hospital." His orders had been to stall. Take her to Williams Lake and declare a problem with the rudder. But, far as he could figure, the best thing to do was keep her happy until he could get her out of his plane. He'd deal with John later.

He set course for Kamloops, and spoke quietly into his mic, got clearance for landing, then turned to Dusty.

"I'll have you there in fifteen minutes. Hang on, okay?"

She stared through the windscreen. "He's hurt."

"He's alive."

TEN

Pain and bright lights bombarded Chase the minute he came to. Then the sounds of an ER seeped in. The slide of cubicle curtains, the beeping of monitors.

He squinted to focus on the tall woman leaning over him. Was almost positive they'd never met.

"Are you in pain anywhere?"

Everywhere. "My head." His voice was scratchy, his throat shards-of-glass dry.

"Here, this will help." Another woman, this one wearing pink scrubs, held a cup of ice chips in his view and said, "Open up."

Not about to be hand fed, he reached for the container and discovered both his hands had IV needles stuck in the back of them, and were tied to small boards to keep his wrists from bending. Not much use to him that way.

"Uh."

The nurse winked and slipped a piece of ice between his parted lips.

"What's your name?" asked the one who seemed to be in charge.

"Chase Mathews."

"I'm Dr. Jones. Do you know what happened to you? How you got hurt?"

"Probably a horse."

Her eyebrows went up. "A horse?"

"Always a horse." At least every other time he'd landed in an ER.

"Not today," she said. "Any other ideas?"

He frowned and dug around in his foggy brain. "Gotta hint?"

"You were last seen in your truck, leaving a filling station near Kamloops after midnight on Monday." This was a new voice, and Chase cautiously tipped his head to look at a man at the foot of the bed.

He held up a badge. "Constable Dufferin. You were found a hundred and twenty-five kilometers from there, two and a half days later, without your vehicle. What do you remember?"

That made it Wednesday.

He'd been heading to Vancouver with the horses. They loaded well, and he stopped to fill up with fuel, grab a coffee and snacks.

It was a great night for driving, cool air, clear sky filled with stars, nobody on the road but him. Then...

He spoke slowly, as the scene came together in

his head. "Car flashed its lights behind me, passed, and a girl leaned out the window, pointing at my trailer like something was wrong." Chase coughed and the nurse slipped him more ice, which he sucked gratefully for a moment.

"You pulled over?"

"Yep. Grabbed my flashlight and went back to check the horses and the trailer."

"And?"

Everything was coming back. He pushed up on his elbows, and the nurse did something to raise the bed behind him, then put a hand on his shoulder and gently pushed him back against the pillows. Adjusted the wires attached to his torso.

"Tires were fine on the near side, tailgate still latched."

He frowned. "A truck. Someone pulled onto the shoulder behind me and hit his high beams— figured he was helping me by lighting up the trailer. Gave him a thumbs-up and circled my rig. Checked the tires on the off side."

He felt the impact all over again. "Something hit me."

"Hit you like what?"

"Like a brick to the back of my head, and I dropped to my knees. Then a punch to the shoulder, and I went over sideways, couldn't move, laid there half out, hearing voices. Then everything faded until I woke up."

"What were the voices saying?"

"I don't know. They were muffled, like I was underwater. But I think it was two men talking."

"What happened when you woke up?"

He told them about coming to on the dirt floor of an old line shack with nothing but a pounding headache, the clothes on his back, and a couple of bottles of water. Then he glanced at the nurse for more ice.

"I wasn't getting any better, kept passing out for hours, and I knew I needed to get moving to either find a road or water. Figured the cow path was my only hope."

"You were found unconscious, sprawled beside a cattle guard."

"I thought about crawling under it to get in the shade, but I stayed on top, hoping somebody might see me. When I woke up there was a guy yelling at me." He glanced at the cop. "What happened to my rig, my horses?"

Constable Dufferin ignored the question and spoke to the doctor instead. "Toxicology?"

"Should have results within the hour."

"Did the water bottle come in with him?"

"Not that I saw. You'd have to ask the paramedics."

The officer abruptly left the room.

Her attention back on Chase, the doctor said, "You're starting to feel better."

"Except the headache." He held up his hands. "When can I lose the IVs and get out of here?"

"I can't give you anything for the headache until I know what else is in your system. And because it appears you've been under the influence of a drug or drugs for several days, I want to see the tox report before I release you."

"Dusty's gonna kill me. I need to make a call."

"There's a pay—" She tipped her head toward the opening in the curtain. "If Dusty happens to be the very determined and intense-looking female headed this way, you won't need a phone."

Dusty marched in and stopped dead. Stared at him. Then shifted her attention to the doctor. "He's okay? Really okay?"

"He is," said the doctor, who then beat a hasty retreat.

"What the hell were you thinking?"

He had no clue what she was referring to, so did the stupid thing and asked, "When?"

"The police say you pulled over because somebody flashed their lights, but that wasn't dumb enough, you had to go and let them jump you, too. How the hell could you let a stupid thing like that happen, Chase? You *know* better dammit."

As she continued to rip into him, the words ran together in his pounding head. There was only one way to defuse this bomb. He closed his eyes, lay very still, and eventually she stopped ranting. Touched his arm.

"Chase?"

He waited, breathing as slowly as he could, until her gentle fingers touched his cheek, and there was a whisper of her breath on his face.

Careful not to club her with the board attached to his hand, he hooked an arm around the back of her neck and smiled. "Don't fight, or you'll rip out my IVs."

His mouth met hers, and he knew everything was going to be okay. His world was back on its axis because of the taste of her, the smell, and the low sound coming from her throat. Now if he could get use of his hands again.

Equally as fast as the comfort had hit, a new and unpleasant sensation washed over him, and he opened his eyes, to look right into those of her father. When Chase went still, Dusty drew back, and John slipped out of sight.

"What's wrong?"

Chase blinked. "What?"

"You look like you've seen a ghost."

"Sorry. I guess the drugs are still wearing off." He lay back against the pillows, and she turned away.

"Where are you going?"

"Murray's on his way. He's bringing you some clothes so you can get out of here as soon as they clear you."

Her voice held something odd he couldn't put his finger on.

"Can't you drive me home?"

"No." Her voice was flat. "I flew down. My wheels are parked at the Casa Mia airstrip."

"Then you'll need a ride too. Wait and go with me and Murray." The stiffness in her shoulders softened.

"Come on. Keep me company for a while. Fill me in on the missing details. What happened to my horses and rig?"

She hovered, as though torn between answering and running away. "Your rig vanished."

"The horses?"

"Haven't been seen, either."

He needed to get out there and find them. Had

101

the ambush been to steal Angel?

She hiked her chin up. "So where exactly were you found?"

"From what I remember about when they were packing me up to load in the helo, we were southeast of Clinton, near the Fraser River, I guess I was damn lucky a rancher was out doing a check on his summer range stock. Otherwise I'd be—"

"Don't even go there." Her eyes flashed anger.

He was sorry he hadn't thought before he spoke, because he understood her well enough to know the anger was hiding fear. If only he could wrap his arms around her and reassure her everything was okay.

"Hey, if you'll pull out these needles and untie me, we could blow this pop stand." The bags were nearly empty.

"Ha, and we'd have to leave here on foot, or call a cab, I guess." She was running her hand up and down her arm. "Do you have any idea how scared I was?"

Oh shit. Don't cry. Not now. Not with her father lurking in the corridor.

"Yeah. Sorry. Do the cops have any idea if I was targeted, or if it was random?"

She sighed. "No, but the one I passed on my way in looked excited about something, so maybe they have a lead." She half-laughed. "Or he was going off shift."

"He and the doctor are convinced I was drugged."

"Really?"

"I'll tell you the whole story, or at least what I

know, later."

"Why wait?"

Because it was neither the time nor the place, and he wanted to let everything simmer for a bit before he started drawing conclusions. He tipped his chin toward the hallway. "Murray's here with my stuff."

Without a word, she left him, only stopping to say to Murray, "I'll be right back. Do me a favor and don't let him disappear.

ELEVEN

Dusty returned about half an hour later to find
Chase sitting on the side of the bed, dressed and
looking rather pale. She dropped her purchases on
the chair. "Where's Murray?"

"Caught a ride back to the ranch to feed and
water, left us the truck." Chase held up the keys.
"I'm not allowed behind the wheel until tomorrow
so you'll have to drive me home." He slid off the
bed, but stayed leaning against it.

"You okay?"

"Sure."

Dusty stayed close to him as they left the
building, and halfway across the parking lot she
slipped an arm around his waist. He stopped to stare
at her. "I'm fine on my own."

"You were staggering."

He jerked away from her. "Like hell." She
followed as he wove his way between cars, leaning
on them for support, and when she spotted the truck

she scooted past him, unlocked the door, and pulled it open.

"Dusty, stop.

"All I did was open the freaking door."

"I can feel you watching, hovering. I'm fine. I can walk on my own, and I can sure as hell open a door without your help."

Dusty wanted to tear a strip off him, but grimly clamped her jaw, telling herself he wasn't well and hadn't eaten in days. Back when he was a rider trying to keep his weight down, lack of food had made him one miserable bastard. Counting to ten, and then twenty, she circled the truck and climbed in.

She turned right leaving the parking lot, and was amazed he let her go a couple of blocks before commenting.

"Where the hell are you going?"

"A quick detour. I'm freaking starving, okay?" Sure, she was lying, but no way was she giving him more ammunition. She knew what she was like when she needed food, and as she approached the drive-thru window, she asked, "Any preference, or do you want me to order?"

"I'm not hungry." He sounded like a sulky ten-year-old, and it lit her fuse.

"Oh, for fuck's sake. You haven't eaten in about three days. If you put some food in your belly, you'll not only feel better, but it might even improve your personality."

Jaw clenched, face still ashen, he glared out the side window. Was he seeing the fading colors of the sunset? Or the earliest stars starting to show in the now-purple sky? Not likely.

"You order."

Tense minutes later, driving away from the bright lights, she passed him a large chocolate milkshake. "Burger and fries in the bag if you want them." She unwrapped a burger for herself and forced it down because she knew she needed it.

Chase savored the icy liquid as it coated his raspy throat, and before long the tight knot in his gut began to ease, and the pressure in his head lightened. He stayed silent and enjoyed watching Dusty drive. Even though she was tiny, and had her seat shoved as far forward as it would go, she drove with authority, the same way she rode.

"Quit staring at me like I'm a bug or something."

"Oh, you're a bug, all right. Pesky one, too."

"Sounds like you're feeling better." He heard the smugness in her voice, but let it go, deciding to change the subject instead.

"Murray filled me in some, and I figure it's highly unlikely Angel and Jake are still in the trailer wherever it is, so searching for it's pointless. If the horses were the target, they'd have been transferred to an unrecognizable rig. And if the truck and trailer were the target, the horses would have been dumped somewhere." He dug the burger out of the bag.

"Which option do you think?"

He wasn't usually a big fan of fast food, but the burger was going down damn easy. "Most likely they were after the rig."

"Why?"

"Crooks all over the country need transportation

for stolen property. And there's been a rash of horse trailer thefts from the racetrack grounds in the past couple of months." He grimaced. "That's why I've been keeping mine at home."

"Ouch. You think the horses were dumped, like a collateral damage kinda deal."

"Yup." He balled up the foil wrapper and stuffed it in the bag after he dug out the fries.

"Since they left clues to help us find you, I wonder if maybe they left a trail to the horses too?"

"Not likely. I think they were just covering their butts by making sure I was found. If you're only stealing rigs, why go up for murder? And if they needed to buy time to change the look of the rig, or get across the border or something, they couldn't just leave me on the side of the road."

"Two days is a long time."

"Exactly. By now the trailer's been painted, maybe modified for smuggling, and hooked up to a different truck. My truck could be in a shipping container headed for anywhere."

Dusty was frowning. "Okay, so if we're only looking for the horses, where do we start?"

"We?"

"We." She kept her eyes on the road, and he wiped salt from his fingers while he thought about how to get around her.

John's words were fresh in his mind. *"You'd be nothing but one more half-breed in a gutter somewhere if I hadn't taken you in. You owe me. You made me a promise, and I'm holding you to it."*

He stared out the side window. "You have better things to do. You know, horses to work, races to win, people depending on you to show up every day. You can't afford to be traipsing around the countryside looking for my horses."

She took a deep breath and let it out slowly. "Angel and Jake may be yours, but they're important to me too, dammit. And because I haven't taken a single day off since April, my agent will cut me some slack so I can help you search."

"You've been up here every Monday." They'd slipped into a routine he loved, even though he knew he shouldn't go there.

"The track's closed on Mondays, but I shedrow two horses early, before I head up here."

His jaw was set. "You still can't waste—"

"For crying out loud, Chase, would you please let me do this? I am not a stupid kid anymore, and I happen to know how to manage my own career just fine, thank you very much."

"Ouch."

"Well, you asked for it."

"What day of the week is this?"

"Wednesday," she spat through gritted teeth.

"Fine, then *we* can spend the whole day tomorrow combing the back country. And on Friday morning you can drive me to Vancouver."

"What for?"

"I need to talk to a friend of mine. A private investigator."

"Oh."

"That's it? Oh?"

"Not much more to say." But she didn't look happy.

"I also need a new vehicle."

When they reached the ranch, an ecstatic Duncan raced alongside the truck, and jumped right in when the door was opened. Pinned to the seat and laughing, Chase waited for the dog to settle down before giving him a shove, then heading for the house.

Everything was fine until he spotted the poster and reality slammed into him.

Dusty touched his arm. "My father had them made, and he called out his pilot friends for an air search today. There were several dozen planes in the sky at first light, and John supplied most of the fuel."

John. Without a word, Chase put the paper down and walked away.

As soon as Dusty heard the shower, she retrieved the T-shirt she'd been using as a nightie, then retreated to the spare room and pushed the door almost closed, but not quite.

Mostly awake since three-thirty Monday morning, she was done. Had nothing left. Fighting with him or worrying would have to wait until tomorrow. She climbed under the comforter and willed every muscle in her body to relax.

But sleep wouldn't come, and she found herself listening intently when Chase emerged from the bathroom and prowled the house. She held her breath while he stood outside her door for too long before going to his own room. Then, through the thin walls, she heard the bed creak under his weight.

Duncan, taking up position outside Chase's door, landed with a heavy thump and groan that made her smile.

Thin bars of light on the clock showed the passing of minutes while she replayed the last part of the day, trying to figure out why Chase had first kissed her like he meant it, then acted like it was no big deal.

He was right into her staying with him before she left—and Murray arrived—but when she got back, he was different. Distant. He really didn't want her with him on the search tomorrow. Would he try to sneak off without her? Hell, yeah.

She sat up. He'd probably take off tonight, as soon as he was certain she was asleep. No way she was going to let that happen. No freaking way was he going to be out there again while she cooled her heels, wondering if he was still alive.

She slipped from her bed and tiptoed to where Duncan was sprawled at his master's doorway. She crouched to stroke the dog's head, then sat down on the floor with him and leaned against the wall. Chase would have to stumble over both of them to get out.

After a while, the discomfort of the wooden floor began to get to her. Thinking she could lie down and sleep alongside Duncan, she contemplated retrieving the comforter from her bed. Then again, the dog had the doorway covered and didn't seem to need her help.

Dusty wandered out to the veranda to stare at Murray's truck. She could hide the keys Chase left in it, but there would be spares somewhere. She curled up on the sofa, and certain he couldn't get to the truck without waking her up, she laid her head down, closed her eyes, and slipped into a light, dreamless sleep.

The squeaking door hinges woke her just before the sound of his feet on the floorboards completed the alert.

"Dusty?" He sounded concerned.

"Over here."

He pushed her legs over and sat, leaning over her with his arm stretched along the upholstered back.

"What are you doing out here?" His voice was soft.

"Sleeping."

"Why?"

"I dunno." How lame.

"Not like you to lie."

She stared through the darkness, trying to make out the expression on his face. Sighed and said, "I was afraid you would try to leave without me."

"Why would I do that after I told you we'd search together?" His voice was flat, sort of.

She swallowed hard. "You went all distant and cold tonight. I felt shut out. I thought you wanted to get rid of me."

Chase turned and leaned back against the sofa. And even though she felt his warmth against her legs, there was an unmistakable coolness coming from him.

"You're doing it again. What's wrong?"

He stayed silent, but took her hand, gently rubbing his thumb across her knuckles, making her afraid of what he might be going to say.

He shook his head. "Not here, not now. Tomorrow we'll have hours and hours for talking, and I promise I won't run out on you."

She didn't say anything, but he kept hold of her hand when he got up, and pulled her to her feet. "You obviously don't trust me. Come on." He led her to his room, shoved her under the covers and crawled in beside her. "Turn over," he said. And when her back was to him, he slid his arm across her waist to pull her in tight.

"Chase?"

"Go to sleep, Dusty. I promise not to leave you."

She closed her eyes, hugged his arm against her, and stayed very still for a long time after Chase's breathing deepened with sleep. Only then did she let herself drift off, refusing to think about what tomorrow would bring.

TWELVE

When Dusty woke alone, her first thought was that he'd taken off on her. But her senses came alive to the smell of bacon and the distant murmur of voices, and she relaxed. He'd promised hadn't he?

She still hurried, just in case. And in less than ten minutes, emerged, showered and fresh in the new shorts and tank top she bought in Kamloops the day before. She looked in the mirror and grinned. Black really was her color.

She found Chase outside with Murray, who was about to get into his truck. "Morning, men."

Chase's smile made her heart flutter. "Hey there, sleepyhead."

"Mornin'," said Murray. "You two stay safe out there today."

"Sure you don't want breakfast?" asked Chase. "It's almost ready. I just have to throw some eggs in the pan."

Murray held up his insulated coffee cup and

shook his head. "Thanks, but this'll do. It'll take me about twenty-five, maybe thirty minutes to shut down the sprinklers in the southeast pasture, then I'll be back to take you to Casa Mia for Dusty's wheels."

Duncan whined, and Chase looked down at him. "Oh, for heaven's sake, go. Hang on, Murray, Duncan's coming with you."

The happy dog hopped inside, obviously satisfied all was well again in his world, and ready to get back to the daily routine.

Dusty headed back inside. "Do you want scrambled or fried?"

Chase's arms slipped around her, held her still. "What I want," his voice was low, "is you."

Slowly, she turned and his hands locked at the small of her back, holding her trapped against him.

Her eyes never wavered from his as his mouth descended, feather light and teasing, silently daring her to respond, and Dusty's answer was to change the pace. Her lips parted hungrily, her body leaned into his, and they were ever so briefly lost together, tasting, reaching, burning. Releasing pent-up fear, anger, and frustration. Her body yearned for release, but she wanted more. Much, much more than sex. She tore her mouth away, and Chase's arms tightened.

She leaned her forehead against his shoulder, with her hands pressed against the taut muscles of his chest, and she could feel his heart pounding.

"Why? Why, exactly, did you wait until now?"

He chuckled, his mouth almost touching her ear, his warm breath caressing delicate skin. "Last night I just wasn't up to the possibilities."

She didn't move. "Meaning?"

"Meaning I wasn't up for rejection if you slapped me away. And on the flip side..." His lips found a sensitive spot on the side of her neck. "I really needed sleep."

By leaning back against the hold of his arms, she could watch his eyes while effectively increasing the pressure of her hips against his. She grinned slowly when his gray eyes darkened, then she swayed ever so slightly. "And now you think you're safe because Murray will be back very soon?"

His hands slid down to hold her hard against his obvious desire. "Don't throw out a challenge you don't intend to follow through with."

She pinned him with a look. "Do not, for one instant, doubt my intentions," she said, as she undid the snap of his jeans and slid her fingertips inside the waistband. "I am more than happy to take you to your knees, right here, right now." She watched his face, trying to decide how far she could push. She was dying to climb inside those jeans with him.

She tipped her head to the side with a smile. "But I think you're expecting that." She slid her hands behind his head and pulled him down toward her waiting mouth. Stretching up to the tips of her toes, she kissed him with everything she had, her entire body moving seductively against his until she almost reached the point of no return.

That's when she put her elbows against his chest and pushed herself free. Took a long, shaky breath, and walked to the stove. "The question," she took a breath, "was…scrambled, or fried?"

She held an egg above the edge of the pan but kept her face hidden.

"Definitely scrambled," he muttered, and she heard his boots clomp away down the hall.

She clenched her fist until egg, shell and contents dripped into the pan together, and she leaned heavily against the stove, waiting for her pounding heart to slow to a more natural rhythm.

***

They spent the morning driving south on an old highway parallel to Chase's route, and stopped at dozens of farms and ranches along the way. But no one they spoke with had seen anything to suggest Chase's rig and or horses had come this way.

When they reached the town where three highways intersected, Chase glanced over at Dusty. "You hungry?"

"Very funny. That breakfast I shoveled in was more than a full day's worth of calories. And I have to ride tomorrow night."

"I seriously doubt you'll have to worry about your weight this weekend. You'll probably have to pack lead."

He was right. It had been a knee-jerk reaction. She'd lost weight over the past few days, which made this a perfect opportunity to throw caution to the wind. No point adding a bunch of lead inserts to a saddle pad if you could eat instead. "I'll have ice cream."

After stopping at a drive-thru, they opted for the

smaller, less traveled highway, one that would take them to where his boots were found.

Dusty waited until he finished his chicken and fries before asking, "Why did you go cold on me last night? *Truthfully.*"

He glanced sideways and took a deep breath. "I'd rather not—"

"You promised to talk to me today, and I see no escape routes available. Guess you might as well get on with it."

She could almost see the wheels turning in his head before he cleared his throat. "I am going to say this in one go, okay?"

"Okay."

"No interrupting or arguing, no matter what."

Chase nearly laughed when she made the childish motions of crossing her heart and zipping her lips. But he quickly sobered and began the story he'd invented while lying awake half the night.

"When I woke up in that shack, my first concern was about you being pissed because I didn't show up in Vancouver, then it sunk in how worried you'd be about me and the horses. Then I drank a bunch of the drugged water and passed out—yes, before I left the hospital, the doc let me know what was found in my system. Not important details at the moment."

He glanced in the rearview mirror, slowed down, and pulled over as far as he could to let a big truck get past. The guy was obviously in a way bigger hurry than they were.

"The next time I woke up, my only concern was me. And from that moment forward, my entire focus, every thought and feeling was about finding my way back from wherever I was. *My* thirst, *my* discomfort, *my* sore feet, *my* headache, *my*, need to survive." He glanced over, but couldn't read her expression. Couldn't tell if he was getting his point across.

"I was focused entirely on myself. I didn't think about what you would be going through, at least not until your dad filled me in on everything that happened after I didn't turn up that morning.

"He was worried, because you completely immersed yourself in the search, and didn't seem concerned about your job, your commitments. He was afraid you were too involved. Warned me to be careful with you. Pointed out how traumatic situations led to behavior that would otherwise be unacceptable, and how easily friendship could be ruined by a spontaneous crossing of the line.

"I knew he was right. We're family, Dusty, and I don't ever want to wreck that."

His lunch sat like a lead weight in his belly, but he had to finish, had to get it said. "I'm sorry I was such a jerk when we left the hospital. Pain, hunger, and self-pity were no excuse, and by the time we got to the ranch, all I wanted to do was put my arms around you, kiss you, and tell you how much you mean to me. But when we walked in, I saw the poster, and it reminded me of everything your dad said earlier. I had no choice but to walk away."

He should have kept walking. But during the night he also decided he owed John nothing.

Dusty's eyes were closed, and her head rested against the back of the seat. Chase waited for her to say something.

"My turn." Her voice was soft. "Yesterday morning, at sunrise, I climbed into a small plane with a man I had only met the night before. I trusted a total stranger with my life, because my only concern was finding you." She braced her feet on the dashboard.

"Halfway through the day, it hit me that there was a chance you'd never be found, and I started to have a panic attack. I tried to distract myself, but it was hard. With the pilot wearing a headset, and not appearing interested in conversation, I had only myself to talk to, and the running monologue worked for a while. But as soon as I let up, the despair I'd been feeling in my heart crept into my mind, and I wanted to jump out the window of the plane so I wouldn't have to face living without you."

His heart skipped a beat.

"In the end, to fight the panic, I did something I've never done before. I prayed. The voice inside my head frantically begged for someone, a god, any god to listen. I told them you were a good man, and far too young to die. I said I needed you, and didn't want to live without you, and soon enough, I began making promises, trying to cut a deal with higher powers."

She opened her eyes and stared at him. "I promised if I ever got a chance to talk to you again, face to face, I would throw caution to the wind and be honest. Tell you how much you mean to me."

Shit. "They won't hold you to it."

"Sorry, cowboy, you're gonna have to listen,

like it or not. But you can relax. This is about *my* conscience and *my* feelings. You are *not* required to respond."

His hands tightened on the steering wheel when she continued.

"For the past few months, I've lived for Mondays. Three hours on the road never seemed like a big deal, because I got to see you and Angel. Yes, much of it revolved around Angel and the work we were doing with her. It was incredible to experience her progress. To sit on her in the starting gate and feel her muscles tense, not in fear, but in preparation to launch out of there when the doors opened.

"When we went riding in the mountains, it was amazing to feel her confidence grow steadily in a completely foreign environment. I always went home happy, and I counted the days until I could be with you again, talking, and laughing, and simply being myself."

Dusty's stomach muscles tightened. It was time to get on with it. Fess up. "I was so busy living in the moment, I hadn't paid much mind to the way my feelings for you had changed." Oh, how she wanted to reach out and touch him, but what if he pulled away?

"You've become a very important part of my life, and this has nothing to do with the shallowness of hero worship, or childhood crushes. There is something deep and endless about how I feel. And the thought of never seeing you again made my throat close and my heart ache. I realized I didn't want to live without you."

She hadn't noticed the Jeep slowing, and was startled when Chase pulled off the road and stopped. He carefully set the parking brake before he turned to her with a serious expression she couldn't interpret.

He took her face in his hands, and placed his lips softly on hers in a kiss filled with gentle emotions, and tears stung the backs of her eyes even before he drew away.

His gaze locked on hers. "Dusty I..." He hesitated. "I think the torture we both went through in the last few days has been rewarded by a deepening of our friendship that transcends what we had in the past." He gave her a quick, hard kiss, turned his attention back to the vehicle and pulled onto the road.

The words, ones he'd obviously rehearsed, hung like a presence in the air while Dusty silently stared out the window on her side.

Right when she'd been certain he was about to declare that he loved her, someone else's voice came out of his mouth, said words that weren't his. Did she feel cheated? Brushed off? Oh yeah. But there was a whole hell of a lot more.

***

It was full dark when they arrived back at Buck Hill. Duncan loped over to greet them enthusiastically, then trotted happily back to Murray's trailer.

"He's certainly gotten over your disappearance."

"And happy to have his life back in order."

"He barely left my side while you were gone. He even slept next to the bed."

"He knew you shouldn't be alone. But I guess now he's good with me looking after you." He was walking behind her with his hand gently resting at the nape of her neck.

"I didn't realize you were guard dog material."

His fingers tightened for a second, and then dropped away when they entered the house.

"You feel like a brandy?" he asked.

"Sure."

Chase reached high in a cupboard for snifters, tucked the bottle under his arm, and led her to the veranda.

They sat in the darkness, quietly savoring the golden liquid for a while before Dusty finally spoke. "You know, as a kid, at night, after you'd bring me back from the bunkhouse, I used to sneak out and sit on the porch for hours. It was easy, with John away so much, and I loved the sound of night in the country. I miss it in town. The subtle things are drowned out by traffic and the ocean."

She shook her head. "Don't get me wrong. I've learned to love falling asleep to the rhythm of the waves, but it's not the same. There's something incredibly peaceful here in the mountains."

Chase's voice was quiet, "And yet some people find it downright boring."

Dusty tried to read his expression, but couldn't in the dark. She'd never met his ex-wife, didn't know much about her. "Chelsey?"

"Good guess."

"Is that why your marriage didn't work?"

"One of many reasons."

"What else?"

"We were kids. Too young to understand what we wanted, needed."

"How did you meet?"

"Her parents were wealthy racehorse owners. When I won the local Derby on one of their horses, they threw a big celebration party at their home. I met Chelsey, we hit it off right away, and it mushroomed from there. We had a lot of fun together. She introduced me to the richer side of life, and I showed her the simplicity of country living. She loved the animals."

"You had this place already?"

"I bought the property and put up one barn a year before she and I met. My home was the trailer Murray lives in now, and Chelsey thought it was a great adventure, coming here with me."

"So she liked it."

"In the beginning."

Dusty waited.

"Her parents bought this house as a wedding present for us."

"I thought you built it."

"I did, but they paid for all the materials, inside and out. They didn't want their daughter living in a trailer."

"Oh."

"It wasn't that they were snobbish. They were nice, and kind, and decent, and over the moon that Chelsey was away from the wild, rich crowd she'd been hanging with. They thought it was more likely she'd stay, and be happy with ranch life, if she had a nice house to live in."

"But it didn't work?"

"It did for a while. She loved the planning and the decorating, but she really missed being surrounded by people, and started to hate living in the middle of nowhere."

"How long did it last?"

"Nearly two years." He swirled the brandy in his glass. "It was a very cold, nasty winter, and when her parents asked us to spend Christmas with them at their place in the Caribbean, I told her to go, even though I couldn't get away—I had horses to look after."

"And that was the breaking point?"

"She met Cameron, nephew of one of her dad's business partners."

Dusty tucked her feet up under her. "He was rich."

"Mostly he had the kind of lifestyle Chelsey wanted. Needed. Lots of traveling and partying. No dirty stalls, or husband that smelled like a horse when he climbed into bed at night."

He stared off into the darkness. "Her parents felt bad about introducing her to Cameron, and blamed themselves for the breakup of our marriage. When I got the divorce papers, I was surprised to see their lawyers had made sure she walked out of our life with nothing. I tried to pay back the house money, but was told that it was their gift to me. Like I said, they were nice, kind people."

"So she left on vacation and never came back."

"Yup."

"Were you devastated?"

"I was mostly relieved, because I knew how unhappy she was here. We'd run out of fun. Kind of like growing up and finding out sometimes life sucks."

"Is she still with Cameron?"

"Last I heard."

Dusty was lost in thought for a while, until Chase's voice brought her back to the present. "We should get some sleep." He tugged her to her feet and, still holding onto her hand, silently led the way to his bedroom.

"Chase?"

"I said *sleep*, Dusty." He reached into a drawer, grabbed a T-shirt, and tossed it to her.

Deciding not to push, she went to the far side of the bed, shed her clothes, put on the T-shirt, slipped under the covers, and turned her back to him.

Chase got in from his side and moved toward her. She waited. He slipped his arm over her waist, pulled her against him, then kissed the back of her neck.

"Chase?"

He didn't answer but his lips continued to make her skin tingle.

Dusty couldn't take it any longer. Rolled over to face him. "I thought—"

His mouth extinguished the rest of her sentence, and she gave in to the pounding of her heart. Her lips parted and a soft moan slipped out. His hands moved under the shirt, and heat rose, quickly stripping away any need for conscious thought.

Lost in sensation she arched against him, and he

abruptly broke away. Swung his legs over the side of the bed. "Dusty I'm sorry... I didn't mean to..."

"Don't you dare apologize. I want you as much as you want me, and there's not a damn thing wrong with that." She danced her fingertips across his shoulders.

"Wanting isn't enough, Dusty."

Oh, for heaven's sake, was he for real? "Last I looked, we were both over the age of consent." She slid closer to taste the smooth, bronze skin of his back. "We've got chemistry, why not enjoy it?"

"We have to be very, very certain." There was something odd in his voice. "We can't rush into what's happening between us."

"You're not into casual, mind-boggling sex?"

"Not with you."

She teased the back of his neck with a couple of less than gentle bites. "I'll take that as a compliment for now. Do you want me to sleep in the other room?"

"No. But I think I'll take a quick shower. Do me a favor and go to sleep, would ya?"

She flopped back onto his pillow. "Okay." She hesitated. "Are you really going to take a cold shower?"

"Yes, why?" He sounded a little exasperated.

"Want company?"

When he turned and found her grinning at him, he kissed her hard. "You stay put, dammit." And he left her there.

She smothered something between a laugh and a sigh, then rolled over, making certain she was on her own side of the bed, and pretended to be asleep when he came back. But she nearly sighed out loud when his fresh, clean scent settled over her like a summer cloud.

THIRTEEN

Chase was at the stove with his back to her, and she couldn't resist sneaking up behind him to slip her arms around his waist.

He jumped. "Don't do that."

"A little touchy this morning," she said, stepping back and grinning when he turned around.

He laughed. "Are you always this sure of yourself?"

"Yup."

"How about a dose of your own medicine?" He crowded her until she was effectively trapped between him and the cabinets. He teased her lips with his for a second before sinking in to kiss her properly, and she got enough buttons undone to slip her hands inside his shirt before he drew back.

"Don't run away now, cowboy," she said with a laugh. "I'm just getting started."

His exaggerated, stern look dissolved into something she couldn't interpret. "Breakfast is ready."

"Coward."

"We have a long day ahead of us. And I'm guessing you won't eat much past noon if you have mounts tonight."

"Always the wise one."

Breakfast conversation was full of teasing and laughter. Senseless chatter for the most part, but then her world paused on its axis—like she'd been hit with a brick—and in that instant she knew. Chase was the man she would love forever…no matter what.

***

Arriving in Vancouver about four hours later, Dusty left him at the investigator's office and drove home to the boathouse. Because she didn't have to be at the track for several hours, she spent the afternoon studying past performance charts and planning strategies for the races she'd ride that night. She had three mounts on the card and, according to the handicappers, two of them were live.

Just as she was arriving in the Jocks' Room at the track, she got a call from Chase. He couldn't get delivery of his new truck until morning. Dusty struggled not to sound excited while she did a little happy dance. "Well I guess you'll have to stay over with me, then. I've got a really comfy sofa."

"What races do you ride?"

"Third, fifth and eighth."

"I'll meet you after the eighth to catch a lift."

"See ya then." She only allowed herself a tiny fist pump, then focused on the here and now. She had horses to concentrate on, her own mounts, and the others in the fields. Race riding was dangerous, and being distracted while she was out there would be stupid.

Her attention to detail paid off, and she won with the two favorites. Better yet, her last mount—a long shot—paid sixty-two dollars to place, and she was in a great mood, walking down the outside fence, already pulling off her silks, when she heard Chase call out to her.

She couldn't resist. Ducked under the guardrail, leaned over the four-foot chain link, fence and planted a delighted kiss on him.

He was laughing as he wiped away some of the racetrack sand she left on his face.

"Meet you at the jeep in ten," she said, and headed for the showers.

***

They picked up Chinese food and sat outside on her deck to eat. The evening was warm, and waves lapped gently against the rocks while Chase told her about the meeting with Tyler, his PI friend. His company was printing handbills, offering a ten-thousand-dollar reward for the safe return of the horses, and Chase was going to plaster every bar, gas station, tack shop, riding center, and corner store in the entire province with them, hoping someone would come forward with information.

Meanwhile, Tyler had some black ops-type

connections in the US who would be accessing video footage from secret sources. If the rig or the horses had crossed into the states, they'd find them.

"With Tyler on the job, there's really little else for us to do."

"Okay." She'd still make her once-a-week trips to visit him, and they could take drives to search, just in case.

"And as for my new truck, it will be ready for me by nine."

"You're leaving then?"

"I'll be on the highway before ten if everything goes well."

"And will you be telling anyone the route you're taking, in case you disappear again?"

"Don't be silly. That was a once-in-a-lifetime event."

"Almost." Her voice was quiet.

Chase frowned. "I promise not to get lost or anything."

Dusty stood up and took his hand. "Come on, it's time to turn in."

Chase followed her into the cottage, but halfway to the bedroom he stopped, and when she tugged on his arm, he pulled her back against him. Kissed her gently, and she wrapped her arms tightly around his middle.

"Dusty, I have to sleep on the couch."

"Have to?"

"I don't trust myself."

Oh, for crying out loud. She jerked away.

This was starting to feel like some kind of weird game, and she didn't like it. No, she didn't *need* sex. But it was a natural progression, and his argument for waiting didn't feel genuine.

"This is getting old, Chase, and I'm starting to think you don't care about me the way I thought you did."

She didn't like the darkness in his expression when he said, "I care—too much, dammit. And Lord love it, I want you. But I just don't—"

"Want to ruin our fucking friendship. I call bullshit, Chase. Bull. Shit." She marched into the bedroom, grabbed the door with both hands, and barely caught herself before she slammed it hard enough to make the walls shudder. Instead, it closed with a soft, and very final, *click*.

Dusty threw herself on the bed and pounded the mattress with her fists. Damn him. Damn him for tricking her again. She stripped off her clothes and stood at the window, letting the night air caress her skin, wishing it was his hands, his mouth. *Stop it. Just stop.*

She dragged a long tank over her head and leaned against the window frame to watch the twinkling lights of the ships at anchor.

An hour passed. An hour of her life she'd never get back. Wasted. With wanting, with waiting for something she felt was inevitable.

Finally, fed up with her inner struggle, she went out to sit beside Chase on the couch. She turned on the table lamp, but his eyes stayed closed.

"Are you awake?"

"What do you think?"

"Okay, this is freakin' ridiculous, Chase. I don't do games, and I won't play along with you anymore."

"I'm not playing games with you, Dusty."

"Then what the hell are you doing?"

"I'm just—"

"No." She stopped him before he could begin to explain, because she could tell by the sound of his voice, he was going to dish out more of the same crap she'd already heard. "Did you hear anything I said to you yesterday? I mean the part about nearly not having a second chance?"

"I did."

"Then I don't get it. We're not children, not even teenagers. We are consenting adults who have an incredibly strong bond, and enough chemistry to blow up a building, and neither of us can probably remember virginity. I happen to be disease-free, and I would hazard a guess you are too. I'm on the pill, but have condoms if you want one."

He threw back his head and laughed. "Do you realize what a reversal of form this is? Your entire argument sounds like something a guy says to a girl he's trying to get into bed."

She shook her head and took a deep breath. "Chase, it's sex, not brain surgery. We'll both feel better afterward."

"You're sure about that?"

"Oh, come on. The relief factor alone…"

"I'm damn sure you can get relief without me."

"Sure, like that's what I'm talking about." She rolled her eyes. "I spent the last hour thinking about the age-old question, *what if*. And I know, it's not usually worth pursuing, but humor me, and think about it for a minute. *What if* you disappear again tomorrow? *What if* you get run over by a bus, or I go down in a spill and spend the rest of my life in a wheelchair, or the earth opens up and swallows us?"

"Dusty—"

"Don't interrupt. What if this is our one and only chance to be together? Are you willing to walk away from that? Too often I've heard people say, 'if I had only known, I'd have taken the time to live more fully.' Or, 'life is not a dress rehearsal.' And it's true, Chase. I have deep and overwhelming feelings for you that go way beyond the hero worship of my childhood. Or lust. I want to make love with you tonight."

When something flickered in his eyes, she added quickly, "But if that's too scary, cowboy, how about we just have hot, wild, jungle sex?" She gently touched his face. "And tomorrow can damn well wait until we're ready for it."

He held up his hands. "Okay, I give. Storying you hasn't done any good, I guess it's time for the truth."

"Well, glory hallelujah, let the birds sing and the banners fly."

Chase cleared his throat. "When I first met your dad, I was at the track walking hots and shoveling shit for meal tickets, sleeping in tack rooms, feed rooms, and the occasional stall. My grandfather had died, and I had no one to look out for me. Well, I did sort of, but it wasn't a good fit."

"How old were you?"

"Twelve, but I lied and said I was fourteen. Your dad offered me a job on his ranch, and I snapped it up. For room and board, I was willing to work dawn till dusk."

"What about school?"

He shrugged. "Never went once I was off the reservation. Anyway, John apparently noticed when you started following me around, and he freaked out. Read me the riot act. Informed me you were not only off limits, but I was to protect you from anyone and everyone else. Your father made it very clear he'd drawn a line, and I was to never step across it, no matter how hard you tried to entice me."

"I'm not a child anymore."

"But you're still enticing me."

She shot him a sizzling look and he continued, "A couple of months ago, when he found out you were coming to Kamloops to exercise Angel, he cornered me for another lecture. Said you were too vulnerable. You were lonely in Vancouver, and if I encouraged you too much, I'd break your heart."

She sputtered, and he shook his head.

"I assured your father I care about you and would never hurt you. I even admitted my feelings had matured to the point where I hoped we'd have a future together."

Her heart thudded.

Chase could still see the older man's face turning purple with rage. "He was furious, incensed. Ranted that you were strictly off-limits, no matter what. Then this week, after my, uh, escape from the mountains, I was determined to tell you how I felt. But John showed up at the hospital and confronted me yet again, adding in that we were nearly brother and sister."

"That's sick."

He'd thought the same thing, but he'd been taught to respect his elders.

"I can't believe you gave in and made up that whole pile of crap you dished out to me."

"I didn't know what else to do." How was he supposed to admit he was being browbeaten by her father—the only family she had?

"If you'd told me the truth, I could have explained why I was such an emotional mess when I came home. The reason Peter kicked me out. Something even John doesn't know about."

"Tell me."

She backed into the corner of the couch, and tucked her feet up under her. "Bear with me, okay? I've never said this out loud before, so it's not easy."

She stared at her hands, and sorrow clouded her face. He caught himself when he was about to tell her to stop. She must need to tell it, otherwise she wouldn't.

"In December, I found out I was pregnant, and was ecstatic. But Peter's reaction stunned me. He was livid. Accused me of trying to trap him into a life he didn't want, and gave me an ultimatum. Get an abortion, or get out of his life. I was shocked, devastated. I begged and pleaded with him to reconsider.

"I told him I couldn't imagine a life without children, but he didn't budge. He was enraged. Grabbed our plane tickets off the bureau—we were supposed to leave for his island house the next weekend—and said he was going early. He tossed mine on the bed, and told me I could use it if I got rid of the baby. Otherwise, I had three weeks to vacate the house. Period. No alternatives. No argument."

"And?" His heart hurt just thinking about what she'd faced then.

"I cried for a while, then I did what I had to do. What I'd been doing for two years. Whatever it took to keep Peter happy, so he wouldn't stop loving me." She wrapped her arms around her middle.

"I made an appointment, and wouldn't let myself think about what I was doing. I arrived early, and had to sit in the waiting room for nearly an hour after I filled out the paperwork and had a consult with the counselor. When the receptionist called my name, I couldn't move, asked for a few minutes more.

"But the minutes stretched on, and she came to sit beside me, told me it was okay to change my mind, or take a few days to think about it, because I was only a few weeks along."

She sighed. "I left, walked around for hours, and a cop picked me up on the outskirts of town in the middle of the night. He thought I was drunk at first, then asked who I was running away from." Dusty half laughed. "I told him no one was chasing me, no one wanted me, my car had broken down, and I was lost. He gave up trying to get me to talk, and eventually drove me home.

"I didn't sleep for a couple of days. Wandered around the house crying, wondering how I had gotten myself into such a mess. And then I saw blood on the floor.

"At first I was confused. I checked my hands for cuts, looked in the mirror to see if I had scratched my face. Then, I saw the blood on my legs, and reality shook my mind clear of the fog I'd been in. The next day, my doctor confirmed I'd miscarried, and gave me the spiel about it being for the best, since something had obviously been wrong with the baby. But I was certain I had willed my baby to die, and I hated myself."

"Dusty."

She held up a hand. "I know better now. But at the time I was wallowing in self-pity and guilt, wondering if subconsciously I didn't want the baby, but was too cowardly to admit it. For a while I believed I was as shallow and disgusting as Peter, and within a few days I left the house and moved in with Mitchell. But I already told you that ugly story." She grimaced.

"Perhaps," she said, "you can understand the state I was in when I came home, and why my father might have been overprotective. And Chase? Here's the bottom line. My father isn't here. He doesn't run my life. He doesn't get to choose who I sleep with, or who I love. I am sure his intentions are good, but I'm not his little girl anymore."

She got up and tugged on his hand. "If I had to make a choice between the two of you, he wouldn't stand a chance. Now will you please come to my bed, so I can make you forget about John and his threats?"

Chase didn't budge. First he'd allowed John to bully him, and now Dusty was calling the shots. Did he have no balls? "Do you lead on the dance floor, too?"

"Only when necessary." she said, taking his other hand, and again trying to pull him up off the couch.

In one quick motion Chase brought his hands toward his body then spread them wide, effectively dropping her onto his chest. His arms slipped down and held her firmly against him. Gray eyes stared into green.

"Do you have any idea how much you mean to me?" he asked.

"I love you too, cowboy."

"You've got to be the cheekiest woman I've ever known."

"Hmmm." Her lips feathered over his, and she said, "I'd rather be the sexiest." She delicately circled his mouth with the tip of her tongue, tantalizing, then grazed his chin with her teeth.

Chase groaned and pushed her away so he could stand up and swing her into his arms. In the bedroom, he peeled the shirt over her head and pushed her backward onto the bed.

She lay still while he stripped off his shorts, leaned over, and balanced his weight with a hand on either side of her. His eyes met hers as he slowly lowered to graze her cheek with his mouth. She turned her head to capture his lips, but he dodged her, instead tasting the edge of her ear, the pulse in her throat. "Roll over," he commanded softly.

"I want to look at you."

"Roll over." He put a hand under her shoulder, and she went halfway, turning her back to him, but stopped, bracing herself.

Amused by her compromise, he worked gentle magic on the nape of her neck until she went limp, boneless, and pliant. He pushed her flat on her belly. His mouth and hands danced together and separately over her skin, moving slowly downward until he was nibbling on the delicate arches of her feet. Her toes curled.

He slid a hand under her hip, gently rolled her again, and made his way back up her body, leaving not a square inch of her untouched or untasted, tortuously pushing her to the brink, then drawing back before she went over.

With deliberate slowness, he raised himself above her and waited for her eyes to open. They were huge and the green, gone nearly black. Her mouth opened, and he could barely hear her whisper, "Please, Chase."

His gaze was unwavering, and his words were clear. "Only if you'll marry me."

Dusty didn't have a lot of brain cells at her command since she was precariously poised on the edge of an orgasm, and would probably plunge over even before he was completely inside of her…and yet somehow the words registered, and the thunder of her heart grew incredibly loud until she could barely hear him.

"I won't have casual sex with a woman I love." He lowered his mouth, but stopped before his lips touched hers.

Her voice was husky, "Nothing casual goin' on here." She reached for him, but he grabbed her wrists and pinned them to the pillow above her head. His mouth continued to tease while he said,

"If I have you once, I'll want you forever."

He sounded possessive, controlling. She heard ownership, and she didn't care. Cold water didn't wash over her, bring her to her senses, and the alarm bells didn't ring. Her body arched toward him. The fire had a life of its own.

"Say yes, Dusty."

"Yes, Dusty."

His mouth took hers as he slipped inside, filled her, body and soul.

***

While Chase slept beside her, she studied his face. Had he meant it, she wondered. Had she? She closed her eyes and sighed. She'd never in her life been with anyone this way. There'd been lots of men. For years she'd believed sex was love, and thirsted for it from every possible source. But sex was sex. Pure and simple. Except with Chase. She'd never been the places he'd taken her, never given up control so willingly, never wanted so badly to give back, leave him breathless in her wake.

Startled when she raised her eyes and found him watching her, she touched her fingertips to his lips, and he opened them to gently capture her with his teeth. A breath caught in her throat, and he took her hand in his, pressed a kiss in the palm, and whispered, "You okay?"

She ran her hand down the center of his chest and followed it with her mouth. "I have never been such a long way from 'okay' in my entire life."

"That's a good thing?"

She lay back and looked into eyes filled with love. "That is *such* a good thing.

FOURTEEN

There was a sense of belonging when she drove through the gates of Buck Hill on Monday morning. And when she spotted Chase stepping off the porch as she crested the hill, her grin matched his. She barely got the Jeep stopped before he was dragging her out and into his arms. Swinging her around and planting a noisy kiss on her lips.

"You two should get a room."

Dusty laughed and glanced over at Murray, who was standing beside his truck.

"Sorry to interrupt," he said. "I'm on my way to Casa Mia for the day, so you'll need to shut down the sprinklers in the south pasture in about an hour."

"What's going on at Dad's?" asked Dusty.

"Separating calves for the auction tomorrow."

But it was only August. "Why's he selling this early?"

Murray climbed into his truck. "He's off to South America soon, and wants the stock gone before he leaves."

"Everything?"

He rolled down the window and closed his door. "Yep."

Dusty glanced at Chase, then back at Murray, "Do me a favor and don't tell him I'm here. I really don't feel like getting in the middle of that dust and mess on my afternoon off."

One corner of Murray's mouth kicked up. "Not much chance I'll see him, because he leaves the dirty work to the hired help. But just the same, your presence is duly un-noted, ma'am."

Wasn't that an interesting turn of phrase? Another tidbit of Murray revealed.

Chase and Dusty puttered around the ranch for a while, doing a few chores, but mostly checking on the horses, assessing foals, and speculating on their potential as racehorses.

Later in the afternoon, when they were relaxing on the shady veranda, Chase asked her if she'd really been serious about wanting to have kids, and her heart did a little bump. This was it. The place and time for her to be who she was, no matter what.

"It's inside me, Chase. Bone deep. I am meant to have children. Be surrounded by young, eager minds I can feed, nurture." She half-laughed. "Doesn't fit the persona, does it? But it's who I am deep down." She knew she could be scaring him away, but had no choice, *had* be true to herself.

"Is it because I was an only child, and grew up without a mother? With a father who was always distant? From watching other kids interact with their brothers and sisters on the rare occasion I was allowed to visit friends?" She shook off the trepidation. "Maybe, just maybe, it's the way I'm supposed to fit in the grand scheme of things."

"You religious, Mel?"

Mel. She liked the way it sounded coming from him. "Been to church twice. For weddings."

"Do you believe in God or anything?"

She frowned. "I don't know. But praying for you to be safe, I kind of threw it out into the universe, begging for some greater power to help me." She tipped her head. "Why the interest?"

"You said, 'In the grand scheme of things.' and I wondered what that means to you."

She tipped her head against the cushions. "I suppose it's that I've always believed things should *fit* somehow. Like life is a big puzzle, and the corner where I am has a bunch of kids in it."

"Do I fit in your corner?"

"Oh, yeah."

"What about your career? How do the kids fit in?"

She laughed. "I'd trade pregnancy for my career in a heartbeat."

"You wouldn't miss the riding, the winning, the excitement?"

She shook her head. "With the possibility of holding our baby in my arms? There would be no room in my life for anything as trivial as riding races." She glanced toward the paddocks. "That said, there will always be horses in our lives, because kids should grow up in an environment like this, filled with love, laughter, animals, dirt, and, of course, work."

"You surprise me."

"Why?"

"You were about the horses, the cattle, cats, all the animals, and I never once saw you with a doll or anything girly."

She felt a bit queasy about his reaction, but had to plow on. "I'm a nurturer. It's the only really grown-up thing I know about myself."

"How do you think your dad will feel about being grandfather?"

That was it? Now he wanted to talk about John? "Who knows? He was never much into fatherhood. Don't get me wrong, he was a good provider and protector, but we've never had a conversation, and he's never put his arm around me, even to give me a simple hug." She thought about it for a minute. "I suppose I was nothing more than one of many items on his shelf of possessions."

"Like Peter?"

She stared at him. "Wow, I hadn't thought about that. I suppose it's what I expected from a man."

"You will never be a possession to me."

"Not a doubt in my mind." Chase was so completely unlike either of the previous men in her life, he could be from another planet.

He took her hand. "I can imagine us, years from now, sitting right here, watching our family, our children and grandchildren, working and playing happily together."

Dusty studied his serious face, then gently touched his cheek. "Nothing in this world would make me happier."

He pulled her into his lap. "When do you want to get married?"

She sat up. "Married?"

"As in, we both dress up in fancy clothes and say 'I do,' and then I kiss the bride."

"No." She tried to hop off his lap but he tightened his grip

"You said yes, Dusty. And if we're gonna have kids, we need to be married."

"Well, technically, we don't."

"Why are you backing out on me?"

There was something like a fist gripping her throat. "I'm okay with *being* married but I don't want to do the wedding stuff."

He made a humming noise, but said nothing, and they sat in silence until Dusty reached up and rubbed a finger over the groove between his eyebrows.

"How about this? I will marry you anytime, anywhere, on one condition."

"Which is?"

"No event. Just you, me, and whoever has to do the official deed."

"No wedding?"

"Exactly. No spotlight, no phony guests, fancy clothes, or cardboard chicken."

"But you don't mind doing the actual legal part."

A smile bloomed from deep inside. "My soul is already committed to you for life. Which means I will die before I ever let you go. *I* don't need the legal papers, but if you do, I'm all over it."

"I need them for a reason you might not like."

"Which is?"

"It smacks of ownership, but not."

"So tell me."

He swallowed hard, "I need to know that if anything ever happened to you, I would be in a decision-making position. I wouldn't have to worry about your dad or anyone else stepping between us."

Startled by his seriousness, she had to ask, "Where did that come from?"

He snuggled her in and rubbed the top of her head with his chin. "Years ago, a good friend of mine went through hell because he wasn't married. He and his girlfriend had been together for years, even had a couple of kids, but when she was hit head-on by a drunk driver, and the doctors pronounced her brain-dead, he had no legal right to take her off life support, even though they had a pact with each other about that very subject. Her parents kept her alive on machines for two years, until her body eventually gave out."

"That's awful." She pressed a kiss against the underside of his jaw.

"If they'd been married, her parents would have had no say. But instead, my friend died a little each day while he watched the woman he loved hang suspended somewhere between life and death. He sat for hours talking to her, knowing his presence was probably causing her to hold on, but he couldn't help it. He had to be with her, see her through it, yet felt he was breaking a promise and betraying her trust."

"How incredibly sad." She leaned back to look

steadily into his eyes, touched his cheek. "No matter what happens in my life, I want *you* to be the person making the decisions that I can't. And I promise to do the same for you." She snuggled into him again and sighed when his lips brushed her forehead.

"I love you, Dusty."

Her heart fluttered. "I know you do." She unbuttoned his shirt and tasted the sweetness of his skin.

Ever so gently, he slid his fingers into her hair, he raised her mouth to his and, while he kissed her, she pushed the shirt from his shoulders, savored the feel of his skin until she reached his belt buckle. Chase's hands closed over hers. "I think we should move indoors, don't you?"

"Are you kidding? There could be no more perfect place to conceive our first child."

"But you're on the pill."

"True." She laughed. "We'll make this a practice run."

Chase lifted the T-shirt over her head, and his fingers played a tingling dance over her skin until she tipped over into the cushions and dragged him down with her. Slowly, one item at a time the rest of their clothes landed on the floor, and the world around them disappeared.

When she woke up it was dark, and Chase's mouth was warm on the nape of her neck. She turned in his arms, and his lips began to take her on yet another journey until annoying ring tones interrupted. She groped around for her shorts, and dug her phone from the pocket.

"Hello." She was breathless because Chase's

clever hands were still at work.

"I just talked to track maintenance about the storm coming in. They're not going to open the main track tomorrow, so all your works are cancelled," said her agent. "Thought I should let you know before you got on the highway."

"Fantastic. Thanks, Marty."

When Chase's mouth closed over her breast, she dropped the phone to the floor. Her back arched and she stifled a moan. "I don't have to go home tonight."

His hand slid downward. "So I heard."

***

The next few days were filled with decisions for Dusty, and hard conversations. She made a deal with Marty to ride one more weekend before hanging up her tack. Would she miss race riding? Maybe later, but for now she was excited to move on to a life with Chase. Which also meant she'd be giving up the boathouse

Linda, Dusty's landlady, was probably twice her age, but they hit it off from the moment they met, like kindred spirits. Which was odd, considering they had almost nothing in common. Linda was born and raised wealthy, had adoring parents, six siblings, and was terrified of horses.

Sitting on Linda's wide patio overlooking the ocean, Dusty struggled to find the right words but gave up. Took another sip of the tart lemonade laced with cranberry juice. "I really love this stuff," she said.

"No small talk. Spill," said Linda.

"That doesn't sound like appropriate shrink talk," said Dusty and Linda laughed.

"Come on, there's something you're busting to tell me."

Dusty's grin got away on her. "Okay, but you have to promise to keep it secret for a while."

"How long, nine months?"

"No."

"But you have that pregnant glow."

"Well, I'm not. At least I don't think I am, but I..." Dusty glanced across the expanse of lawn to the boathouse cottage where she and Chase made love for the first time. "Well I…"

Linda laughed. "You should see your face. You look like a schoolgirl caught making out in the back seat of her dad's car."

Dusty's mouth fell open.

"And you're going pink."

"I am not. Okay, here's the deal. I've quit riding—as of next Sunday—and I'm moving to the interior."

Linda's sudden smile and wave made Dusty look over her shoulder to see Chase was coming across the lawn toward them.

"Ladies."

Linda glanced back and forth between the two of them, then asked, "Are you the man who has this woman blushing?"

"She doesn't blush."

Linda tipped her head toward Dusty, and both she and Chase laughed out loud.

"Well, would you look at that," he said.

"What did I tell you?"

Chase planted a cheery kiss on Dusty's pursed lips, and she pushed him away saying, "Okay, you two, enough picking on me."

"When's the wedding?" asked Linda.

Dusty groaned, "I don't do weddings. We're getting married at the courthouse."

"I'll help you get a dress."

"I don't need a dress. I came to tell you I'm moving to the ranch, but I don't want to leave you in the lurch next week." They were heading out on their sailboat, expecting Dusty to be there to look after the cats.

"Oh, damn."

"We could swing it to stay here while you're gone," said Chase, catching Dusty completely by surprise.

"We could?"

"That would be terrific," said Linda.

"Then it's handled. When do you take off?"

"Next Wednesday, and we'll be gone about ten days."

"Great. That'll work for us," Chase said with an enthusiasm that had Dusty studying his face for a minute before she was distracted by Linda's questions.

***

The following Wednesday, about half an hour before Linda and Rick were due to depart on their trip, Dusty and Chase were on their way across the wide expanse of lawn to see them off when Chase asked quietly, "Would you like to get married right now?"

She stopped and stared at him. "Right now, like, I mean, as in this minute?"

He nodded, and she was stumped for an answer.

"I have a license, and Linda's friend Henry is here to marry us if you're willing."

"We were going to do it at the ranch."

"We need two witnesses, and there's only Murray at home." He touched her cheek. "None of the phony stuff, just us and our two friends. Over and done with."

Dusty's smile came unbidden. He got her. "I love you."

"No, it's, *'I do.'* But with practice…"

She gave him a light punch, and he countered with a quick kiss on her smiling mouth.

Ten minutes later, with no fuss and no muss, they were married, and the only moment she remembered clearly was when Chase said, 'I, Timothy Mathews.'

As soon as they were alone, she had to ask, "Timothy? How did you get Chase out of Timothy?"

"Your dad hung it on me. At the track, people called me Tim's kid from Chase. John dropped the rest of the line and called me Chase. It stuck."

"Tim's kid?"

"Apparently my father's name was Tim."

"You don't know for sure?"

"Exactly. Tim was a blacksmith who conveniently traveled around the interior shoeing riding horses and picking up women. I guess he had a pretty effective line of bull."

"Will you want to continue what your mother started, and name one of our sons Timothy?" When he shrugged, she said. "Funny, in all my daydreaming about having kids, I've never thought about choosing names for a dozen kids."

"Dozen?"

"You said you wanted lots."

His brow furrowed. "Lots felt like five or six when I said it."

"Okay." She took his hand and led him toward the bedroom. "We can start with a half dozen, and if we like them, we'll make more..

FIFTEEN

British Columbia, Early Fall 2001

Bob was drying glasses and listening to the chatter of deer hunters having a cold beer and shooting the shit with each other. The weather was unseasonably warm, making it less than ideal conditions, and the camp owner had already thrown in a couple of free nights to keep the men from heading to an area higher in the mountains.

"Came across about fifty squirrels and a few doe tracks, but that's as close as we got to real game," one fellow complained.

"Hey, we did better than that. A chipmunk, a badger, one gray wolf, about four hundred squirrels and two horses."

"Wild horses?" asked Bob, ready to call bullshit.

"Naw, they were pretty tame. Stout brown and a flashy red. Kept bumping into them, and started thinkin' there must be a cabin close by, figured we better get the hell outta there. Not like it was posted or anything. We weren't trespassing if we didn't know, right?"

"I'll put up a notice for others. Where exactly were you?" asked Bob, and the men described the area in great detail while he tried to appear nonchalant.

Once they headed back to the tiny cottages on the edge of the river, he dug out the poster he'd been given weeks earlier, and made a call, but there was no answer. He waited for the beep. "I might have found your missing horses. Name's Bob, I'll call back in an hour."

Thirty minutes later Chase and Dusty were staring at the answering machine, listening to the message for the fourth time. Because it came from a payphone, they couldn't even call the man back.

"You could contact your PI and get him to trace the number to wherever the phone's located."

"True, but let's wait, just in case."

At exactly the hour mark, the phone rang and Chase grabbed it. "Hello."

"Is this the outfit lost a couple horses a while back?"

"Yes. Have you seen them?"

"Nope. But if I know where to find them, do I get the reward?"

"If I see the horses, you get the money. Where are they? How do they look?"

"Like I said, I didn't see 'em myself, but a coupla hunters run into them up in the hills here."

"How do I find you?"

He gave Chase directions to a small town about four hours away, and they arranged to meet in the morning. Then Chase made a bunch more calls before plans were firmly in place. An undercover officer would go with Chase and carry the reward—no chances would be taken with lives or money.

At daybreak, Chase headed for the new truck and trailer already hooked up and parked in front of the house.

Dusty waited until he walked around the back of the rig before she made her move. In a split second she reached the truck and jumped in.

Chase opened his door and stared at her. "I thought you agreed to stay home."

"No. You said you wanted no argument, and I agreed not to give you one. Besides, I brought ammo." She held up a bag of carrots and he sighed.

"I may love you to death but—"

"Come on, we need to get rolling. You can lecture me on the way if it will make you feel better."

What was the point? He had no defense against her.

They were halfway to where they'd pick up the officer when she broke the silence. "Are you really mad at me?"

"Yes. But don't worry," he winked, "you'll pay for it later."

She made a face at him, then laughed. "If we find Angel and Jake today, you'll forget about being mad at me."

They picked up the plainclothes cop a few minutes before seven, and by eight they were pulling into the gas station. A man got out of a pickup truck parked at the pumps and walked toward them. Chase rolled down the window. "Hi, there."

"I'm Bob."

Chase stuck his hand out. "Pleased to meet you, Bob, I brought some friends just in case the horses are hard to catch."

Bob nodded, then said, "The hunters claimed they saw the same two horses more than once, just north of here. I'll lead you to the area, but can't stay. If you find them, you can stop at the restaurant there," he pointed to the small building next door, "and pay me on your way past."

"What if we're late coming back? How long will you be there?"

"I'll wait."

"Okay, Bob, let's get started."

After driving for what seemed like hours, he pulled over and waved them alongside. Pointed to a fork in the road. "I'm going right. I'll keep an eye out while I work my way back to town. If you take the other side, you'll come to a wide meadow where you can either turn that rig and continue on foot, or drop the trailer and go on with the truck. The horses were spotted not far from the meadow. Follow the creek that runs alongside it and it's about a ten-minute hike upstream."

"Thanks." Chase waved.

"I don't think it's wise to unhook," said the officer.

"I agree. Makes the trailer easy pickings," said Chase. "How about I turn it, and you can stay with the rig while Dusty and I cover some ground."

It didn't take long to reach the meadow, and only minutes after heading out on foot they spotted all the proof they needed in the soft ground beside the creek. A perfectly clear print of a horseshoe with a toe grab and block heel. Exactly the kind of racing plate Angel had been wearing.

"Not bad," said Dusty. "She's still got one hind shoe on."

"Remind me to give my farrier a bonus."

They followed the creek for a while, then Chase stilled. "They're close by."

"I can smell them," Dusty whispered. She turned a slow circle, searching for the slightest hint of movement or color and her breath caught in her throat. "There," she whispered. Angel was half hidden behind a small clump of trees.

Chase called to her softly, and her head lifted, her nose searching for his scent.

"Good girl, Angel. Come on, mama, you can do it." The filly's ears swiveled back, as though she was listening to something behind her, and finally Jake appeared.

"Jake," Chase called, and the big horse never hesitated. Lumbered past Angel and right to Chase, reaching out his soft muzzle, looking for a treat. Chase snapped off a piece of carrot for him, and Angel crowded forward for the other half.

Looking ridiculously calm, Chase rubbed the filly's face with one hand and scratched Jake under the chin with the other, while Dusty's heart hammered with excitement, and fear the horses could spin around and take off at any instant. "Do

159

you want the ropes?" She was wearing them wrapped around her waist, because if a wary horse didn't want to get caught, having a rope in your hand was sure to send him running.

"I don't think I'll need them, and too much movement could be a problem. I've got enough carrots and peppermints to keep Jake interested until I have him in the rig, and Angel will go wherever he does. What you could do is scoot ahead and warn Jack to stay in the truck. No point having them pick up the scent of a stranger. Who knows what they've been through, and what might spook them?"

Dusty went ahead, spoke with the officer, then took up position to close the back door of the trailer as soon as they were in. Smooth as silk it went, and once Chase hopped out the side door, she let out a squeal and did a little dance.

Laughing, Chase lifted her up and spun her in circles.

***

After a long day of excitement, they settled on the porch to watch Jake and Angel wander contentedly around their paddock, apparently happy, well, and unfazed by their adventure.

"Did you think this day would ever come?" Dusty asked.

"I did, actually. But I hated the thought of them out there at night, alone and defenseless, especially when I heard coyotes or wolves howling.

"Well, it looks as though they did alright alone.

Aside from a bucketload of burrs, chipped-up feet, and being covered in bug bites, they look as healthy as the last time I saw them."

"Amazing, isn't it?"

"Yeah. Now what?"

"Meaning?"

"Now what do you do about Angel? Will you try to run her, or just let her sit here until January when the lease runs out?"

"I don't know. I guess I'll have to wait and see what she wants."

"Can I still be her rider?"

"You retired."

"Please? I'll stay fit galloping and working her. If you're gonna put tack on her, please let me be the one in it."

"It's too late for her to run in Vancouver. The meet will be over in less than a month, and it will take longer than that to get her ready to run."

"How about taking her to California?"

He tipped her face up. "You can't ride if you're pregnant."

"Actually, I can for the first few months. And because I'm not pregnant yet, and January is only three months away, there's a good chance the timing will be perfect. But if it's not, then I'll be grounded, and someone else will get the pleasure." But she hoped she'd be the one to ride the filly.

"By the way, are you still mad at me for coming along today?"

"Yes."

"Why?"

"Because you didn't care about how worried I

was for your safety."

"I *did* care, but I was scared to death I could lose you on a mountain road in the middle of nowhere, because maybe the same bad guys were trying to lure you out there."

"And you were going to rescue me even if the cop didn't?"

"No, but I could be with you." She gazed into his eyes. "You're my reason for living, Chase. If I lost you"—her voice cracked—"my heart would simply shrivel and die."

He pulled her closer. "Stop that kind of thinking. I have a confession of my own." He planted a kiss on the top of her head. "I'm glad we were together when we spotted them."

"It was sort of magical, wasn't it?"

"Yeah, it was."

"What a perfect day. I could get used to this," she said. But deep inside something lurked that made her afraid this kind of happiness was only borrowed, and not really hers to keep.

SIXTEEN

Ranch Country, British Columbia,
Late Fall 2001

Angel was even stronger than she'd been before her adventure in the mountains, and when she was ready to run in late November, preparations were made to take her to California. Stabling was arranged, and a contact found them a furnished apartment close to the track. The Coggins tests and health certificates were done, and they were almost ready to go.

After power-washing the rig and bedding it down with fresh shavings, Chase and Dusty were ready to hit the shower when they came indoors, but Dusty noticed the blinking red light on the answering machine. Pushing the play button on the way past, the sound of her father's voice stopped her dead in her tracks.

"Chase. Do you know where the hell my

daughter is? Is she with you? Call me."

Chase studied her face for a minute, then said quietly, "I guess John's back."

She frowned. "He didn't sound very happy."

"I'd better call him."

"I've got it." Dusty punched redial.

"Chase."

"No, it's me, Dad. How was your trip?"

"Where are you?"

"I'm at...Buck Hill." She nearly said, *I'm at home*.

"Why?"

"Ah, Dad, I need to talk to you."

"I'm here." And the connection was cut.

Dusty glanced at Chase. "I'd better go explain things to him before he jumps to conclusions."

"I'm coming with you."

"Thanks."

He took her hand and said, "I meant it when I promised I would always be at your side, and have your back, no matter what."

Dusty wove her fingers with his. "I love you, too. And I meant what I said months ago. You come before him."

They were at John's kitchen door in less than fifteen minutes, and when he opened it, he stared over Dusty's shoulder at Chase.

"Why was she at your place?"

Dusty pushed past him. "Why don't we sit down and talk?" Out of habit, she opened the fridge and took out three cans of pop, handed one to John. "Sit, please, Dad."

John chose his customary spot at the head of the

table.

Chase opened his soda and sat at the opposite end, while Dusty took a seat between them.

For a few minutes they sipped cold drinks, John staring at Chase with an unspoken message, Chase not backing down, and Dusty unexpectedly feeling uncertain about what to say. This was far more animosity than she expected. Even the air was dark and nasty.

She cleared her throat and dove in. "We have news, Dad. The best kind ever. Chase and I got married a couple of months ago." She recognized the displeasure in his clenched jaw, and tried to fix whatever was wrong. "We fell in love, Dad. The real kind of love, the kind—"

"Fucking ridiculous."

"It's not. You'll see when the babies start coming. Chase and I were both only children, but we're going to make a big family, and fill Buck Hill with kids and dogs and horses. You'll have grandchildren…"

The color working its way up John's neck was a sure sign of trouble, and Dusty was determined to head it off. She would shut him down with calm and determination. She lowered her voice in both tone and volume.

"I am Chase's wife, and we both believe in 'til death do us part.' We're not playing silly games. We're adults, and we love each other the way we've never loved anyone before."

John started to speak, but Dusty interrupted him firmly. "Let me finish. You of all people know what a good person Chase is. He will be a great father to your grandchildren."

Even though she didn't understand it, she recognized the animosity filling the air and cut to the chase.

"You need to understand this is a done deal and, although you are my father, and I will always love and respect you..." She swallowed hard when John's hands started to shake.

"...Chase is my husband, and I will stand by him until the day I die."

Chase laid a hand over Dusty's. "John—"

Like an explosion, the older man shot to his feet, shouting, "Don't touch her."

Enraged, he slammed both hands on the table. His face had gone past red and was headed for purple, while fury clung to every word he shouted. "I told you to stay away from her! I drew the line, and you promised to never cross it!" He pounded the wood with his fists. "You have betrayed me, and you will bring my daughter nothing but heartache!"

He sucked in a breath. Was maybe getting an edge of control, thought Dusty, but she was quickly disabused of that idea when he snarled, "Get out of my house."

"John, you have to listen."

"I HAVE TO DO NOTHING! OUT!" Spittle flew. "Get out of my house!" He flung a hand toward Dusty, "And take this trash with you. You're both dead to me."

Chase tugged on her hand until he was between father and daughter, then shoved her out the door.

They climbed in the truck, and again he took her hand. Held it until they got home. Slung an arm around her shoulders while they walked inside, and once the door closed, he wrapped her in his arms and held on. Pressed his face into her hair. "I'm sorry, so very sorry."

She leaned back to stare at him. "What do you have to be sorry for?"

"Creating a rift between you and your father."

She laughed and shook her head. "You don't get to own that."

"If it wasn't—"

"If it wasn't for you, I wouldn't be as happy as I am. He's made his choice to be a miserable old man. That's not on you, and it's sure as hell not on me, either. *I'm* sorry I misjudged him and led you blindly into that buzz saw."

"All he could see was betrayal and disrespect."

She held his face between her hands, stared into his eyes. "What he *imagined* was betrayal and disrespect. And don't you dare forget that part. He wants total control, we both know that, and won't be giving it to him, which is pissing him off royally." She shrugged. "Maybe he'll soften his stance when he meets his first grandson."

Chase quirked an eyebrow, and she shook her head. "Like maybe in a year or ten."

Looking both relieved and disappointed, he said. "You really are okay with his attitude, aren't you?"

"No, I'm not okay with his attitude, but I can accept it for what it is, and I can live without his approval. One day, when he gets his shit in order, he'll realize how wrong he was."

"Do me a favor, baby, and don't hold your

167

breath waiting for it to happen."

Dusty laughed. "I know, he's a stubborn cuss, and that will never change. God, I hope none of our kids take after him."

With a spark of humor in his eyes Chase said, "They'll get plenty enough stubbornness from you."

"Well, at least I'm not unreasonable."

"No, but somehow you always get what you want."

She grinned, reaching for his hand. "And right now is no exception." She led him to the veranda. With agonizing slowness, she undid buttons and pushed the shirt off his shoulders. Once his belt and jeans hit the floor, she tipped him onto the sofa and, in no hurry at all, she slipped out of her shorts and T-shirt.

She explored every inch of him, touching, tasting, teasing, until he finally pulled her onto his chest and with a raspy voice said, "Enough."

She smiled slowly and replied, "Never," And her mouth descended to his.

John sat staring at three soda cans on the table, smug because the answer to everything was right in front of him.

SEVENTEEN

California Racetrack, Late Fall 2001

Angel was on post parade for the first official start of her life, and Dusty was in the tack.

Monitoring the filly's body language through binoculars felt every kind of wrong to Chase, and he regretted letting Dusty talk him into watching from the grandstand instead of riding Jake alongside them. Nothing he could do about it now.

He studied Dusty, perched on the chestnut filly's back, looking like any other jockey, except for the heavy black braid between her shoulder blades. Chase smiled to himself when she slid a reassuring hand down the filly's neck.

As much as he had looked forward to this day, now he couldn't wait for it to be over, and not just because all first starts were nerve-racking. Technically this was Angel's second, but her first had been many months ago, and she was still slightly unpredictable. Granted, she rarely spooked these days, but in his gut he knew she was still capable of digging her toes in at a full gallop, anytime, anywhere.

When he tried to talk Dusty out of riding Angel, they had one hell of a row. She'd been furious with him for even suggesting another jockey could ride the filly, and when he tried to explain he was concerned for her safety, she snarled back that he sounded like her father.

At that point, Chase had removed himself. Gone for a long walk and, in the end, conceded because, as Dusty had pointed out, it was a matter of trust. Trust in *his* ability as a horseman, and *hers* as a jockey.

They'd schooled Angel over and over at the starting gate, and impressed upon everyone how much she depended on routine and familiarity. The starter assured him that Nico, the man who worked with her in the mornings, would handle her today for the race.

Chase jumped when a disembodied voice blared through dozens of enormous speakers, announcing that the horses were approaching the starting gate.

This was it. His stomach did several impressive flips, and he rested his elbows on the grandstand railing to help keep the glasses steady.

The first few fillies were loaded without incident, and it was finally Angel's turn. Nico slipped his lead-up into her chin strap and reached up with his other hand to rub her face. She dropped her head, calmly followed him into the stall, and stood looking straight down the racetrack while he climbed up alongside her, and the rest of the field was loaded.

Number ten, the last horse in, hopped forward in anticipation of the start, but when the gate didn't open, she threw herself backwards, rearing, and tossing her rider out over the tailgates while she continued to fling herself around, frantically fighting the man at her head.

In spite of all the commotion only five stalls away, Angel appeared to be calm. However, when the starter officially scratched the ten horse and called for the entire field to be unloaded, Angel shot out the backs so fast she nearly ran over the groundsman behind her.

Nine fillies circled behind the gate with their lead ponies while the fractious troublemaker was led off the track through a backstretch exit.

When the loading began again, the number two horse refused to go in, and Nico passed Angel off to another handler while he went to help out with the two. When Angel tried to follow him, the man on her head checked her hard, and she stopped instantly.

When he was ready for her to move forward again, she didn't move. The groundsman waiting to close the tailgate behind her swung the end of his leather lead-up, tapping her gently on the butt, and she shot forward, missing her stall opening, and driving her chest against the edge of the open tailgate.

She backed away with her head up and her ears jammed forward in the way that always spelled trouble, and Chase's breath caught in his throat.

Again the man hit her with the leather strap, and when she crashed into the tailgate a second time, the pieces clicked together in Chase's head at the speed of light. His heart slammed into his throat.

No. Oh God, no.

He bolted into action, sprinted down the stairs to the tarmac, flew through the crowd, ducking and weaving, bumping, not caring, not hearing anything but the voice in his head and the announcer calling the horses' numbers as they entered the gate.

He could finally see his goal—the phone in the winner's circle—a direct line to the stewards on the roof. Only they could stop the race.

"They're all in." The announcement stilled the crowd.

Chase grabbed the phone and without even a ring, there was an answer. "Stewards."

"Stop the race. You've got to stop—"

"THEY'RE OFF!"

Too late.

"Hello?"

Not too late. "Tell the outriders the five horse is blind, and the rider doesn't know." He dropped the phone and ran to the edge of the track.

Angel was already two in front, drawing away from the field, and Chase started to pray, "Please, God..." but his throat slammed shut, and he could do nothing but watch.

It would be the longest sixty seconds of his life.

Dusty had Angel hugging the rail, sweeping around the turn all alone, while the other horses were a solid pack of eight, four lengths back. Angel's brilliant red coat glowed in the sun, and

Dusty was down so low on the filly's back she was barely visible.

At the head of the lane, Angel switched leads, and Chase held his breath when her head came up ever so slightly. She'd never heard the roar of a crowd blasting out of the grandstand before, and he didn't know how she would react, but by watching the big screen in the infield, Chase saw Dusty move in a way that made him suck in a breath.

She lowered herself into a position that dropped her elbows down either side of the filly's withers, her forearms and hands flat against the sides of Angel's neck...as though to steady her.

Chase's heart pounded against his ribs and blood thundered in his ears. His world was reduced to one woman and one horse thundering toward him. Flying down the lane as though they'd done it together a hundred times before. He couldn't take his eyes off them as they won by clear lengths, then galloped out around the turn.

Angel's blindness was still a threat to Dusty. The filly could at any instant be frightened by something she couldn't see and stop suddenly. Dusty's short stirrups put her body in a position so high above the horse's center of gravity, she would become the ultimate lawn dart if Angel hit the brakes.

Please, God.

The outrider galloped alongside Angel to take the reins and rescue Dusty, but Chase could see her waving him off. The man shook his head and stayed beside her while Angel came to a slow and graceful stop, then he reached for the rein, turned them around, and brought them back to the winner's circle.

Chase let a long breath out slowly. A passing jock's valet slapped him on the back. "Congrats, man, been years since that record was set."

When the meaning clicked, Chase swung to look at the tote board, where the message was flashing. *New track record.*

And by a blind horse.

When they arrived at the winner's circle, Chase dragged Dusty to the ground, wrapped his arms around her in a fierce hug, and then he was kissing her like it was his last chance.

The hoots and applause eventually got his attention, and he pulled away to find they were surrounded by a cheering crowd, and the outrider was still patiently leading Angel in circles.

Chase thanked the man and snapped a lead onto the side of her bit, then took her into the winner's circle, where he stood with his arm around Dusty to have their picture taken, then they got moving in opposite directions.

Dusty headed back to the Jocks' Room, and Chase hustled to get his hot horse to the test barn, where she could cool out properly. A racing official kept pace with him. "Stews want to talk to you."

"I've got a horse needs my attention for the next few hours." And he was feeling all kinds of guilt he needed to deal with.

"They get that. Said for you to be in their office at eight sharp tomorrow. Meanwhile, the track vet will come by your barn after the last to examine your horse."

Chase nodded. "Sounds fair."

He'd finished Angel's bath and was walking her when Dusty joined him and took the filly for a few laps.

"One question," said Chase.

Dusty shook her head. "Can't it wait until we get back to the apartment? Why not enjoy what we have right this minute, and put her to bed happy, instead of getting dragged down by a bunch of negative energy? She broke a twenty-two-year-old track record, Chase, and I wasn't even asking her. Didn't dare."

"You knew."

"When she rammed into the tailgate the first time, it pissed me off. I snapped at the gateman." Dusty ran a hand down Angel's powerful shoulder. "But when she did it again, hitting the other side, everything fell into place. I knew she'd run into it because she couldn't see it, and was compensating for the first mistake."

She stopped at the bucket to offer Angel another drink. "I could have said something, hopped off, whatever, but I knew she trusted me, and I trusted her."

Once Angel didn't want any more water, she was taken to the test stall, where they warned the techs that she couldn't see them.

Chase watched her on the monitor. "She's taking everything in stride."

"Same as during the race. When we hit the wall of noise at the head of the lane, I got as low as I could to make sure she remembered I was with her, and she powered on without hesitation."

Dusty's eyes glistened. "I thought my heart would burst from the sheer joy of being on her back, Chase. It was like nothing I'd ever experienced before. She was all power and confidence, and it was effortless. Oh God, it was just so incredible." She threw herself into his arms. "I wish you could have felt it with me."

His heart lightened, and he actually laughed. Couldn't help it. Her excitement was contagious, and that was one of the things he loved about her. He kissed her then. Had to. And his world felt a lot steadier on its axis. "Everything's going to be okay."

"More than."

Once Angel's pee was collected for testing, they took her back to the barn to finish cooling her out. And after the vet came by to examine her, they did her up in standing bandages, mudded her feet, and she was tucked into a belly-deep bed of straw.

Dusty added extra apples and carrots to her dinner, and gave a bunch to Jake as well.

Hand in hand, Dusty and Chase made their way to the truck. "Fancy restaurant or burgers?" he asked.

"Burgers. Let's hit the drive-thru and go home."

To a rented apartment where they'd eventually have no choice but to talk about Angel's future.

Racing was no longer an option.

The dream was over.

EIGHTEEN

California, December 2001

After two days of rigorous questioning by racing officials, and the press draining them dry, it was finally over. Chase and Dusty could relax and get on with their life together.

But they'd just started packing up the apartment when there was yet another knock on the door. Prepared to tell whatever reporter was out there to go away and leave them be, Dusty wrenched it open, and was astounded to see her father standing there.

He didn't bother with pleasantries. "This." He shoved a newspaper at her. "This embarrassment, has forced my hand." It only took a glance to recognize the now-famous picture of Chase kissing her brainless in the winner's circle, with Angel and the outrider in the background and a headline that read, "Love is Blind."

Dusty said nothing.

"May I come in?" Even though the words were polite, the nastiness in his voice was unmistakable.

No. Why couldn't she say no? "If you like."

He scrutinized their place in seconds flat, but the disdain vanished from his expression the moment Chase came around the corner and said, "Please sit down and tell us why you're here." He dropped an arm across Dusty's shoulders...in a show of solidarity? Or just comfort. She'd take either. Both.

John perched on the edge of a chair while Chase and Dusty sat together on the couch.

"You have to get a divorce."

"Not in this lifetime," Dusty said quietly.

With a tightening jaw and flaring nostrils John ground out the words, "You *can not* be married."

Dusty shot to her feet but Chase was quick to wedge himself between them. "You need to leave, now."

John ignored him and spoke directly to his daughter. "I'm doing this to protect you."

"From what? From happiness? From the kind of life I've always dreamed about?"

His fists clenched. "Why are you making me do this? Why can't you obey me for once? I don't want you sleeping with him."

An incredulous laugh burst from Dusty and she backed up a step. "You don't want me sleeping with my *husband*? Isn't that rich." Defiance put fire in her soul. "Where the hell were you when I was"—she used air quotes—"*sleeping with,* any man who wanted me? Married, single, old, young, I didn't care. It was a way to actually feel close to another human being for minutes, maybe even hours. Where were you then, John?"

"Enough," he ground out.

"No. Not nearly enough." She kept her voice low and controlled. "If you'd ever been half a father to me, maybe I wouldn't have been so fucking lonely that nothing else mattered." She took a breath. "But then I stopped feeling sorry for myself and found more. Found love. And no matter what you have to say about it, Chase and I will be together for the rest of our lives."

With a sneering half laugh he said, "Oh, you think so? Well, I know different."

Dusty sighed. "Time for you to go away, John. Get out of my life. You have no control over me. Us. You've made your pitch, and I'm not going to fight with you anymore. Ever, for that matter."

"I don't care if you fuck every man breathing. Don't fucking care." The suddenly venomous look on his face made her skin crawl. "But you can not be married to *this man*, or have his children."

Chase finally spoke. "And why, for the love of God, not?"

John's eyes went to slits. "Because she," he stabbed a finger toward Dusty, "is your half-sister."

Dusty's jaw dropped, and she groped blindly for Chase's hand while she stared at John, waiting for whatever insanity he'd spew next.

But silence filled the room, thick, sour-smelling silence, and she found herself blinking as though it might help her see more clearly.

"Explain." Chase was the first to speak.

John cleared his throat. "When you showed up at the track years ago, I saw a boy with the kind of drive and determination I had at that age. Then, a couple of months after I hired you, when I found out where you came from, I suspected you might be my son. That's when I took you to the ranch to live and work."

Dusty's thoughts flew back over what Chase told her about his mother giving birth alone, at the age of fourteen and dying shortly after. She'd been found dead in a pool of blood, with the baby tucked alongside her.

Raised by an elder he called his grandfather, Chase led a life rich in the ways of his people until the old man passed away. That's when Chase went to live with distant relatives, but then he found his way to the nearby racetrack, where he lied about his age, and John eventually hired him.

Gave his *son* a lousy bed in the bunkhouse. Ordered him around like he owned him.

"Why didn't you tell me?"

"I saw no need. You were told right from the beginning to stay away from Dusty, and I trusted you to respect my wishes. Besides, it was your mother who lied to you, or didn't know for sure who your father was. It wasn't my place to tell you and make her look bad."

"She died when I was born."

"I have respect for the dead."

Dusty could no longer take the pressure building in her head and the incredible fury erupted. "Respect? Why you self-righteous, phony, immoral son of a bitch. How the hell old were you when you got a thirteen-year-old girl pregnant and then turned your back on her? On a *child* who died giving birth because of *you*." She closed her eyes and swallowed hard, fighting the rage grabbing her by the throat, while memories flashed and brought life to a horrible realization.

"I remember listening to you with your buddies, joking and laughing about the girls you'd had. I *thought* you were referring to women as girls, and I didn't know what it meant to 'have' them."

How many nights had she sat hidden from sight, lonely, and listening to the men having such fun, laughing, joking? "All that stuff about bagging a fresh one…" Her stomach lurched but she fought the bile and plunged on. "You were raping children, *virgins*, and keeping score. Get out. *Out. Get—*"

"Don't you dare speak to me like—"

"I'll dare, damn you." She lowered her voice, "I used to wonder what kind of woman would walk away from her newborn. How my mother could have left me behind. But now I understand why she had to run. To get away from you, no matter what it cost her."

"Your mother *died* when you were born."

"No, that was Chase's mother."

"Your mother."

"You lying bastard. Did you really think I could be a part of the racing community all these years and never hear the stories about my mother? How the poor little thing fled from you, forced to leave her baby girl behind? I thought they were exaggerating. I believed she chose her career over me."

"She lied to me. Said the baby was a boy. She was nothing but a drunken squa—"

Dusty flew at him, arms swinging, and a growling sound coming from her throat while Chase's arms wrapped around her and dragged her away.

"She was nothing but Reservation trash."

"You filthy sonofabitch. *I'm* half Native, *Dad*. How would you like to have men talk about me that way, *fuck* me that way?"

"Enough." Chase's voice was low and calm, but she could hear the tension. "Before our lives are *completely* blown apart, we'll get DNA tests done."

She wrenched herself free in order to see his face. "He can't break us up with his filth, Chase. Nothing is going to change. I don't care if you are my brother, my cousin, or my freaking aunt, it is *no one's* business but our own. We love each other, and that's the bottom line."

"But if we can't have children, Dusty…"

"A bridge we'll cross when we get to it. Kids all over the country need parents. We can adopt a dozen if we want. Give them the parents they need." She shot a look of disgust at John. "Parents they can *trust*."

"You will never be approved to adopt when they find out you both have the same father. And it's against the law for you to be married, so I certainly won't be able to keep it a secret." He hesitated an instant for effect. "Such an ugly word, isn't it? In—"

Dusty lunged at him. Wild for the sound of his pain when she clawed his face. But Chase hauled her back, held her close.

"Let me go," she growled. His grip around her middle tightened. He wrapped his other arm around her shoulders and spoke to John through clenched teeth, "You've got about ten seconds to get out that door before I let her go."

John beat a path to the door, pulled an envelope from the inside breast pocket of his jacket and tossed it at their feet before disappearing from sight.

When Chase let her go, crossed to close the door and locked it, Dusty's legs refused to support her and she sank to the carpet. "How can this be happening?"

He picked her up and sat on the couch holding her, their stunned silence the only sound in the room for a very long time.

Dusty was the first to move. She leaned back and looked into his face. Seeing her own sadness mirrored there, she sighed, and he pressed his lips to her forehead.

"I don't care about anything but loving you," she said. "And living without you is not an option."

"I love you more than life, and I'm not going anywhere." He kissed her hard. "Nothing can ruin what we have, Dusty. We're going to grow old and gray together, no matter what anybody else does or says. We might have to move to the moon or Alaska or somewhere else remote, but we'll be okay. As long as we have each other, we'll be okay."

"I don't trust him."

"Neither do I, but we can't hand him the power. We'll make our own decisions, no matter what he says." He reached for the envelope still on the floor.

It was addressed to them, as though John had planned to leave it, whether or not they were home.

He ripped it open and pulled out several sheets of paper. The first was a cover letter from an investigative agency. The second had the date of the submission of a soda can for DNA testing, information on the extraction procedure, and several signatures. The test results followed.

Chase finished reading and handed the last page to her.

Dear Mr. Torino,
We conclude, without doubt, that the DNA sample we obtained from the soda can submitted is that of your offspring.

"What? Wait a minute. They used a soda can—from the night we were over there telling him we were married, right? How can we be sure John didn't give them mine instead of yours?" She jumped up, excitement overriding the horror of the last hour. "What's the name of the PI you used when the horses were missing? We'll contact him and have the test redone." She waved the papers. "Have the results compared to these."

Chase grabbed his phone, made the call, and before long arrangements were made and they were out the door, headed to a lab about ten miles away.

Once again they were on the uphill of the rollercoaster, with hope and excitement building, but it sucked to know they wouldn't get results for several weeks.

In the meantime, there was plenty to keep them

busy. Stumpy, the filly he'd leased to travel from Kentucky to Buck Hill with Angel nearly a year ago, would have to be shipped to California for the return trip, and Jake transported home to the ranch. Only then could Chase and Dusty load up and make the trip to Kentucky to return the two fillies to their owner.

NINETEEN

Road Trip to Kentucky,
January 2002

Lying awake beside Dusty, and not letting himself touch her, while listening to taunting voices of elders past, had become penance for Chase.

If only he'd shown respect, done as he was told, none of this would have happened, and she would be safe from this turmoil now.

But instead, he'd sentenced her to a life without the children she had a soul-deep longing for. His lust, and lack of respect for his elders, had stolen her chance to be the mother she was meant to be.

A man with a backbone would give her what she needed, what he'd taken from her. A man of integrity would take her pain upon himself, suffer for her, and set her free.

On the second morning of the road trip, Chase spotted a deer lying motionless on the shoulder and pulled over.

"What are you doing?" asked Dusty.

"Just a quick check, in case she's only injured."
He put a hand on Dusty's knee when she
immediately began stuffing her feet in her boots.
"Stay warm. I'll shout if I need a hand."

He twisted around to access the emergency kit
strapped to the back of his seat. Grabbed a black
blanket and a small length of rope before heading
around the rig. He talked to the horses while
unfolding the blanket, and stopped once he could
see the deer. Watched, and saw no rise and fall of
her ribs, but still he held the blanket ready to drop
over her head if he found he was wrong—sudden
darkness was often enough to make a wild animal
freeze, and blocking their view of a scary human
was never a bad idea.

But this deer was long dead. He did a quick
search of the ground around her and saw nothing of
concern, then climbed back in the truck, and Dusty
ran her window up.

"Brrr." She held up a hand. "I know, you said
stay warm, but I needed to be able to hear if you
called for me." Her mouth twisted. "And I'm still a
bit gun-shy. What if someone had been hiding in the
bushes, waiting to rob whoever stopped?"

He could have said she was being silly, or
shouldn't worry, but he understood her concern.
He'd also been on full alert. He touched her hand.
"Thanks. Never hurts to be vigilant."

While he got back on the road, and up to speed,
his complete attention went to the way the rig was
pulling, whether there was a weight shift or jerking

motion to indicate an imbalance caused by the horses being restless. But all seemed well.

"Dry doe," he finally said. "Probably died on impact late last night."

"I'm glad she was dead and not suffering." Dusty kicked off her boots and put her feet flat against the dash. "Could you have finished her if she'd been injured?"

"Maybe she'd have been savable. Then I would have hog-tied her and put her in the tack compartment to get her to a vet."

"A wild deer?"

"Yeah." He glanced over at her. "I rescued one once. Rehabbed her, too."

"Really?"

"Yup. Seems like a hundred years ago."

Dusty wasn't sure what it was she was seeing in his face. Longing, perhaps? "Tell me about it."

He took a sip of coffee from the insulated cup she handed him. "I was about seven, and living with my grandfather in a tiny cabin in the woods. The trail I took to get to the school bus wound through the trees, and there were curiosities, distractions of every imaginable kind. I laughed when squirrels scolded me for being in their territory. Got lost occasionally when following wolf tracks, and I was constantly mesmerized by the sound of ravens' wings. I had trouble remembering why I was supposed to leave such a place and go somewhere I'd have to sit indoors for endless hours."

Dusty could see the little boy, dressed warmly in canvas and leather, scooting along trails, staring up into trees. She could imagine big gray eyes in the child's face, and promptly tamped down the longing and the frustration of waiting to get the DNA results.

"I heard a small sound I didn't recognize, but I knew something was wrong. Standing perfectly still as my grandfather taught me, I continued to listen carefully, pinpointed the direction it came from, and headed off to rescue whatever creature was in trouble." He sighed. "As a boy, I had no doubts, ever. Always forged on, as though I knew everything." He took another swallow of coffee.

"I found her near the creek. A tiny doe with her leg caught in the steel jaws of a trap. The snow was scraped down to dirt because of her struggles, and there was blood everywhere. It only got worse when I tried to help her, because she became frantic, and fought even harder to escape, and I was terrified the leg might rip right off. I raced home to my grandfather, crying, begging for him to help.

"He didn't hesitate, didn't ask why I wasn't in school. Simply gathered supplies into a gunnysack while explaining he would do everything possible to help, but if her injuries were too severe for her to survive, he would *spare her soul the suffering*."

He glanced at Dusty. "I've always remembered those exact words, and I understood what he meant. Had seen the knife. And was no stranger to death."

He was quiet for a minute before continuing. "By the time we got to her, she'd already begun to weaken. Grandfather covered her eyes with the blanket, used one leather thong to hold her three healthy legs together, and another to tie off the injured one and stop the bleeding. Then he released her from the trap, wrapped the leg, used his knife to split the gunnysack down one long side then cut a hole in the end. He slipped it over her head and the sack molded to her body."

Chase stopped talking while he navigated through a small town, and once out the other end, when Dusty thought she'd have to prompt him to get the rest of the story, he began again. "When we got her to the vet, he shook his head and told us she had less than a ten percent chance of living, and advised euthanasia. But Grandfather insisted he set the leg anyway, saying, "Might as well give her a chance.""

Chase's face softened. "We took her home and made her a bed in the shelter behind the house, and I spent the next few months caring for her, and convincing her I was, in fact, a friend, not an enemy. Can't tell you what a thrill it was the first time she walked up to me."

"And you've been gentling wild creatures ever since."

"My calling, according to my grandfather."

"He sounds like a wise man. How old were you when he died?"

"Twelve."

"Where did you go? Who looked after you?"

"There were some relatives on the reservation who took in anyone and everyone. I stayed with them for a while before I found my way to the racetrack, where I discovered I could sleep in a tack room, and earn enough to feed myself."

"What about school?"

"I went on and off until your dad gave me a job

at Casa Mia."

Barely any formal education, but he had an innate wisdom she'd been drawn to from day one.

***

When they approached the impressive nursery barn in Kentucky—the one where Angel and Stumpy were born—Richard Selby was waiting for them, waved at Chase to open his window.

"You can back right up to the main entrance here to unload, and their doors are open on the left. I've had dividers taken out so they'll share the space of three box stalls until Angel becomes acclimated."

"They'll like that," said Chase. "But once she settles, knows her surroundings, and trusts the staff here, she won't need any special handling." He swung the rig, then backed into place, and they climbed out.

"Richard, this is my wife, Dusty, Melanie Mathews."

"I can't tell you how often I've watched the replay of the race." Selby pumped her outstretched hand. "You did an outstanding job, and the filly obviously trusted you completely."

"Thanks. We did a whole ton of schooling hours together. Her trainer was a hard taskmaster." She winked at Chase, but he was busy sliding the ramp out from under the rig and getting it secured. He didn't always use it for Angel, but Dusty wasn't surprised he did today. The setting here could have memories, triggers they couldn't possibly know about.

Unloading went smoothly, and two grooms joined the threesome watching the fillies nibble on hay, and stare out wide, screened windows at the rolling pastures. Hard to believe only one of them could actually see what was out there.

Chase filled the workers in on the best ways to introduce Angel to new things and areas. "As long as you always have a companion horse with her in the beginning, she'll be fine. Doorways, and stuff on the ground, or changes in footing, are the only things to really be careful about. But she's smart and resilient. Survived in the mountains for weeks with only an old racehorse to follow."

It was going to be hard for him to leave Angel.

Once the grooms had gone off to do other things, Selby said, "Mr. Sanderson, Angel's owner was both horrified and impressed by what you accomplished with her. He wanted to thank you and apologize in person, but is swamped with meetings this week. He asked me to give you this envelope, and explain that if you would like to talk to him tomorrow, the arrangements have been made."

"Arrangements?"

"He's in Hawaii. You'll have to fly there to meet with him."

"Hawaii."

"It's a central point in his world. He has business interests in North America, South America, Canada, Australia, and New Zealand. His jet is here in Lexington, waiting to take you to Hawaii, where he will put you up in a private beach house for a week. Then you can fly back here on his aircraft, or, if you would rather fly commercial to your home, he will have your truck and trailer transported for you."

Chase looked stunned, and Dusty could only say, "Wow."

Richard shrugged, and said to Chase, "Mr. Sanderson is an extremely tough businessman with a very big heart. He was already blown away by your ability to tame his wild filly, but when her blindness was discovered, and he realized what you must have gone through while you watched the race, he said he wanted to do something special for you and your wife."

"Well, this certainly qualifies as something special." Chase said with a grin. "Got somewhere I can park my rig for about a week?"

Richard laughed. "Back it up alongside the barn there, and I'll give you a lift to the hotel. There's money in the envelope to cover any extra expenses. Your plane leaves at ten in the morning."

***

When they landed in Hawaii, they stepped off the plane and into a limousine. Dusty was dropped off at a gorgeous beach house, and Chase went on to meet Mr. Sanderson.

Truly alone as she hadn't been in weeks, she kicked off her shoes and padded across cool marble floors, running her fingertips along lovely rattan furniture and glass-topped tables, one of which held a bottle of champagne on ice and brightly colored dishes filled with candied fruits and chocolates.

Continuing to explore, she found his and hers silk bathrobes in the massive bathroom, and several outfits for each of them laid out on the king-sized bed. Swimsuits, shorts, shirts, and even a pretty dress made from the lightest, most delicate fabric Dusty had ever seen. There was a whisper of memory from back in her life with Peter, but she quickly banished it.

In the tiny kitchen, she found a fully stocked fridge and pantry. And throughout the entire house there were white candles of every possible shape and size.

She'd had a refreshing shower and was sitting on the patio, sipping fruit juice and watching the waves roll in when Chase returned.

He never said a word, simply picked her up and carried her inside. Laid her gently on the bed, removed the creamy-colored bathrobe, and kissed her with such incredible tenderness, it made tears well. He shifted and paid homage to her breasts, then his mouth slid across her soft belly. Her back arched toward him, and she touched his face, drawing him up until she could see his eyes, and for the briefest of moments saw sadness flickering there.

"What's wrong?" she whispered.

"I'm overdressed," he said in a voice edged with tension. His eyes stayed locked on hers while he stripped off his clothes and their flesh finally met. Souls intertwined, and nothing mattered but being together. Being one. While the world slipped away.

Later, when she stirred beside him, he said, "I

will never stop loving you, Dusty."

Tears stung the backs of her eyes, and she didn't know why.

For the next six days, in the warm turquoise ocean, on their private beach, and inside the beautiful house, they were like dying lovers, trying to savor every last moment of lust and loving that the gods would allow.

TWENTY

*Ranch Country, British Columbia,
February 2002*

When they got home, the test results were
waiting for them, and it was confirmed. John was
Chase's father.

It was a fact they couldn't change, but Dusty
refused to let it affect her. Sure, it meant there
would never be children of their own, but she
started researching adoption.

Chase's reaction to the news, however, was
troubling. He blamed himself, claiming he'd let his
heart rule his head when he should have been
respecting John's wishes. Even insisted it was his
fault she wasn't still riding races and falling in love
with someone who would give her the big family
she longed for.

Dusty vehemently disagreed, but couldn't shake
him from his position, and as spring came and went,

the distance between them widened. It began slowly and subtly, but like the heat of summer, became a tangible entity in their lives.

Chase rarely laughed anymore. Never shared his thoughts or feelings. Even their sex life—the one thing she'd been able to depend on from the beginning—had disintegrated. There were no more long, passionate afternoons of lovemaking. Instead, he would occasionally wake her in the dark of night, and their coming together would be fast and frantic.

He wore a cloak of desperation she couldn't penetrate. He refused to talk, shrugged her off, and spent every waking hour with the horses, as though they were the only comfort he could find. Originally there were twenty to break, but when word spread he was accepting more, there was a steady parade of vans dropping off yearlings.

Leaving their bed at four in the morning, and staying away from the house until he fell exhausted into bed at night, became Chase's routine, and the harder Dusty tried to connect with him, the more he pulled away.

Chase was driving a wedge of distance and frustration between them…with a sledgehammer. But Dusty wasn't budging.

She could have hung out in the barn to be close, followed him around like when she was a kid, but she cared too much about him. He needed the space, and couldn't afford to be distracted when working with green horses.

Instead, she stayed in the house day after day. Pacing from window to window, talking to Linda on the phone, and following every bit of her advice, but nothing changed how hopeless she felt when she looked into Chase's dark and troubled eyes. The man she loved was slipping away from her, and apparently there wasn't a damn thing she could do about it.

Two days before Christmas, after the last of the client horses shipped out—finished and ready to go into training in the spring—Chase said, "We need to talk."

He led the way to the living room. Sat on the edge of a chair, propped his elbows on his knees and folded his hands together. Stared at them.

When she took a seat across from him he said, "I've had an offer I can't refuse."

It wasn't the words, but the tone that sent a chill through her.

"Angel's owner, Mr. Sanderson, has asked me to run his breeding and training operation in Australia. I have a two-year work visa."

His eyes finally met hers and she saw a stranger there.

"I've put the ranch in your name, and my lawyers have the paperwork if you need it."

A done deal. "You're leaving me." Her voice was barely a whisper. Where was her anger? Her backbone? She needed to fight this. Change his mind.

He took her face between his hands, threading his fingers into her hair, and she choked back a sob. How long since he'd touched her this way?

"If I don't go, you'll never have children, and you were meant to be a mother, Dusty." The strain in his voice was palpable.

"I've applied to—"

"We were turned down. I intercepted the letter. John has made it impossible for us to be approved as parents."

"Then we'll have each other."

"It is your destiny to raise children." He swallowed hard, and she was sure he didn't realize his fingertips were biting into her scalp. "There is someone out there who is worthy of your love and will stand beside you. But as long as I'm here, I know you will never try to find what you need to make you whole."

"Don't do this. I can't live without you."

"You can and you will, because you're the strongest woman I've ever known."

Silent tears dripped off her chin, because nothing she could say was going to change his mind. He'd built his case and lived with it for as many months as it had taken to put the plan together.

"When? When did you get the offer from Sanderson?"

He looked away.

"Don't lie to me, Chase. It was when we went to Hawaii, wasn't it?"

He nodded, and she wondered if a knife in the belly could be any more painful.

"I don't understand."

"I made a promise to keep you safe, to never cross that line, and I not only let John down and broke my promise, but I let you down, too, by disrespecting an elder. I forgot who I was, and now it's cost both of us."

It took great effort to get her voice past the lump in her throat. "Please don't do this. I'm begging you, please reconsider. We can survive, Chase. Rise above it." She touched his cheek and he turned to put his lips in her palm.

He squeezed his eyes shut, but tears leaked out, slid down his face. "I will always love you," he said, his voice a mere whisper. "But I have to leave before there's nothing left of me, and your life is over too." He pressed his lips to her forehead, then hurried out the door.

Gone.

Unable to move, Dusty cried until she was so empty she might as well be invisible. Her throat ached, and her head pounded, until she finally fell into a deep and exhausted sleep.

In the morning, she woke to ghostly quiet, and glanced around the living room. Nothing had changed. Only her.

She went to the bedroom and stared at the empty bed. When she made it the day before, she had no idea life as she knew it would be over in less than twenty-four hours.

Chase was gone, and in her gut she knew the two-year visa was only a beginning, because he'd never be coming back, even though his clothes still hung in the closet. He'd taken nothing with him.

An envelope with her name on it was propped against their wedding picture on the dresser. In the photo, they'd both been wearing shorts and tanks, and laughing because Linda wanted them to be serious.

Chase's note was short.

I will always love you, and I will understand if you never forgive me. I will never forgive myself. Forever yours, Chase.

She tipped over and buried her face in his pillow, inhaling his scent and dying inside.

TWENTY-ONE

Vancouver, British Columbia,
December 2002

After dumping the whole story on Linda, Chase waited for her to speak. He needed her to understand why he'd done it. How he'd screwed up, and Dusty had suffered. That she would need Linda for support now.

"Why, exactly, do you think this is your fault?"

"I disrespected my elder. John tried to do the right thing. Warned me, right from the beginning, to stay away from her."

"He was a father worried about his child in the midst of a bunch of rough stable hands. Absolutely understandable. The kind of warning that becomes irrelevant when the child is an adult. And then perfectly natural for you to disregard."

"He maintained his position with repeated warnings. Went so far as to predict I would break her heart if I disobeyed him. He was right."

"Stop that foolish thinking, right now. John Torino doesn't deserve anyone's respect. How can you even consider leaving Dusty simply because he told you to?"

"She needs children, a family. A life I can't give her."

"And what does *she* think about this decision?"

"She hates it, but I still have to do what's right. I was raised by an incredible man, who was wise and giving, and firm in the lessons he taught. If he was alive today, he would tell me I am being punished. I have failed Dusty by failing myself, and thereby failing my grandfather's spirit."

"Your grandfather would not want you to be unhappy for the rest of your life because of one mistake."

"I ignored the ways of my people."

It was still only one mistake, but Linda was at a loss to figure out how to make him understand. The man was stubborn and locked on.

She worked hard, asking him questions that should lead him to understanding his position from a different angle, but he didn't budge, and she gave up. Male reasoning, no matter how professional she was, sometimes frustrated her no end.

And she wasn't equipped to walk in the shoes of a man questioning his own spirituality—which was at the root of Chase's problem. She could see by the look on his face and hear in his voice that there was no argument he was willing to accept. He had tried and convicted himself.

She gave up, because nothing she could say

would change his thinking. "I believe, in my heart, you two belong together." She held up a hand to silence Chase when he tried to interrupt.

"I'm the shrink, remember? And it's my turn to speak." She smiled grimly. "I know I can't change your mind, and that saddens me deeply. I understand your reasoning—even though I disagree with it. Your conscience and your heart are telling you what to do, but does it have to be a life sentence? Would it not be wise to revisit this in, say, a year? Two? What if Dusty never meets someone else she wants to have a family with? What if she's still sad and lonely, pining for you, in five years?"

Hoping his frown meant he was actually listening, she plowed on. "Do you think she deserves an entire life of emptiness? Are you aware that the punishment you give yourself you also, unfairly, condemn her to live with?"

"It has to be a complete break. I've got no choice."

"Don't give me that crap. You *are* making a choice."

His eyes reflected what she thought must be the bleakness of his heart. "If I came back and found her up to her neck in diapers and laughter, I would truly be happy for her...but my heart would be ripped open again."

"I could be the go-between. Let you know how she's doing, if she needs you—"

"No." He stood up. "I have to walk away and never look back."

Linda gave up, went to him, put her arms

around him. "I will always be here, my friend. Maybe one day you'll call."

"I won't. Please, don't make me let you down, too."

"Then send me a Christmas card every year, to let me know you're alive." She laid gentle hands on his shoulders and said softly, "Oh, how I wish I could reach inside your head and fix what's broken, turn off the switch to your wrong thinking and let you see clearly again."

Chase wrapped his arms around her. "Please, just help Dusty get over what I've done to her."

With tears running down both their faces, Linda kissed his cheek, and Chase left quickly.

***

Profound sadness wrapped itself around Dusty's soul the day Chase walked out, and she was defenseless against it. For the first time in her life, she had no interest in anything at all, as though her spirit had died.

She was driven to keep moving, hoping to outdistance the pain relentlessly dogging her. She tromped the snow-covered fields and pastures of the ranch, often crying out to the sky, begging to understand why this was happening. But nothing changed. Chase was still gone, and her soul still bled.

She kept her distance from Murray and Duncan, and slowly felt herself disintegrate. Became afraid to sleep, because her dreams were filled with trying to find Chase, calling out his name and running to the edges of cliffs, looking down, seeing him twisted, crumpled, and broken below her.

To avoid the dreams, every evening, when the lights went out in Murray's trailer, she slipped out her front door, hiked through the field and into the foothills on the other side of the road from the ranch. Her destination was always the same, a spring-fed watering hole where dozens of wild animals came to drink at night.

Chase had built a small blind there years ago, for watching the animals without disturbing them or scaring them away. He showed it to Dusty when they were riding the horses in the hills one day, and now it was her place, where she'd crawl in and sit in frozen silence for hours, watching deer, moose, coyotes, and wolves approach with extreme caution and sip from the clear pool. Occasionally even a lynx ventured by.

Before dawn every day she'd unfold herself from her hiding place and return to the ranch, flip on the lights in the kitchen, so Murray would know she was there, then head out to walk among the horses.

One morning when Murray woke up, there were no lights on at the house, and when he went to check on her, he found each room empty and cold. He and Duncan searched every inch of the property. But there was no sign of her.

Murray called Linda, and Linda called the police, telling them the missing woman was distraught and could be a danger to herself.

***

At the sound of men and dogs approaching, the large gray wolf unwound himself from the sleeping figure and slipped silently into the forest.

Ten minutes later searchers found her, unconscious and dangerously cold, and she was airlifted to the Kamloops hospital.

When Linda arrived three hours later, Dusty was recovering nicely, and gave her friend a grim half smile.

"No lectures, please. I know it was stupid and careless to fall asleep out there, but...."

"They say you were also seriously dehydrated."

She stared down at her hands. The doctors were amazed she had no frostbitten fingers. "I guess I haven't been looking after myself lately."

"No kidding," said Linda.

Dusty was startled by her friend's less-than-kind response. "This was not a ploy to make Chase come back, if that's what you're thinking, nor was it an attempt to hurt myself."

Linda's reply was quick. "Then where did those two ideas pop up from?"

Dusty sighed. "The resident shrink here has been quizzing me since I woke up, trying to decide if I should be in a rubber room."

"And how did you convince him you were okay?"

"I told him the truth. The whole ugly story, right from the beginning."

"Since I already know most of it, up until you stopped answering your phone, why don't you enlighten me about the last two weeks?"

Dusty told her about the nightmares and fighting sleep by going to the watering hole. "And then last night, I guess everything caught up with me, and I simply nodded off."

"I can think of better places but..." She looked her friend in the eye. "Being overwhelmed by self-pity doesn't allow one too much room for intelligent or logical thinking."

"Ouch."

"You know me, girl, I call 'em as I see 'em."

Dusty nearly managed a whole smile. "I think I feel better already."

"I imagine the sleep and several bags of IV fluid helped. Along with the bottom of the pool."

"Pool, as in water?"

Linda sat on the edge of the bed and everything about her softened. "You've been going through hell for months, Dusty, and what you've experienced is like a slow emotional drowning."

She touched Dusty's hand. "Once you begin to sink, there is a place in the middle where you don't know up from down. You're overcome by the loss of control, and simply hang there, in limbo, feeling unable to help yourself. But there are two ways out. One, you can kick to the surface and keep treading water, hoping for a helping hand. Two, is what you did. You kept sinking until your feet actually touched the bottom of the pool, which is when you instinctively pushed off, and the journey back up to the surface was rapid."

Dusty shuddered. "The middle place was scary, like living in a bubble, unable to see or hear what was around me, and not even certain I existed anymore."

"And now your eyes are wide open again, aren't they?"

"But I didn't do it. Didn't push off. Searchers found me."

"And you responded to treatment vigorously. Trust me, you pushed off. If you hadn't, you wouldn't be talking to me about it."

Dusty nodded.

"And you're ready to join the living again? Get on with your life?"

"I guess I don't have a choice, do I?"

"Ah, there's a trigger word for you."

"Meaning?"

"Choice, Dusty. You will *always have a choice*, and don't you *ever* forget it." She cocked her head for a minute, listening. "Unlike that baby I can hear crying out there. A child is completely dependent on someone else to meet its needs. It has no control over its present, the way it hopefully will someday in its future."

Dusty stared at her hands again for a few minutes, then asked quietly, "What makes you so smart about everything?"

Linda laughed out loud. "Let's see, maybe it was the years in university, or the ones I've spent trying to help people play effectively with the cards they've been dealt. I've had a lot of exposure to other people's anguish."

Dusty took a deep breath. "Okay, coach, what's my next move?"

"Think about how you can begin to live again. Find a corner you can tuck your pain into for at least part of your day. And," she held up her hand to stop Dusty's interruption, "I am not saying that you won't have Chase on your mind twenty-four seven. But do yourself a favor and *try* not to dwell on the terrible ending between you. Savor the good times instead."

"It sounds easy, but—"

"It won't be. You'll have to work hard. Set yourself some goals, minuscule ones at first."

"Like what?"

"Maybe make a promise to yourself that you'll read five pages of an inspirational book every night before bed. Start a gratitude journal, foster kittens for the SPCA, or read to the elderly at a care home. Find a way to bring comfort to someone besides yourself. I know how fragile, how terribly breakable you feel at the moment, but your strength will come back. Slowly at first, but it *will* come back. And when you feel really strong one day, try flying right into the face of your pain. Challenge yourself."

"How?"

"Your dream life was going to be with Chase and a house full of happy kids. If you can't have Chase, find a way to bring joy to children. Become a birthday party clown or teach kids to ride, be a big sister, or volunteer in the pediatric ward."

Dusty's gut clenched and tears threatened.

Yet again, Linda put her hand over the one lying still on the bed. "Dusty, if kids are truly your calling in life, someday you *will* find a way to reach that place, whether it's one year or ten before you take the first step."

Dusty turned her hand over and squeezed

Linda's. "You're a pretty good shrink, you know?"

She shook her head. "I'm talking to you as a friend, not a psychologist, Dusty. If you were coming to my office, you'd be doing all the talking, not me. And I'd be giving you specific homework, not throwing out a bunch of ideas, hoping you'd find one that might help you."

"Thank you for your friendship." Tears threatened to spill over, but she managed to speak. "I'm not ready to be anything to anyone right now. Especially not to a child. But one day I will be. Just as soon as I figure out how to be whole again."

Linda nodded. "Your journey has already begun.

PART TWO

Discovery

TWENTY-TWO

In the place Dusty intends to build her future.
Fall 2004

Comfortable, stretched out with nothing but a blanket between her and Mother Earth, Dusty slowly opened her eyes, as though they had been closed for a very, very long time. Nothing seemed to have changed, yet she felt different. There was no weight on her chest. Peacefulness permeated her soul, and her spirit was finally, truly, hers.

The brightness beyond the heavy branches of the tree above her was more than sunlight. She blinked, trying to find the lesson. Concentrated. Each branch was laden with long needles bursting forth from their root with excitement, standing tall and proud, identical to thousands of brothers, yet uniquely singular. Delicate. Strong. Purposeful.

She shifted her gaze to the scarred trunk of the tree, the heart, the mother, supplying nourishment to all.

Trees. The most indestructible entities on earth. They are survivors, no matter what man does to destroy their uniqueness. Pavement and concrete can surround. Smog and dust can smother. Each arm can be sheared, every branch torn away, and still new growth will appear. Even if the lifeblood and flesh are cut all the way through, and a tree is tossed on a truck or into a river, it lives on. It lives on, washed ashore as a place to sit near the fire. It lives on as part of a structure for living things to take shelter. Milled, rolled, sliced, kiln-dried, it lives on as a chair, a table, a piece of a house, or paper to write on.

Even fire, while it seems to take everything from a tree, leaves behind ashes to feed the tiny seeds released by the heat of the blaze, and a new tree will be born.

Hundreds of bits of trees in the lives of everyone, and yet they're given little thought. People marvel at the beautiful old table in the antique store, admiring the labor and love someone put into its creation, yet does anyone celebrate the tree who gave birth to it all?

She smiled up at the tree and whispered, "I love your strength and tenacity. I acknowledge you are one more elder for me to respect and learn from. I will see more clearly now, the purpose which is not in front of me. My thoughts won't be consumed by questions. My mind will be open to answers—to see, to learn, to become more."

She stayed still for a while, then silently rose from the hand-woven blanket, folded it with care, and gently ran her fingers over the trunk of the giant pine before winding her way back down the rugged trail.

When the view suddenly opened up before her, she was truly amazed. Hiking up the mountain, she hadn't seen this sight, but now, from the opposite direction, the gift spread out before her. Not only an unobstructed view of where she would build her new home, but there was the most beautiful big, flat rock near the edge, inviting her to sit, rest awhile, and absorb her surroundings.

Dusty used her blanket as a cushion, and settled there, waiting for something. Her eyes drank in the scenery, one blade of grass, one tree, at a time. Her nostrils flared, seeking the comforting scent of sunbaked earth and the freshness of pine she could actually taste. She acknowledged the sound of delicately strong wings cutting through the air, and the soft padding of wild toes on the earth.

She closed her eyes and lay back on the sun-warmed rock, surrounded, enveloped by those she could not see. "Thank you for walking with me. For giving my spirit this sacred place."

The sun on her eyelids was warm, the brightness glowing through her skin. She lifted splayed fingers into the air above her, reaching for the heat.

As though in slow motion, she opened her eyes, then sat up, amazed to see clouds hiding the sun. Yet she could still feel the warmth, and she smiled. "I understand." Her voice was soft, "I celebrate being a part of such a complete existence, and offer my spirit to those who cannot yet soar."

Eventually she felt compelled to move, gathered herself, and stood, tucking the blanket under her arm. Once again Dusty began to descend the mountain.

The solemn gray wolf rose from behind a giant pine and padded quietly in her wake.

That night she sat at the tiny table in her camper, parked on the land that was now hers, working on her drawings. The buildings had to face east and form a circle of sorts, while maintaining the integrity of the land. Everything must *fit*.

Fit. The word stirred memories just beyond the edge of her consciousness. Memories she had no desire to revisit, but they were insistent, and finally, grudgingly, she let her father's irritated and dismissing voice in. "Don't be stupid, Melanie, a house has to *fit* the people, not the land."

She remembered the look on his face, his disdain. She had only been about ten years old when she saw a new house on a property not far from them, and she'd innocently made the comment that it didn't 'fit.'

Dusty laid her pencil down and leaned her head back against the cushion. Even with the discovery of her Self, and the wonderful awakening of her Native spirituality she still had the past to deal with. So much to learn, to face up to.

She closed her eyes and allowed her mind to wander back two years, to when she realized she was ready to give up all hope of Chase coming back and making a life with her.

Buck Hill Ranch, Spring 2003

The days were hard and the nights harder, but Dusty plowed on. Worked side by side with Murray through foaling out the mares, and prepping the rest of the horses for the April sale, but by the end of May there was little left to do. The mares and foals were on pasture until the fall, the barns and paddocks had been cleaned to stand empty for the summer, and miles of fence rails had been oiled.

There was barely enough work left to keep Murray occupied, which left Dusty with nothing to do.

Lying in bed one night, staring at the ceiling, she was surprised to realize she was ready to make a move. Buck Hill, without Chase, was no longer her home.

She climbed out of bed and stripped off her nightshirt in front of the full-length mirror. What she saw gave her hope. A future.

She tugged on clothes, grabbed a pen and a pad of paper, and sat on the veranda to put a plan together. Worked out the details, backwards, forwards, and sideways, then at dawn was pounding on Murray's door.

He opened it, coffee cup in hand, looking relaxed, but as always there was something assessing about his gaze. "What's up, boss lady?"

"That. Can I come in?"

"Sure, coffee? Duncan, get out of the way, would you?"

"No, thanks. I'm already revving." She sat at the small table, and rubbed Duncan's ears.

Murray took his usual chair on the other side and asked, "What's got you goin' at this hour?"

"I don't want to be boss lady."

"Meaning?"

"I'm leaving."

His eyes narrowed, but he said nothing.

"I'm going take the money we got from the sale, buy a brand-new truck and camper, stash whatever's left, then pack up and head south or east."

"What about the ranch?"

"It's yours."

He blinked. "Dusty—"

"Honest. The only thing I ask is that you keep Jake safe and well to live out his days. That's it. I'll see the lawyers and get the paperwork done today."

Murray stared out the window behind her. "What if I don't want it?"

"Oh."

He smiled in typical Murray fashion—eyes mostly, with just a twitch of his mouth. "Hadn't thought about that one, eh?"

"I'm sorry, I assumed, because you love the place, you'd want to stay here. I wouldn't sell it and put you out of a home, and I don't need the money."

He took a deep breath. "Chase and the ranch were here when I needed a place, and a purpose. But I'm past that now, and if both of you are gone, I don't know if I want to stay."

"Oh." She cocked her head. "How long have you been here?"

"Long enough."

"What did you do before?"

His gaze traveled to the view outside the window. Or was he seeing anything at all? Had his thoughts made him blind to what was in front of him?

"Traveled a lot. Worked at odd jobs. Needed a place to be still, and Chase gave me one."

"You knew him before you came here."

"Met in a sweat lodge, and the rest is history. My plan is to eventually retire to a lakeside cabin and do nothing but fish for the rest of my days."

Okay, so he didn't want to talk about his past. She could certainly understand and respect that.

"I'll put the deed in your name, and you can sell the whole works tomorrow for all I care, and buy that cabin you want. I'll just have to find somewhere to board Jake."

"You can't make snap decisions about your future and the ranch. It's too soon, Dusty. You're still getting over the loss. And you can't give the place away." He hesitated. "What if Chase comes back?"

She squeezed her eyes shut for a second. "He won't."

"But—"

"Murray, it is yours. Keep it, sell it, bank the money for Chase, do whatever you want. The land, the buildings, the horses—everything is yours."

She let her shoulders sag then. "I need to be free, Murray. I have to walk away, and I would much rather give Chase's ranch to you than sell it to a stranger right now. But once I've gone a mile down the road, it really won't matter to me what you do with it."

"Chase gave you the ranch to make sure you'd be financially secure. He wanted you safe."

Hearing the words rattled her a bit, even though she already understood the sentiment. "He said that to you?"

"Yes. You were his only concern." Of course he'd have talked to Murray about his plans, even though he kept them a secret from her. She rubbed her knuckles over the ache in her chest.

"I will never be free of his shadow if I stay here, and I'll only be half alive. I think I can be whole again if I go back to riding. There's a good living to be made anywhere I choose, and with a good truck and camper..." She blew out a breath. "I need to cut ties and be free.

TWENTY-THREE

Dusty spent a couple of hours doing paperwork with Chase's lawyers, bought a nice new truck and camper, packed herself up, called Linda, and was within two hours of a clean getaway when the phone rang.

"Hello?"

"Is this Melanie Torino?"

Her first thought was, Melanie Torino doesn't exist, but she answered, "Yes, who is this?"

It was a social worker at the Kamloops hospital. Her father had been brought in by ambulance that morning, it looked like he'd had a stroke, and she should come.

Dusty didn't go. As far as she was concerned, her father was already dead, had been since the day he walked into their California apartment. The man in the hospital was a stranger to her. But she put her plans on hold anyway.

The family doctor Dusty remembered from her

childhood called the next morning. John made it through the night, but his long-term prognosis wasn't good. He had full paralysis on his left side and partial on his right. Was barely able to swallow, and could not speak. His condition might improve with intense physical therapy, but it was doubtful he'd ever be able to look after himself.

She still didn't go to see him, and another day passed before she got a call from the hospital's legal department. There were papers to be signed by John's next of kin, and perhaps his attorney should be contacted.

Attorney. Brilliant idea. Dusty finally had a direction. And someone to hand the reins to. But because she had no idea who John's legal rep was, she was forced to drive to Casa Mia, her childhood home.

Bombarded by dread, she paused on the road outside the massive wrought iron gate, but quickly shut down her emotions. There was no time for such foolishness. She needed to get the information to hand off an obligation she didn't want, and then she could get on with her own life, free and clear of even the slightest hint of guilt.

Driving slowly, she took in the long, low racing barns where she used to play with kittens, where she learned how to properly offer a treat to a horse, and later, where she met Chase. Followed him around like a needy puppy.

She shook off the memories, and when she arrived at the house, parked right in front of the wide entranceway.

With fingertips, she traced the figure of a

galloping horse carved into the smooth, wooden door. It should be warm from the sun, but like everything else at Casa Mia, it was cool to the touch.

Dusty moved quickly through the cavernous entry, her footsteps on the ceramic floor echoing in the chilled air. She could almost hear John bellowing to close the door, but silence reigned, like it did when he spent hours—days, it seemed— locked in his office.

That's where she should be headed, but couldn't resist poking her head into the bedroom she occupied from the day she was born until she left at sixteen, and was surprised to find it unchanged.

Not a speck of dust marred the ornate headboard, night table, or desk—family heirlooms imported from Italy, like the rest of the furnishings in the house—and she could smell the lemon-scented polish.

Dark brown, floor-length curtains she'd been trained to keep closed made the small window appear much more grandiose than it was, and a matching bedspread was perfectly smooth and lint-free.

For years, one of the games she played when trying to fall asleep was imagining what her room would look like if only her father would let her be a real girl. She wouldn't have pink and frills, but she'd paint over the pea green walls, and hang pictures, her bedspread would be the color of the winter sky, and she would have pretty clothes in the closet. She glanced at the folding door, slid it open to find western-style shirts and jeans hung in a neat row, and boy's pajamas and underwear stacked on the shelves. Everything exactly as it had been.

Dusty spun and left the room, clicking the door shut carefully and quietly, as she'd been taught.

She made her way to his office. The small, freestanding building had been off-limits to her— which didn't stop her from sitting in the chair behind the humongous black desk when he was out of town. She would stare out the picture window at the sprawling acres and imagine calling this room her own one day. She would paint and decorate using desert colors of pale orange, green, and blue, with a sand-colored desk, and plenty of shelves for her books.

John hated books, made her leave them in the barn.

When Dusty eventually pushed the door open, she half expected to find him sitting there as always, glaring, demanding she quit bothering him.

But the chair was empty. Shoved awkwardly against the huge black safe, leaving a large, empty space between the desk and the wall where a small cotton square—the kind a paramedic would rip from a sterile foil wrapper—and a discarded surgical glove told the story.

This was where it happened. Where he had the stroke. Where his life had been irrevocably changed.

She knew what that was like, waited for a wash of emotion, but felt nothing. Tossed the trash in the wastebasket and pulled the chair over.

First she tried the desk drawers, for a card, or a

personal address and phone book, but came up empty. Then she shook the mouse, and when the computer came to life, was surprised to discover it wasn't password protected.

Her amusement at his foolishness...or was it arrogance?...evaporated when she accessed his emails. There were sixty-two waiting to be opened. And three of them were from Mr. Sanderson. The same man Chase had gone to work for? Suspicion buzzed.

She opened the most recent and found only three words. "No data available." Opened the others, and she had confirmation. John had been trying to locate Chase through Sanderson.

In for a penny, she thought, and scrolled through folders. Found correspondence between John and Mr. Sanderson dating back to about when Chase borrowed the training gate for Angel.

Dusty was sickened, yet not surprised to learn it was John who asked Sanderson to offer Chase a job in Australia. John who pulled in a favor to get the work visa approved in record time. And there was more. So much more Dusty, could no longer look at the screen.

How much did she really want to know?

She paced the room, racking her brain. What should she do? She looked at the computer. What exactly did it hold? She sat down again and went to the internet, searched for a private investigator named Ty in Vancouver. Scrolled through results until she found the address where she dropped Chase off many months ago.

She made the call from her own cell, and ten

minutes later, she was unplugging the computer and carrying it out to her jeep. Tyler would search every last inch, byte, pixel, or whatever, for any information she might want or need. Then maybe, just maybe, she could find Chase and convince him to come home.

Back in the office, she studied the safe.

John had loved that old thing. He'd spin the dial as though it was magic, and she would watch through the barely open doorway. She reached for it now, and held her breath while she imitated his moves the way she'd done so often before. Then pushed down on the big handle and, with a barely audible click, the door swung open. Dusty gathered all the papers, contracts, envelopes and such together. She would take them home and go through them. Surely there would be legal papers with his attorney's name.

She looked at the metal cash box on top of the pile, and curiosity got the best of her. How much money would he keep in it? She knew he always had a wad of hundreds in his pocket. Whether he was buying bulls at the auction, or a truckload of feed, it was always cash. She opened the lid and found exactly what she expected. Filled to the brim with hundred-dollar bills, neatly bundled like they were freshly made. She lifted them out and laid them on the desk. Ten bundles. Lord, that was an awful lot of money, and wouldn't she love to donate it to a charity he hated?

Not that she would, but thinking about it lightened her heart somehow.

Glancing at the empty box, she quickly realized

it had a false bottom. She pushed and pulled, prodded and shook. Could hear something inside. The giant magnifying glass John always kept on his desk helped her find a thin slot, and, using his letter opener, she quickly popped the bottom off, spilling the meager contents on the olive-green blotter.

There were several keys, a folded sheet of paper covered on both sides with names and phone numbers she didn't recognize. A worn, yellowed envelope barely held an old birth certificate—John Torrence Smith had been born on exactly the same day as her father, in White Pine Springs, Alberta.

Dusty turned over another envelope and was shocked to see it was addressed to her, Melanie Torino, c/o John Torino. The print on the upper left corner read, Desert Life Hospice, Hataseeh, New Mexico. It was postmarked last September 25th. The envelope had been ripped open across the top, and her heart thumped hard in her chest when she pulled out a single sheet of hospital letterhead.

Dear Melanie,

I am writing to tell you I have breast cancer.

My doctor insisted you be informed, as it is now part of your medical history.

I am not looking for sympathy, money, or to make contact.

Nurse Finley, who is doing the writing for me, will not mail this letter until I am gone, which should be soon.

Sincerely,

Myrya

P.S. you should also know that John Torino is

not your biological father. I only said he was to get even for what he'd done, and I was trying to get him to pay for my abortion.

The paper slid to the desk and her hands fell limply into her lap. For endless minutes, she stared at the words, her brain trying to compute the reality.

Last September.

He had known he wasn't her father, last September. Long before Chase left.

He knew, long before he drove Chase away, and yet had still been determined to destroy them.

Whatever she'd eaten that morning churned sickly in her gut.

She could never again tell herself her father had done it because deep down he loved her—only wanted what he thought was best for her. The last tiny drop of little-girl hope she hadn't even realized was still there bled from her heart.

Her father truly hated her. A sound came from her throat, half sob, half laugh. He wasn't even her father, and he hated her. But he was. He was the only father she'd ever known.

Bits and pieces of her childhood flicked through her mind. Odd snippets, like the night she'd come running in from the barn, excited about a new foal, and thrown her arms around his legs, to look up at him all excited. He was so tall, and her head barely made it to his belt buckle. She must have been around five or six.

He'd instantly flown into a rage and yelled, "For God's sake, Mel, don't do that." Then shoved her violently across the room.

And one night when she'd lain in bed crying because of a bad dream, he came to her room. "Daddy," she'd cried, and held her arms out to him.

He stopped, and stared at her as though she was an alien. "Daddy, I'm scared," she sobbed. But he never came to her, made no effort to comfort her, instead bellowing, "Shut up, dammit. For the love of God, shut up."

He stormed out, slamming the door behind him, and she heard his truck start up, drive away.

From then on she slept with her door closed, making sure he couldn't hear if she cried.

She gave herself a shake and said out loud, "You are not a helpless child anymore. Big deal if neither of your parents wanted you. At least one fed and clothed you, left you alone to grow up as you wished." *And he waited until I was an adult before he really fucked up my life.*

Hours later she was sitting on the porch at Buck Hill, with Murray.

She told him the story, and showed him the letter.

"Maybe God is punishing him now," he said.

"Sure. He'll live out his days in comfort, with someone waiting on his every need."

Murray said nothing for a while, then he reached over and put his hand over hers. "Nothing will ever change who you are in your heart, Dusty. You're a good person."

"But not a very smart one." She shook her head. "When we did Chase's DNA test in California, why didn't we do mine, too?"

"Because what you were focused on was

whether or not John was Chase's father."

"And we had John's DNA profile right there on paper. We were so caught up in hoping my DNA had mistakenly been identified as his." She closed her eyes. "One swab of my mouth, and our lives would have been right back on track. I'd be sitting here with him right now instead of you."

Anger and sadness danced together in her heart. "I guess I'd better phone Linda before you do."

"Good idea," was all he said before he slipped off into the darkness.

Duncan, sitting by her feet, whined softly. She stroked his head, gave him a hug and said, "I'm okay, pal. You can go."

He licked her hand before following Murray into the night.

TWENTY-FOUR

The next day Dusty drove directly to the hospital, signed the necessary documents, and then shocked herself by asking for his room number. It was as though she wasn't in control of her body. Her feet were taking her to John while part of her mind screamed, NO.

But apparently she needed to do this. Tell him she knew. Tell him she didn't care if he rotted in hell, because he was getting what he deserved. She would tell him it didn't matter how much he hated her, because she would always hate him more. She would spit in his face if he so much as *tried* to speak. She would....

And then she was frozen, motionless, barely breathing, just outside his room. Staring in at the shell of a man in the bed. The olive skin of his Italian heritage gone pale and lifeless. The hair flat against his head was thin and colorless, too long, and the neckline of the washed-out blue hospital gown hung crookedly across his bony chest. His mouth hung open like a baby bird while a woman in bright yellow scrubs inserted what looked like a spoonful of thin pudding. Then she pushed up on his bottom jaw to close his mouth, and Dusty watched the exaggerated movement of his Adam's apple. Up, then down. The simple act of swallowing made visible.

Dusty's anger was gone, the fire in her gut evaporating like a puff of steam.

Maybe Murray was right. Maybe this was his punishment. She walked away.

***

On the drive to Vancouver, Dusty thought about what she and Chase had been through because of John, and when she eventually handed everything over to Tyler, files, computer, tin box of money, the birth certificate, and a copy of the letter, she was ready to let go of everything. To leave her past behind.

Somehow giving him the responsibility allowed her to breathe more easily, and after about twenty minutes of conversation, she walked back out onto the street feeling like a huge weight had been lifted from her shoulders.

For nearly a week, Dusty stayed with Linda. They talked for endless hours, shopped, ate, drank margaritas on the patio, and simply hung out. Linda made sure Dusty had a clear view of her options, and didn't mince words.

"What happens when John dies, Dusty, and you

inherit his fortune?"

"I don't want his money. I don't want anything to do with him."

"Then what? Who gets his money? The government?"

"I don't know, don't care."

"What about doing some good with what he leaves you?" She smiled in response to Dusty's frown. "Sleep on it."

"No pressure."

"You could always arrange to put the money in trust until you can find a worthy cause."

"Maybe I'll use it to find Chase. That would be payback to John in a big way, wouldn't it?" Dusty said, and heard the bitterness in her own voice.

Linda's lack of response made Dusty very uncomfortable. Then the words came slowly and clearly.

"Maybe you should search for yourself first."

Dusty's tears were sudden and unstoppable, as though they'd been trapped under the surface for too long. Linda moved over, opened her arms, and Dusty fell into them.

Eventually, when the storm subsided, Dusty pulled away, and her voice was hoarse when she said, "I really don't know who I am anymore."

Linda nodded. "It will come. You're a smart woman, not to mention stubborn. I have no doubt you'll find the answers you need."

"You." Dusty hesitated. "You're everything I would wish for in a mother."

Linda scowled at her. "I'm far too young to be your mother."

Dusty's smile finally came back. "Okay, then a big sister."

"That I can live with. How about some chocolate ice cream?"

They were halfway to the kitchen when the phone in Dusty's pocket sang a tune.

It was Tyler. His report was finished, and he needed to hand-deliver it to her. She gave him directions, and he was there in less than thirty minutes with two large brown envelopes.

One was addressed to John's attorney, who, per Dusty's wishes, had been identified by Tyler, and then apprised of the situation. The package contained the information needed to look after John and his business for the duration.

The other envelope was addressed to her, and was stamped several times with the word, CONFIDENTIAL. He held it out to her, but didn't let go when she tried to take it from him. He waited until she met his direct look, and then, in a very serious tone said, "There is *nothing* in this envelope that you will like, and my advice to you, as a fellow human being, would be to burn it unopened and get on with your life."

"Nothing to help me find my husband?"

"Nothing.

"And if I don't take your advice?"

He shook his head "Your life will be forever changed. Your perspective altered."

"Are you trying to scare me?"

"I'm being dead honest. What you'll learn from reading this report will only add to your sadness and disillusionment."

234

Well. That was certainly straightforward. "I understand."

"No you don't, not yet. What I found is protected by client confidentiality. However, it is my professional responsibility to advise you to go to the authorities with the information."

Dusty appreciated his desire to protect her, but there was no need. "Tyler, I learned long ago that my father was a rapist. And I will not protect him. I'll be reporting anything you found because it's the right thing to do, and I *will not* have his crimes, whatever they are, on my conscience."

"Then it's up to you how the reporting is done. I have a contact I can call, or you could simply walk into a police station and ask to make a report."

Dusty struggled to think, to reach for logic and reason within herself. She took a deep breath, closed her eyes, and waited. Let it come, she thought, let the answer surface from the jumbled thoughts. She concentrated on square breathing, in for ten, hold for ten, out for ten, hold for ten. Soon she was up to a count of twenty. Calm deep breathing always helped. The brain couldn't function without oxygen. She opened her eyes, met Tyler's squarely, then said, "Are you in a hurry to leave? Do you have any other business this afternoon?"

"Nothing that can't wait."

"Then why don't you call your contact and ask him to come here?"

Linda's nod confirmed she'd done the right thing.

An hour later, they were a group of five

gathered in Linda's living room. Two detectives listened to Tyler as he spoke, and the tiny microphone clipped to the collar of his shirt captured every word. He was thorough, began at the beginning, walked them through to the end. Explained how he found what he did, and why he believed the man in question was beyond prosecution.

When they began to question Dusty, it became real. Had she ever seen him with young girls, had he ever behaved inappropriately with her, with her friends? It went on and on. Had he ever touched her in a way that was uncomfortable?

She laughed then, and everyone stared at her. She sobered quickly, and explained. "I spent most of my childhood wishing he would put his arms around me and hold me like fathers I read about in books." She shook her head, "I think he may have actually touched me less than half a dozen times in my entire life. I craved his affection, but never once did I experience it. I can safely, honestly, and with complete confidence say he never ever did anything to me that would be remotely considered inappropriate."

"And you are certain you haven't repressed anything."

"Officer, my father came into my bedroom only once in my life. I'd been crying because of a nightmare. He stood halfway inside the room, raging at me to stop crying. For years I've remembered the horror on his face, and assumed it was because he found me abhorrent." Had he simply been afraid to touch her?

She thought of herself as a little girl, hugging his legs—while eye-level with his belt buckle—

Linda's voice cut into her thoughts. "Dusty, wherever you're going with this, stop. Don't make assumptions or excuses. Do *not* invest your heart where there is nothing but a wasteland."

Dusty's mouth went dry "How did you know?"

"I could see your heart beginning to bleed for him. Take back the anger for a while instead. It's healthier. Think of those young girls. Feel their pain first."

Exactly the reminder she needed.

The next hours were a blur. There was so much to be said, and so little. And then, finally, she was alone. Linda was in the kitchen fixing supper, talking quietly to Rick. Dusty stared out over the ocean while her fingers played with the edges of the brown envelope in her lap. She'd already heard the horror, the cops had the tape and the computer. What could possibly be any worse? Of course, in the end, she needed to know.

It was a fourteen-page document. The first three pages were a chronological outline of her father's life, beginning with his parents' marriage in England.

It was a sad story, information Ty gathered from John's journals, and an interview with a member of his birth family.

While flying with the RCAF during WW II, Jack Alexander fell in love with and married a handsome English woman named Charlotte, and brought her home with him to the huge family ranch homesteaded by his great-grandparents in southern

Alberta. There were five homes on the property, all somewhat isolated from each other.

Jack's family was shocked by the arrival of Charlotte, and by the marriage, because they expected him to return from the war and marry his high school sweetheart. They felt he'd been tricked by the slick English woman.

Life was difficult for Charlotte, living in isolation on hundreds of acres of pastureland, with only Jack's unfriendly family members for neighbors. She was a vibrant, wealthy socialite, and her romantic adventure to Canada was not turning out as she'd pictured it. Two years went by before the birth of twin boys gave her blessed relief from the loneliness. She doted on them until, at the age of six, they were old enough to escape from the house and help with the work of ranching.

Once again she was alone, and Jack grew weary of her constant whining and complaining. He stayed away from the house as much as possible, and she apparently found companionship elsewhere.

The arrival of her third son, John, was not a good thing. Even her older boys, hanging over the edge of the cradle, asked why the baby looked different from them. His hair and eyes were nearly black and his skin was more golden than white. Charlotte quickly explained that, although she was blond and blue-eyed, her own father had black hair and dark eyes. It was her mother she'd gotten her coloring from. But as the baby became a toddler, his skin darkened even more, and Charlotte changed.

No longer reserved and correct, she became agitated by the smallest of things. Her voice was shrill while she constantly scolded the boy, and she made a point of keeping him confined to his room.

Jack had managed to pretend things were fine in their house until the boy was nearly two. But when confronted by his own brothers and told he was the laughingstock of his family, he had to do something.

He made a trip to town and withdrew his life savings from the bank. When he got home, he told Charlotte to pack her things, and the boy, the one he knew wasn't his. He drove her to the train station in Calgary, bought her a ticket to the West Coast, and handed her the rest of his money, two hundred and twenty-three dollars.

For nineteen months she lived in a one-room apartment above the greasy spoon restaurant where she waited tables. She bought an old wooden playpen for the toddler, and turned it upside down over the mattress on the floor to keep him contained while she worked.

At night she took money from the men who visited her bed, and after more than one was displeased by the child's eyes watching them, she draped an old tablecloth over the sides of the cage.

Then, early one January morning, she gathered the money she'd been hiding behind a loose piece of wall paneling, quickly penned a note to leave behind with John's birth certificate, and walked to the train station. Thirty minutes later she boarded a train to cross the country. She would be almost home then, with only an ocean left to cross.

Four-year-old John Alexander was found alone when Charlotte didn't come downstairs to work her shift. He was taken to the local orphanage. The administrator was given the note which read: *The boy's name is John. His father doesn't want him, and I can't take him to England with me.*

John's life in the institution was unpleasant, to say the least. He was called half-breed. Didn't fit with the whites, didn't fit with those called Natives. After years of isolation and abuse, he took off when he was thirteen, and was in trouble with the law shortly after. Theft and assault landed him in juvenile detention more than once. At fifteen, an attempted sexual assault on a young woman who refused to date him because she said he was an Indian nearly sent him to adult court, but the lawyer pleaded with them, saying the boy was an orphan and needed guidance, not punishment.

He was sent to a work farm, and his two-year sentence there set him up for life. When released, he went to cattle country and never looked back. He worked, saved, changed his name to Torino, and eventually became a respected rancher. He told anyone who would listen that his father was an Italian count, hence his dark coloring, and the name of his ranch, Casa Mia.

A solid member of the community...with a secret life. John Torino was a pedophile, and more. Dusty scanned the details of how John arranged for Angel to be stolen, and his assumption that once the horse was gone there would be no ties left between Chase and Dusty.

But the plan backfired.

The men who were to drug Chase and leave him in a mountain cabin threw in a twist of their own by drugging the water bottles, and he didn't show up alive and well the next day like he was supposed to. John was forced to go to dramatic lengths to make sure he was found, but in the meantime, Dusty became far too involved.

John had not only refused to pay his henchmen the balance of their fee, but, being a vindictive man, he had set them up for a fall, making sure they went to jail for a completely different crime, one he had no traceable connection to.

When John saw the picture of Dusty and Chase embracing in the winner's circle in California, he was enraged, incensed, and had no choice. He produced the DNA proof and expected them to bow to his wishes, but it didn't happen. He contacted Mr. Sanderson, Angel's owner, asking him to help. The letters back from the man were interesting. He would only agree to offer the Australia job to Chase, but refused to have any further business dealings with John after that.

And then there was the list. The threats he would use on, or had made to Chase. They were numbered, and the first eight had ticks beside them. They were horrible. Number five stood out as particularly horrid, a detailed description of how Chase's fingers would be mailed to Dusty, one by one.

TWENTY-FIVE

Dusty drove back to Kamloops the next day, directly to the office of John's attorney. Signed the documents they had ready for her, gave him the envelope from Tyler, and told him she was leaving town. No, she didn't want to be notified if John died. If there was an inheritance? Put it in trust. Emergency contact? Linda.

Thirty minutes. Over, done with. Close the door. Walk away.

Six days later, she left Buck Hill Ranch. Truck, camper, and determination her only companions for many hours of soul searching, and endless miles of pavement. Her first destination was the hospice where her mother had died.

There she spoke to nurse, Anna Finley, who had spent many hours listening to Myrya ramble on about her life, her triumphs. Anna was unable to tell Dusty what she wanted to hear—that her mother had regretted leaving her baby with John—because it wasn't true. In fact, Myrya had been very clear about her feelings towards her daughter. She was glad she hadn't had an abortion, because it had saved her the agony of facing, later in life, that she had done something so despicable. But she never wanted a child, never longed to be a mother. Even at the end was glad she was alone in her death, with no responsibilities except for the one the nurse took care of in the letter. Simple biology, nothing more.

Anna said Myrya's death was peaceful.

Dusty only asked one question which brought her a satisfactory answer, one she could build on. Did Myrya have family? Parents? Siblings? Yes. In fact, she was born on an Apache reservation nearby, and her parents still lived there. They had come to visit Myrya only once. She had told them about the child she'd given away at birth, a girl named after her grandmother. Then she asked them not to return, and they respected her wishes.

Dusty thanked Nurse Finley, and moved on to her next destination. To the place where she would discover her Self.

***

A diminutive woman opened the door, and a slow smile moved from her eyes down to her mouth, and lit her whole face. She held out her hands. "Welcome, my child." Her voice was beautiful, low, melodic.

"I am looking for the parents of Myrya," said Dusty.

An elderly man joined the woman in the

doorway, and he, too, smiled with genuine warmth. "MaLainie. Your name is MaLainie. Welcome to our home. Your home." He backed away to make room, and the woman pulled Dusty inside.

"My name is Melanie."

"Myrya named you after your grandmother." He nodded toward the woman still holding onto her hand. "Her name is MaLainie."

Dusty opened her mouth to speak, but the woman quietly interrupted with words that seemed to be spoken more to herself than to them.

"Myrya's image, if not for the green of your eyes, and the reddish glow in your hair. But your voice is hers." She looked down at the hands she held and turned them over. "The calluses show you are not afraid of work, yet you care for your nails." Her thumb rubbed over the white gold wedding band. "And there is a man who loves you, something Myrya never had." She looked up with hope shining in her eyes. "Will you be able to stay with us for a while?"

There was a tightness in Dusty's chest that she didn't understand. "I would like to get to know you. To learn about my heritage."

They both smiled widely, and he said, "Then you will stay. And I shall call you Lainie…if I may?"

They accepted Dusty into their home, opening their arms and their hearts with a quiet warmth, never doubting who or what she was. Only she did that.

Dusty learned her grandparents were a crucial part of their community, because they were Elders, and revered for their wisdom, life experience, and patience. They held a position of great respect, and everyone came to them, thirsting for knowledge. Dusty among them.

After long hours of words and equally long hours of silence, she began to understand, ever so slightly, the peace in their souls. She loved to watch them listening to the children. Could see love and respect in their eyes, and in the touch of their hands. Every fiber of their beings showed how much they cherished the young souls. And when the Elders spoke, a respectful hush blanketed their listeners.

Dusty had traveled a vast distance to learn about her mother, but instead she discovered the beauty, the peaceful intensity, and the completeness of Apache spirituality—something her mother hadn't found.

Dusty came to understand, with great clarity, where she came from, where she fit in the world, and why. And she accepted that not only was she on this earth for a purpose, but everything she'd been through thus far was for a reason.

In July, she was invited to attend a *Sunrise Ceremony*, the ritual of a girl's rite of passage into womanhood. Dusty, like the girls participating, never slept during the four days and four nights of the Ceremony. She didn't miss even a moment of the process.

There were endless hours of dancing, praying, sacred rituals, and running—each morning, for a greater distance, the young women ran into the sunrise. This required such great physical endurance and preparedness that most of the participants had spent at least six months in training so they would be able to complete the Ceremony. Their ultimate goal, to achieve and embrace the spiritual, healing, and physical powers of *The White-Painted Woman*—the most revered female figure of the Apache people.

By the end of the Ceremony, Dusty came to know her own physical and spiritual selves, found her power, and understood where she belonged.

Dusty shut down the memories then, shuddering her way back to the here and now, the fall of 2004.

She opened her eyes, grabbed a coat and stepped out into the night. From under the camper, she retrieved a folding chair. Positioned it so she could see nothing but land and sky while she reflected on the good she'd found—no, *created*—in her new life.

Even though she discovered great strength, peace, and tranquility among her mother's people, and in the light and openness of their desert, it was not her home. Her spirit longed for the weight of the mountains and trees far to the north.

Leaving behind the wonderful people she had become very close to, Dusty followed her heart back to the interior of British Columbia, to the land where she had been born, and had grown into a woman. To a sunrise her soul recognized.

Then she spent months driving miles of back roads until she found this place, where she fit so well. Where her spirit guide the wolf belonged, and the lookout rock welcomed her.

The land was raw, and she would take great

care settling into its open arms, asking for permission and guidance from the many spirits there. She would build a place of happiness in the shape of the *circle of life*, where peace and harmony would thrive within its power.

Dusty stretched her arms in the air with her fingers spayed wide, and spoke with a voice that belonged in a place of worship. "This...is my home… My spirit is peaceful here. And I promise to respect and love this land that I can feel without touching, and see without opening my eyes.

"Here," she went on. "Here is where I will bring them. The children must have a place to feel their own spirits, to heal. And it is my destiny to share what I have learned."

Her eyes went to the northern sky, and she sighed, replete, watching the movement of pale yellows and greens. The northern lights, from here, were barely a hint of what they could be, but still she heard the voices of the sky, and felt the power of such wondrous light.

This is my destiny. This is what I can give to the lost and forgotten children.

A wolf howled nearby, and she was complete— held close by the spirits of her ancestors.

PART THREE

Celebration

TWENTY-SIX

Twelve years later.
Sunrise Ranch, British Columbia,
Fall 2016

Staring out her kitchen window at the unfamiliar vehicle coming down the long, bumpy, and very private road, Dusty muttered, "You have got to be kidding."

All three dogs waited at the door, wearing expressions of concern and excitement. "You guys have to stay home," she said, before she opened the door and hopped across the porch on one foot, struggling to get her second boot on. The German shepherd and two border collies scooted to the edge of the wide porch, and took up position to watch the dozen or more wild-looking horses poking their heads over the sides of an open stock trailer.

When Dusty got to the cab of the truck, the door opened, and a short, round man plopped to the ground. "Ma'am," he said, and held out a couple of slightly dirty and crumpled papers.

She read the bill of sale listing names, registration numbers, and prices of fourteen racehorses. The total on the bottom was five thousand, eight hundred dollars. The second page was a hand-scrawled note that read, "Deliver to Dusty Mathews, Sunrise Ranch," and she recognized Murray's scribbled signature on the bottom.

Well, hell. Not much she could do now. She shrugged her shoulders in defeat and asked, "Does this thing have a ramp on it?"

"Yup."

She pointed. "Could you back it into that pen over there?"

"Yup." He hoisted himself into the cab, and Dusty cringed when he revved the engine with a roar and a puff of nasty black exhaust.

She closed her eyes for a moment. This wasn't what she'd pictured when Murray called and asked if she wanted a few ex-racehorses to retrain.

The gears of the truck protested loudly before it was turned around and backed toward the row of pens. Dusty sprinted to the gate, swung it wide, then watched as the lumbering transport was deftly maneuvered through the opening in one swing.

They worked together to get the ramp lowered, then she stood clear while he removed the single two-by-four holding the horses in.

The first thoroughbred started down the ramp quite peacefully, but was nearly trampled as the rest felt the pressure of their crowding ease, and moved quickly toward what had to feel like freedom.

Dusty pasted herself against the fence as they stampeded past her, then backed out alongside the truck. Dust swirled as the nervous bunch milled around in the small space, quickly discovering solid fence rails keeping them from the green fields.

Then the truck jerked forward, and Dusty had to scurry to get the gate closed as the rig pulled out and rumbled its way down the driveway. She shook her head. "Well, this is certainly crappy timing."

Tossing her annoyance aside, she got busy filling the water tub, but scuffles over who'd get the first drink quickly made it apparent she needed to open the two adjoining pens to ease the pressure of the large group, and prevent fighting.

Dusty pulled out the separating rails, filled three tubs, tossed hay into the pens, and headed back to the house. She had less than an hour to get to town before the post office closed.

Every Thursday she made the trek to civilization to pick up mail, fresh fruits and vegetables, and Billy, her oldest, who was in his third semester at culinary school, and had Fridays off.

She quickly changed into clean boots and jacket, opened the back door of the big blue pickup for Justin, her German shepherd, to jump in, climbed into the driver's seat, and shot down the long driveway, only stopping long enough to close the gate when she reached the main road.

Barreling toward town, she pushed the dash buttons to speed dial the built-in phone, and after four rings, the recording came on and she listened impatiently. "Murray here. If it's a nice day, I'm probably out on the lake. Otherwise, I guess I'm busy. Leave a message if you must..."

"I must," she muttered, waiting for the beep, then, "Dammit, Murray, you said a *couple* of horses, and fourteen is a hell of a lot more than a couple. Call me. I need to yell at you."

The bugger was likely listening and laughing at her.

He knew how much she hated September, when the ranch became an empty nest and messed with her heart. To give her something else to think about, keep her busy, he'd dumped this bunch of horses on her. She didn't mind, really. But she wouldn't tell *him* that. Not for a while, anyway.

Murray had been a good friend to her for a very long time. He sold Buck Hill a year after she returned from New Mexico, used half the money to buy himself a smaller place—fifty acres right beside a lake teeming with fish—and put the other half in a scholarship program for foster kids.

The only horses he kept were retirees, ex-racehorses, and pensioned broodmares who didn't require too much attention, and he could devote himself to fishing. In the summertime he'd take half a dozen Sunrise Ranch kids at a time and spend hours teaching them about casting and flies and things, and they would always come back before supper with fish to share with the others.

It was easy to imagine Murray right this minute floating around on his lake, chuckling about how perfectly he'd set her up.

TWENTY-SEVEN

Watching Billy step off the bus brought joy to Dusty's heart, and the tiniest wisp of sadness. At twenty-one, he was beginning to look more like a man than a boy, and oh, how she had adored that freckle-faced boy.

He appeared years ago, when she was working with the fencing crew, an adorable pre-teen with curly red hair and a backbone. He'd hovered at the edge of the trees, watching the men work for a while before boldly approaching to ask about a job. The foreman pointed at Dusty. "Talk to the boss lady," he said.

The youngster looked stunned by the fact that under the overalls, plaid shirt and crumpled straw cowboy hat, what he'd thought was a small man was actually a woman, and it was the first time in his life he'd ever seen green eyes like his own. He'd stammered, "M-ma'am, I'd like a job. I'm strong, and a good worker."

Dusty had struggled to keep a straight face. "Well, you certainly look strong," she said. "But if you're under sixteen, I'll need your parents to give permission for you to join the crew." His shoulders tensed, and he bit his lower lip. Dusty's voice softened, "What's your name?"

"Billy O'Dell, ma'am, but my dad's not feeling good, so I know he couldn't come and sign for me today."

"Do you live nearby, Billy?"

"Just over the hill, ma'am."

"Then that makes us neighbors." She held out her hand. "My name is Dusty, and I'm pleased to meet you."

"Yes, ma'am."

She grinned. "You can call me Dusty."

"Yes, ma'am. Dusty, I mean."

"Have you ever worked on fencing before, Billy?"

"Yes, ma'am, Dusty, ma'am, I fenced with my dad lots."

"Maybe your dad could come by tomorrow and sign for you to work."

Billy mumbled, "Maybe. What time do you start?"

Dusty hadn't missed the subtle change that came with mention of his father. She was curious, but didn't want to scare him away. Instead, she talked to him about the ranch she was building, and the kids who would come every summer to stay.

"Suppose I could get work next year too, then? I don't have much to do in the summers."

"I bet there will be lots for you to do next year."

Once the boy went home, she talked to her foreman and found out Billy's dad was a good rancher, husband, and father up until his wife died of cancer. Then he'd fallen into the bottle. Rumor had it he barely got his morning chores done before he hit the booze, and the boy was left to his own devices.

Dusty drove over the hill at eight o'clock the next morning and met Billy's father. Lucas O'Dell was a pleasant man, probably in his forties, but looked sixty-something. When she talked to him about the place she was building as a summer camp for children, and explained how she needed a kid's input into some of the building and designing, he willingly signed the necessary papers. He obviously loved his son, and wished for him to be happy.

A very grown-up Billy laughed when she told him about the arrival of the new horses that afternoon.

She scowled and grumbled, "It's not that funny."

"Come on, Dusty, admit you're excited about having a bunch of thoroughbreds handed to you." He shook his head at her frown. "How many hours have I listened to you going on and on about the racehorses you used to ride? Your face always lights up, and then you get a faraway, dreamy look."

"Oh, for heaven's sake. Dreamy looks are for the girls you know at school. I'm an old lady."

"Huh. The bus driver calls you hot, and Bobby's dad was asking the other day—"

"Not another word." She laughed. The years

had been kind to her, and she didn't look or feel forty-three. As fit and trim as she'd been as a jockey, she still looked damn fine in a pair of snug jeans, and she liked the sparkle of gray hairs she noticed when she wove her raven black hair into a single long braid every morning. Mostly it was her inner serenity, the peacefulness of her soul, that gave away her age.

She and Billy talked and joked for the rest of the trip home, or at least until they saw Ben and Flower, her two border collies, sitting where the main gates were swung wide open.

At least half a dozen of the new thoroughbreds were grazing alongside the driveway, and it looked as though the dogs had kept them from escaping onto the road at least.

She pulled in slowly, and Billy scrambled out to close the gate behind them.

Dusty climbed out to praise and hug her dogs.

"Do you expect anyone tonight, or should I put the padlock on?" asked Billy.

"Lock it up. I'm gonna leave these horses alone until I check things out." *There must be a fence down.*

Once they were alongside the pens, it was easy to see what happened. The gate on the last pen was wide open. She didn't remember checking it when she took the dividing rails out, and the main gate…well, hell, she must have missed the latch. She was shaken by her own carelessness. Being in such a hurry to get to town could have made her responsible for a deadly accident.

If a horse had been hit by a car—she

shuddered—people could have died, because impact occurs at the upper leg level of the animal, thus sending the body squarely through a windshield to crush the occupants.

She shook her head at the gruesome picture in her mind, and thanked the spirits for watching over her and keeping her dogs vigilant.

"Are you sure they're all here?" asked Billy.

Dusty counted, then counted again. "I get fifteen."

"Me too."

Dusty dug the bill of sale from her pocket and held it out to him.

"Says fourteen," he said.

"That's what I thought. But I never stopped to count them before I left. I'll call Murray later to find out who the extra is." She still needed to yell at him. He expected it from her, and she'd be happy to oblige.

They unloaded the truck and shook grain into a bunch of wooden feed boxes and rubber buckets, and before they were finished, twelve of the loose thoroughbreds calmly walked back into the pens, happy to have a meal provided.

The three still grazing the sides of the driveway were locked out, away from the grain and water while Dusty and Billy went about the evening chores and setting up for the weekend.

Billy was in the lodge kitchen getting supper ready when Dusty went back to check on the horses. Two of the loose ones were standing calmly beside the pens, looking longingly at the water trough. Dusty slipped them each a piece of carrot from her pocket, opened the gate, and they quite happily followed her in.

The last one, a black mare stood alone, halfway between her and the barn. When Dusty took a step forward, she turned and sauntered farther away before again facing Dusty.

Laughing to herself, because the horse was unwittingly putting herself in a corner, Dusty kept moving toward her slowly, talking in a low voice, and maintaining eye contact. "You are certainly a handsome girl. And there's no need to be afraid. I just want to give you this piece of carrot, then I'm gonna leave you alone."

When the mare turned away again and realized she was cornered, she snorted, spun, and squared off against the woman standing between her and escape.

Would she try it? Her eyes were pretty wild. Dusty waited, praying the nervous mare wouldn't attempt to bolt past her, because she'd have to let her go by, and then they'd be off to a bad start.

The black had the barn at her tail and corral fences on each side. Between her and freedom stood the woman with the outstretched hand. After she spun around again, as though confirming her situation, a deep, frightened, nicker of uncertainty rose from her throat.

Several of the penned horses whinnied in response, and her ears flickered toward them. Then from inside the barn came a high-pitched noise that sounded vaguely like a cartoon donkey's bray.

Dusty held her breath and waited. Even though she never took her eyes off the mare's face, she sensed a change in her body language when she was momentarily distracted from being trapped.

Again the wheezing hee-haw cut through the air, and this time the mare turned her back on Dusty, lowered her head near the barn door, and nickered softly in reply.

Caesar, the miniature donkey, called out again, and the nervous black reached for the door latch, working at it frantically with her lips and teeth. She pawed the ground in frustration while continuing to fiddle with the metal handle until the door swung inward. Without hesitation, she jogged right into the dark barn, and put her head over the stall door where only the tips of long, gray ears were visible.

Dusty waited quietly in the doorway, watching her apply her gate-opening skills to the one holding Caesar in his stall. With determination, she worked that latch until it, too, slid open. She used her head to swing the door outward, away from the donkey, then without a backward look, marched out of the barn. Dusty scrambled to reach a wide paddock gate and swing it into the breezeway so they would have no choice but to enter the open pen on the left.

She held her breath when the mare stopped briefly to wait for Caesar to catch up, then the two of them calmly sauntered in side by side.

Dusty closed the gate quickly, slid the latch into place, tied it with a bale twine, then scurried into the barn to retrieve a piece of chain and several double-ended snaps, in order to prevent the next escape attempt.

Billy arrived as she finished fastening the chain, and she told him about the new horse's determination to free Caesar.

Billy leaned over the fence. "Well, mighty Caesar, you appear to have a girlfriend."

"And she's an escape artist, likely the culprit responsible for the open gates today."

"A regular Houdini," said Billy.

"That she is."

Dusty's gaze traveled over the horse, and she sucked in a startled breath. "Look at her hide."

The fronts of her legs were completely hairless. The skin was black, as it should be, but shiny and thick.

Her face was sprinkled with quarter-sized spots of bare skin, the edges of her ears were hairless, and her chest had hand-sized bald areas. There was a deep groove about four inches wide and a foot long halfway between her withers and her belly.

Dusty's eyes met those of the mare, and she was transported to a place of great heat, riding bareback at a full gallop, bale strings wrapped around her wrists, pulling two horses along on each side of her. A fiery branch was lodged between her inner thigh and the mare's body.

Her leg was pinned by a filly pressing against her on the left, so she turned her toe outward to jab the offender in the side with the point of her boot, but in the middle of such panic there was no response.

She let the strings fall away from her wrists, and they galloped on blindly, relying on adrenaline and survival instincts until pain and lack of oxygen won. She collapsed over the mare's wither, looped her arms around her neck, laid her face in the thick mane, and held tightly to her own hands, praying she could stay on until they found their way out of the thick brown sludge hanging motionless where the air used to be.

But consciousness slipped away, and her grip loosened. There was no more strength, no more reserve to draw from. And when her limp, charred body slid off the horse's back, the last few burning embers of the branch fell away too.

"Dusty? What's wrong?"

She shook her head to clear away the images. Shuddered.

"Nothing, just hungry I guess."

The mare blew out a sharp breath, and Dusty felt it dance across her skin. This wasn't the first time she'd seen into the soul of an animal, but she'd never been a part of the images before, and it was disconcerting, to say the least.

She would always wonder what had happened to the woman riding the mare through the fire. Perhaps one day she'd find out. Or not.

TWENTY-EIGHT

Dusty woke to the frantic wheezing sound of Caesar's brays, and within seconds she dragged the shotgun from under her mattress, stuffed bare feet in her boots, and ran out the door, headed for the pen.

Strong arms grabbed her, and when a hand clamped firmly over her mouth a scream exploded in her throat. Dusty fought, but the effort was futile.

An odd, raspy voice right beside her ear penetrated her panic. "Wait. Allow her to protect him."

With her heart slamming against her ribs, she made garbled sounds behind his hand until binoculars were held in front of her eyes.

"The wolf is hurt and hungry, but trust me, your donkey is safe."

Dusty's heart continued to pound hard and fast while she watched through night vision lenses and admired the mare's defensive stance. She'd placed herself sideways between Caesar and danger. Whenever the wolf moved to duck under the fence and into the pen, she either kicked at him with her hind feet or struck at him with her fronts. The stranger was right. Caesar wasn't in danger.

As Dusty relaxed, the hand dropped away from her mouth.

"I'm sorry to frighten you, but I couldn't let you shoot him."

"But if he's injured? Shouldn—"

"Let him fight for his own life."

"I meant shouldn't we help..."

The wolf stopped and turned, stared directly at Dusty, and she could have sworn he looked right through the lenses and into her eyes. She sucked in a startled breath, and released it slowly when he limped away from the pen. Dusty held the field glasses herself now, totally absorbed in watching the sleek creature jog awkwardly along the edge of the field toward into the trees.

But he stopped limping before he disappeared from sight. Dusty used the glasses to check Caesar and the mare, then turned to speak to the stranger.

He was gone.

She spun completely around once, looking quickly, then again, searching with the binoculars, but there was no movement, nothing. He had vanished.

A cold chill ran down her spine, and she backed up until she felt the edge of the porch behind her knees and plunked down on the cedar decking. The dogs gathered around her, curiously quiet.

Dusty wondered if she'd been dreaming. But

the rifle was balanced in her right hand, and the binocs hung from a strap in her left. She set them on the porch, then walked toward the pens to check the horses, but glanced over her shoulder at the sound of the dogs whining.

"Release," she said, and all three bounded off of the porch and stuck close to her side while she visited with Caesar, reassuring him he was safe. Then she turned her attention to the mare.

"Well smarty-pants, now do you understand why he was locked in the barn? Do you get it, that he is small and defenseless out here?"

The black ears flickered, all her attention on Dusty.

"You did a masterful job of protecting him, though. Thank you."

She was tossed up about putting them both in the barn for the night, but in the end decided they might as well stay where they were.

"Dusty?" Billy's voice came from the dark space between her and the house.

"I'm here."

"What's going on?"

"There was a wolf trying to get to Caesar, but the mare scared him off."

He saw the gun in her hand. "You didn't shoot him?"

"No."

"He'll come back."

"I don't think he will."

"What makes you so sure? Did she hurt him?"

"Ah, sort of. He looked like he was limping." Dusty hoped that would be enough explanation to appease his curiosity.

"Are you okay?" Billy was obviously picking up something from her, and she could feel his scrutiny through the darkness. She assured him she was fine, and he headed back to his own cottage.

Dusty plugged in the electric kettle and went to her room to put on some clothes, only now realizing she was wearing nothing but thin, silky pajamas— the top being little more than a camisole—with bare feet in her boots.

Once she donned jeans, heavy socks, moccasins, and a thick sweater, the kettle was singing, and she poured the water into the teapot, then stood inside her back door staring out into the darkness, waiting for it to steep. She'd sit outside for a while.

She was still on the porch in the blackness of night an hour later, snuggled deep in the leather-covered lounge chair, where she had gone over and over in her mind every second of her encounter with the stranger.

He wasn't overly big, but he was extremely strong. She felt absolutely helpless against his strength, yet once the initial shock wore off, she hadn't felt threatened. And thinking about him made her admit she'd actually felt safe in his arms. Almost peaceful.

She shivered. Was he real, or a ghost? She'd heard plenty of stories about Spirits protecting people and animals. But he had such an earthy scent, a rich mixture of wood smoke and dirt and leather, that was very real. And she could still feel the roughness of his jacket against her bare shoulders, the warmth of his hand over her mouth, on her arm. His breath had tickled the fine hairs on her neck when he spoke.

When Dusty dozed off, Justin positioned himself alongside her chair before laying his head down on outstretched paws.

Cold air had her dipping her face inside the blanket, looking for warmth, and drinking in the scent of the wool. She was caught in that place where sleep doesn't want to let go and awake is still a distant illusion.

The gentle sound of horses shuffling about in the pens began to permeate her consciousness, and she opened her eyes to see the wonderful, misty light of morning that happens just before the sun rises with the birth of a new day. She groaned and stretched, then slowly swung her feet to the porch, momentarily encountering the softness of Justin as he scrambled to move out of her way.

Dusty reached to fold the blanket and froze. Slowly, she ran her fingers over the distinct pattern of blues and browns, then raised it to her face and took a deep breath. She closed her eyes while feelings washed over her.

"Dusty."

Her eyes snapped open. "What?"

"Geez, I thought you were asleep sitting up. I called you, like, six times."

"Sorry, Billy. I'm a little stunned, or frozen, or something this morning."

"Did you stay out here all night?"

"Apparently." She shrugged. "Hey, I had to watch over Caesar, you know."

"Yeah, right, you coulda put him in the barn."

Dusty gestured toward the horses in the pens. "You going to keep nagging, or help me feed this bunch?"

"You feed, I'll get breakfast ready."

She smiled. He would always choose the kitchen over outdoors. "Deal. I'll be back in twenty minutes."

Dusty left the blanket she'd never seen before on the lounge and placed the binoculars on top of it.

After breakfast, she and Billy opened pens, rearranged the new thoroughbreds, and set off on ATVs to gather the saddle horses still enjoying summer grazing fields about a mile away. A completely self-sufficient bunch, but the thought of a hungry wolf in their midst concerned her until they came into sight.

As always, at the sound of the ATVs, Jake ambled toward the gate, and the other thirty-six followed, anticipating the grain and alfalfa waiting for them at the barn where they'd spend the weekend. They didn't appear to be spooked, but she would still check them over carefully to be certain there had been no wild encounters.

Memories of her brush with a stranger crowded her thoughts, and she hoped Billy hadn't noticed when she nearly drove into a tree.

By midafternoon, everything was as it should be, and Dusty was sitting in her office, looking forward to the order and predictability of the afternoon before her. The saddle horses were resting their full bellies in the shade of the pine trees lining their paddock. Billy was happily ensconced in the lodge kitchen, cleaning and prepping fruits and vegetables, and the dogs and cats were sleeping in the sunshine, resting up.

Around five o'clock, when an old yellow school bus lumbered its way up the driveway, all hell would break loose for about an hour, because her six foster kids would be home for the weekend.

TWENTY-NINE

Like clockwork it unfolded. Three excited dogs and six laughing, happy kids ran headlong into the house with backpacks full of homework, an endless supply of hugs, and lots of stories to tell. It was always like this on Fridays, and Dusty's heart filled to bursting.

The youngest, Molly, was eight, although she was so tiny, many guessed her to be only five or six. She wrapped her arms around Dusty's legs and looked up, her face brimming with happiness. "We had races with worms today."

"Where *did* you find jockeys small enough?" asked Dusty with a straight face.

Molly dissolved into laughter, and the other kids giggled. "They didn't have jockeys. They were in a cardboard mace that had food at the end."

"Maze, Molly. Who won?"

"Marsha. Her mealy worm did it in ten minutes, but mine was a slug. He finished last."

"Well, heavens, why did you race slugs against worms?"

The giggles were renewed, and Molly stomped her foot. "You aren't listening. They were *all* mealworms, but mine was as slow as a slug." Her face became very serious, and she sighed. "It was my own fault. We weren't supposed to feed them last night, so they'd be hungry this morning. But I couldn't do that. I didn't want my worm to be hungry, 'cuz then he'd be sad."

Dusty gave her a big hug. "Good for you, Molly. Always go with your heart."

"Worms can't be sad," muttered Daryl.

Dusty wiggled her eyebrows at him. "Do you know that for sure?"

"Everybody knows worms don't have feelings, they're just dumb things."

Dusty's voice was soft with love and understanding. "I heard that about kids once, and I'm sure glad I didn't believe it."

Daryl's eyes locked with hers, and she winked. His serious expression relaxed, and a glimmer of a smile appeared.

Dusty looked at all the faces, then spoke in the sternest voice she could manage. "Okay troops, enough goofing off. Get washed up and put your school things away. Dinner will be on the table in twenty minutes." They vanished down the hall and three—usually well-behaved—dogs completely ignored her and galloped madly after the children.

Dusty went to the kitchen with a warm heart and a smile on her face. She learned long ago that kids needed their bellies filled before you could even begin to feed their spirits. That's why today, like every Friday, when they came through the door, the smell of food was in the air—thanks to Billy— and the table was already set for nine.

In the beginning, kids were curious about the extra place, and Dusty explained it was because there was always room for one more at her table. No one would ever be turned away. Now, whenever a new child joined them, it warmed her heart that yet another extra place setting appeared without her prompting. Dusty stroked the polished pine. There was room for twelve chairs around this beautiful table, which meant she was good…for a while at least.

Daryl was the first to appear in the kitchen, and she could tell something was troubling him. She carefully turned to the sink and began washing her hands, "How's things, Daryl?" she asked without looking at him. "Anything new and exciting happen this week?"

Silence.

"Could you pass me the towel, please?"

He quickly handed it to her, and then stood silently at her side.

She watched his reflection in the window over the sink. He wasn't moving. She tried some gentle openings. "Any tests next week to worry about?"

"Nope."

"Everything okay at the Butterwicks' these days?"

"Yup."

Perhaps he needed more time to think about what it was he wanted to say, to stew over whatever was bothering him. Maybe tomorrow he'd open up. She turned to him. "I was wondering if you could help me with the new horses in the morning." His eyes lit up, but faded as she continued, "I have to make some observations about their temperaments. You know, decide which ones will be suitable for kids."

"What will you do with the ones that aren't?" He looked worried.

"Sell them to experienced riders instead. Horses, are like people, not all of them are suited to the same job, but I'll make certain they get good homes, no matter what."

"Oh." He took his seat at the table. Daryl had only been with her for about a year, and he still had some major issues to sort through. First his father had walked out, then his mother remarried. His stepfather was big on corporal punishment, and sadly, the grandmother who eventually agreed to take him in, died. By a very young age, Daryl had learned an awful lot about not being wanted by the people who were supposed to love him.

Once in foster care, he became withdrawn, not allowing himself to get close to anyone, either physically or emotionally. Dusty knew she had only a slim chance of reaching him, and worked hard to connect on his terms.

Since school was back in session, and the children were staying with the Butterwicks during the week, she'd sensed a change in his body language, a softening of his stance, and she suspected he was almost ready to let go of some of his distrust. Perhaps the solid routine of his life was allowing him to believe in the people looking after him. Maybe her plan was paying off yet again.

***

Years ago, when Dusty returned from New Mexico, she became a volunteer in the children's ward of the local hospital. She read to kids, helped them with homework, played games, and simply sat talking to those too sick to want much else. She considered going back to school to become a nurse or physiotherapist, but was impatient, and unwilling to wade through the education system.

Passing the emergency department one day, she heard a child crying, and when she went to investigate, she met Leyla. The little girl wasn't sick or injured, but had been brought to the hospital with her gravely ill grandmother, her sole caregiver. Leyla was going to be handed over to social services unless a family member could be located.

Dusty talked to the social worker, and learned the child's bumpy road would likely be a never-ending journey. She would become a ward of the courts, and there was no telling if she would grow up in one foster home or be moved countless times. Permanent adoption of First Nations children was complicated.

Dusty's heart had been touched by the child with the big brown eyes. She wanted to do something…somehow. Looking into the foster care system, she learned two important facts. One, children were mostly placed in foster homes based on availability, not ethnicity.

And two, a single woman living in a camper would never be approved as a foster parent.

Dusty spent a week being haunted by thoughts of Leyla, wishing there was something she could do to help her. And then, as soon as she realized there could be hundreds of Leylas out there, an idea began to jell.

If she couldn't help one child for the long haul, what about giving a whole bunch of them a regular, fun, and uplifting experience by providing a summer camp for First Nations kids in the foster system? A camp which embraced their cultures. Gave them a couple of months every year during which their own heritage and spirituality could be explored. Dusty's own experience on the Apache reservation had been life-changing. She had found love, direction, and a spirituality that made her feel whole. Maybe she could share that gift.

Using the money sitting in trust since her father's death, Dusty built Sunrise Ranch, and less than two years after meeting Leyla, fifty-seven kids experienced eight weeks of great fun, friends, family, horses, Native ceremonies, arts, crafts, languages, and endless laughter.

But it ate at Dusty to hear so many of her kids tell horror stories of being bounced from one foster home to another. The reasons were endless. But the only important thing was that too many kids had absolutely no security in their lives. They never knew for sure when they got up in the morning if this would be the bed they would go to sleep in that night.

They became accustomed to changing schools,

and often gave up trying to make friends. Some had great placements, some not so great, while others slipped through the cracks completely. And of course, the worst problem—good foster parents were getting burned out, too.

Like the Butterwicks.

Dusty met them in the middle of the summer, when they brought several kids to the ranch for ceremonies.

They lived in the small town about an hour's drive away, had been fostering First Nations children for more than thirty years, and were getting tired. It was okay during the week, when there was school, but on weekends and holidays, keeping up with healthy, rambunctious kids needing outdoor activities and twenty-four-hour supervision was taking its toll.

Their situation lit a fire in Dusty. Gave her the idea to team up with them and have their kids spend weekends on the ranch. But Children's Services had to be convinced first. It took long hours of writing proposals, then attending classes and meetings, before everything came together, but now there were six kids living much better lives.

They lived in town Monday through Friday, with the Butterwicks, a kind, loving older couple. There, they had a safe home, responsibilities, help with their homework, and lots of love. They learned about their own cultural history, language, crafts, and dance.

Then on the weekends, while the Butterwicks rested up, the kids were at the ranch with Dusty, where they had open spaces, horses to ride, chores to do, dogs and cats to play with, and all the fresh air their growing lungs could suck in.

Now, laughing, they tore into the dining room and scrambled onto their chairs.

Dusty waited until everyone was silent, then gave thanks to the spirits of animals, earth, and sky who had provided the food they were about to eat. There was a quiet murmur of thank-yous around the table just before she asked, "Who's hungry?"

The noise level grew exponentially while she dished out the meal, and then it fizzled while they tucked in.

This, she glanced from face to face. *This fills my soul.*

Saturday morning began with chores at six am. Daryl and Dusty fed and watered the new horses, while Amber, Jamie, Jonas, and Lucie looked after the saddle horses. And Molly took care of feeding and watering the three dogs and six barn cats.

Twenty minutes later, everyone converged on the dining hall for the hot breakfast Billy had ready for them. Once they finished eating, there were dishes to be washed, and horses to brush and saddle. Manure to be picked from the paddocks and added to the pile behind the barn. The kids negotiated who would do what, and tackled their assignments with gusto, because as soon as they finished, they could go riding.

Shortly after nine, Dusty was standing at the fence with Daryl, studying the new thoroughbreds. "What do you think's going on with the bay gelding in the corner? He's not eating," she said.

"He's scared. Doesn't look like he's used to

being in a big crowd like this."

"Should we give him a paddock of his own?"

"Then he'll never adjust. Maybe start slower. Put him in with one other horse, then in a few days, if he seems comfortable, add another."

"And another and another and..."

Daryl laughed at her. "Yeah. Like that, but real slow. Give him a chance to get his confidence."

"Who should we put him in with?"

Daryl scrutinized the horses eating hay spread out on the ground. He concentrated on observing each one, and Dusty kept a poker face while she watched. She wanted to grin because, know it or not, he was using his ticket to freedom. Was able to make a solid decision on his own, with total confidence, because of the time he took to respect each individual. He might not trust the human race quite yet, but he had learned to trust himself.

Watching the horses for their behavior and natural traits was exactly like what she did with the kids who came to her. Feel them out from a distance, let them come to her, identify what they needed even before they had it figured out for themselves.

She swallowed the growing lump in her throat. This was a moment she'd save to write down later. She kept a journal for every child, a simple story of their progress, kind of like a baby book in a way, only the first steps and first words had a myriad of deeper meanings.

The pictures she added told their own story. Faces changing from sad, uncertain and distrustful, to peaceful, confident and happy. Their woes seemed to fade into the paper.

There were fourteen journals on her shelves...so far.

***

It was noon on Monday before Dusty was able to put any thought into her encounter with the stranger on Thursday night—the binoculars and blanket were gone when she returned from bringing the horses in from pasture on Friday morning.

She sat on the porch with a coffee mug in her hand, wondering why she'd been so moved. Had she really been visited by a Spirit? Was it in her heritage, in her blood, to believe in such things? Or was she being foolish?

Dusty gave her head a shake. He had night vision binoculars, for crying out loud. He was probably some eccentric animal behaviorist who spent his entire life following wolves around. She'd seen documentaries done by such people, and they truly were incredible. Every detail of the workings of a wolf pack caught on film in a way that left you in no doubt the person telling the story was almost an actual pack member.

Yes, she thought, her mystery visitor must have been one of those. She wasn't ready to admit to herself that his arms around her had made her think of Chase, and the colors of the blanket...

Dusty jumped up and headed for the paddocks. She needed to do some work with the new thoroughbreds. Needed to reduce the numbers quickly by getting them into new homes.

For the next few weeks, she struggled to choose which horses to sell. Each one she rode had qualities she liked—mixed, of course, with things she didn't care for. In the end, she simply penned an open advertisement. She was offering thoroughbreds for sale. Previously raced, doing well in their training to be saddle horses.

But one horse she kept separate. The black mare was not for sale. She had adopted Caesar, and Dusty wouldn't separate them. Even when she rode Houdini, Caesar had to be visible, or the mare fussed and fumed, refusing to cooperate in any way. Yet, when the little donkey was there, she was not only a stellar pupil, but was fast becoming the teacher's pet.

Dusty didn't have the heart to put a saddle over the nasty scar, instead riding her bareback, careful not to press her leg against the old injury.

Since Dusty began riding, there was always a saddle between her and any horse she'd been on, and stirrups for maintaining balance—which made her nervous about climbing on bareback the first time. But as soon as she slipped onto Houdini's back, she felt right at home.

Warmth penetrated through her jeans, and she could feel the muscles flex and move beneath her. When the mare moved, Dusty felt like they were connected. Not just together, but one.

The best part of her day was sliding onto the black mare and heading for the hills. Mighty Caesar's short legs got quite a workout, but he didn't seem to mind skipping along behind them.

Some days, when turned loose in the field,

Houdini would gallop in big, sweeping circles around Caesar, and Dusty would marvel at her grace and athleticism. It was very clear this one could run. But she didn't have a tattoo on the inside of her upper lip, which meant she'd never been raced. What a waste of talent, she thought sometimes, galloping around in my field when she could have been a star on the track.

But, she was happy and healthy living at Sunrise, so the lack of a career was no great loss.

Eventually ten of the original fourteen horses were sold, two were given away, and two stayed on at the ranch. She'd kept the timid gelding Daryl had taken a shine to, and the one it had been paired with.

Murray laughed at Dusty for selling them so cheaply she barely broke even, but said he expected nothing different from her. He only sent her the horses to give her something to do on the days the children were in town.

THIRTY

December 2016

It was Christmas. The one day in three hundred and sixty-five she allowed herself to look at her past, and to feel sad.

The landline rang several times, but she didn't answer it. The kids had her mobile number for emergencies.

Dusty spent the morning looking after the animals, chopping firewood, and setting the stoves with kindling while snow fell gently and gradually covered the cold ground. At noon, she carefully packed her saddlebags with water, food, a flashlight, candles and matches. She pulled heavy woolen pants over sweats, and fastened a hand-tooled leather case containing a very sharp hunting knife to her belt.

She donned a wool-lined canvas jacket, tucked her satellite phone into the inside pocket, and shoved half a dozen shells in the outer pockets.

From the gun safe hidden carefully behind a wall in her bedroom, she pulled out her shotgun—the same one she tucked between the box spring and mattress of her bed every night.

The dogs followed her to the barn and milled about while she saddled Jake, the wisest and smartest horse she owned, and her last connection to Chase.

Fully prepared for any possibilities, she led the spry old gelding through the gate to the mountain trails, and ordered the dogs to stay home.

Dusty smiled ruefully at their dejected faces, and promised she'd be home for supper. She swung up into the saddle, and she and Jake slowly made their way across the field and into the woods, to the trail that climbed gently up the side of the mountain.

It was peaceful among the trees, and the fresh snow made everything brighter, with new covering old.

When they reached the plateau, Dusty dismounted and led Jake toward the huge, flat rock right on the edge of the mountain. This was her favorite place in the whole world, had been since the first time she sat here imagining the ranch she'd build, the children who would come to stay.

She untied the handwoven blanket, a gift from her grandparents, from the back of her saddle, and laid it on the rock, then settled herself there to take in the view of her ranch—her gentle and thoughtful mark on the earth.

Sunrise took years to complete, and was worth every ounce of sweat, and hour of planning. The house, cabins, dining, and great halls were set in a circle, with intersecting walkways which divided it into four quadrants to resemble the Apache Circle of Life.

The barns, paddocks, riding ring and storage sheds formed another circle, also quartered by intersecting paths.

Jake's head went up suddenly, and he tugged against the reins in Dusty's hand. He turned his head and stared farther up the trail, his ears straight forward, and his nostrils flared wide, searching for scent.

Dusty rolled to her feet, watched, waited, but eventually he calmed, as though deciding there was nothing to be alarmed about…no immediate threat...and turned his attention back to her. She rubbed his face, and he leaned into her hand.

"Probably nothing but a squirrel, old boy."

His head lifted quickly again and startled her. Now his attention was focused down the path they just climbed. He snorted and backed up a step.

Without taking her eyes off the trail, Dusty slid the shotgun from the scabbard she wore across her back. Slipped her fingers into her pocket to close around two shells. She loaded them into the chamber, but didn't cock the gun.

She could hear something, too.

At the sound of a faint whistle. Jake's body language changed abruptly, and she patted his shoulder. The whistling grew louder, and a bundled figure came into view.

Dusty removed the shells and shoved them into her pocket.

Billy looked at the shotgun and asked, "Were

you really gonna shoot me?"

"I should, as punishment for scaring poor Jake."

Billy laughed. "And what did you think was coming up the trail, a bear? They went into hibernation a month ago. A moose? Not likely to care much about you this time of year. A cat? No self-respecting cougar would ever make that much noise."

"Thanks for the wilderness lesson. But mostly I was prepared to deal with the unknown." She sat back down and looked at him closely.

"What brings you up here?"

"Tracking you."

"Why?"

"When I got home, the dogs were moping around, and I found your footprints leading into the woods."

"I thought you were spending the whole day with your dad."

Billy shrugged. "He passed out, so I left."

"I'm sorry. I know you were hoping—"

"I was stupid to think he'd stay sober for a whole day. Even though he promised."

She sighed. "It is not easy for him, Billy."

"Well it's not easy for me either." His jaw was tight, and she could see his anger so clearly it hurt. "How would you like to have a dad who prefers vodka to his only kid? How would you feel?"

"Vodka is a choice he made many years ago, Billy and he's entrenched in something he can't find his way out of. He loves you, but the alcohol is his lifeline."

Now he sighed. "Sometimes I get so mad I

almost want to hurt him. That's why I have to leave."

"Leaving is a smart choice. But it would be better if you could find a way to understand, because then you could avoid the anger altogether. Strange as it seems, you might even feel compassion for him. Not," she held up a hand, "that you will ever have a dad who is any different from the way he is now. And I know it sounds like a stretch, but someday you might even be proud of him."

"What the hell is there to be proud of?"

"In spite of his addiction, he's made some impressive decisions, Billy. He allowed you to come to me when you were only a boy. Then he swallowed his masculine pride and allowed me to pay for your tuition so you could follow your dream and become a chef. It takes a good man to put his child before himself, and even though he seems to put the alcohol before you, when the chips are down, he does what's right, drunk or sober."

"You think it's right for him to get loaded on Christmas Day when he promised to spend it with me?"

He was an adult now, and the time for making everything better was long past. "One day, even you will make a promise you will know you can't keep." Dusty took a deep breath, held it for a moment, then exhaled very slowly, stared out over her land.

She could feel Billy watching her for a few minutes, and when he spoke again, his voice had not only lost its edge, but he sounded concerned. "I'm sorry. I didn't mean to sound ungrateful, and I promise I'll try to understand him."

"Thanks, Billy." She closed her eyes.

"Something else is wrong. Why are you sad?"

For some strange reason, she answered his question instead of brushing it off. Her voice was barely a whisper at first, but it grew stronger as she went on.

"Many, many, years ago, I was in love with a very special man, and we planned to raise a huge family together. We talked for hours on end about the future, and how we would sit on the porch, watching our children—and eventually our grandchildren—playing happily on our land. But something terrible happened, and I lost him." She was surprised her breath still caught on those words.

"I was devastated. Wanted to die. Wallowed in self-pity for a long time. But then, with the prodding of a friend, I stepped back into my life. I went to a place I had never been, found family and love among strangers, and eventually discovered the core of my Self. Was able to celebrate my spiritual heritage." Sometimes she was surprised she could even remember who she'd been before the Ceremony.

"Then one day, in a hospital, the sound of a crying child reached out to me, and as cliché as it sounds, my life was changed forever. I knew how it felt to be alone and abandoned, even when I had control and could make choices for myself. But that child, she didn't have any of those choices. She was not only frightened and alone, but also completely dependent on strangers to look after her. When I went to her bedside, she looked at me, and a smile shone through her tears. I pushed the hair back out of her face, and she said 'momma.'" Someday she hoped Leyla would find out that her fear that day had changed the lives of several hundred children.

"A social worker scurried in and demanded to know who I was and why I was touching the little one. We talked then, and I learned there were many like Leyla who had no parents."

Billy finally spoke, "I'm glad I wasn't one of them."

"You were lucky to have a dad who loved you and struggled through his own pain to make sure you had a decent life."

His attempt at a smile was grim, and his voice was low when he said, "I wish he'd been different."

Dusty laughed. "Oh, how I understand that."

"Why?"

"My father and I didn't speak for the last years of his life. I often wished he'd been different. But he wasn't. And eventually I actually understood him."

"Was he a drunk, too?"

"No. He was much worse. He was the warped product of a terrible childhood, and he took it out on the innocent. Besides that disgusting side of his life, he was a self-righteous, arrogant bastard, who tried to run the lives of the people around him. He thought he was smarter than everyone else. He actually believed what he was doing was in our best interest. I once accused him of ruining my life."

"But he didn't really?"

"My life's path was altered because of him, but I wouldn't be here with you if my father hadn't done what he did. I even built this ranch with his money, which means, in a very twisted way, every child who climbs on a horse or sits by our campfires has him to thank."

"Do you think that would make him happy?"

"Not likely. But if someone had cared about his childhood, he might not have been such a destructive and hateful man. Maybe he would have been a good and decent human being." A small half laugh escaped her. "He's probably rolling over in his grave as I speak."

"And that makes you happy instead?"

"Ouch. Guilty as charged, I suppose." She needed to own that and put it away.

"My dad isn't awful like yours." Billy interrupted her thoughts.

"Your dad is a very, very good man. He never left your mother's side while she was dying a long and painful death, but he felt helpless, and less than a man, because he couldn't do anything to change the course of her illness. He only reached for the bottle to drown his feelings of loss and inadequacy *after* she was gone, and keeps using the alcohol to get past his memories. And then, of course, he lets *you* down, which makes him sad, and then he drinks more. It's a vicious cycle."

"Did you get past losing that man, the one you were in love with?"

"It doesn't hurt as much anymore." An invisible fist gripped her heart, but she didn't regret the lie. It was based in truth at least.

"Why not?"

"I found peace, because I've come to believe

there is a greater power directing our lives, and we have to find a way to follow comfortably."

"You mean God?"

"I mean a greater power of some kind."

"Don't you wish there was a man in your life? Aren't you ever lonely?"

Dusty shook her head with a small smile. "How could I possibly be lonely? I'm where I am supposed to be. My life is filled with young souls needing my love. I guess that's why there is no man for me. I had my great love already." She laughed. "Besides, who'd want me, with seven kids year-round, and several hundred over the summer?"

"You could dump us. Heck, I'm not even a kid anymore, and the rest are growing up too."

"And as each one leaves this nest, another comes. There will always be children who need me, and that, my friend, is what gives me breath."

They sat side by side for a while, each occupied with their own thoughts, until Jake began to fuss again. They looked around and could see nothing. "Maybe he's tired of standing here," said Billy.

Dusty watched the horse's eyes and knew it was more than that. He could hear something, but couldn't see what it was. It reminded her of the look Angel used to often wear. A jab of pain put a hitch in her breath.

"What's wrong?"

"Nothing. I guess we should be getting back."

"You never told me why you rode up here."

"You're right." She looked at her watch "Let's get a move on." She slid the bridle off Jake and hung it on the saddle horn so he could walk along freely, and she turned to lead the way down the narrow trail with Billy and the old horse following.

When they were clear of the woods Dusty whistled, and the dogs sitting at the gate streaked across to greet them.

"What a faithful trio you are," she said laughing at their antics.

"Life is simple for dogs," Billy said quietly.

"Your life can be as simple or as complicated as you want it to be, Billy. It's your choice to make."

He was silent for a while. But once they reached the barn and unsaddled Jake, he said, "Dusty?"

"Yes, Billy?"

"Would you mind if I left?"

"Of course not. I had every intention of spending the evening spoiling myself. It's my Christmas ritual."

"We were supposed to go to Aunt Rosa's for supper, and maybe I'll stop and see if my dad still wants to go."

"He probably won't," she warned.

"I know. But I'll ask anyway."

She gave him a hug. "Be gone." Planted a kiss on his cheek and said, "Go live your life and enjoy."

An hour later, with her evening chores done early, just in case, she put a halter and shank on Jake, and led him into the woods, leaving the dogs, once again, at the gate.

The sky had darkened by the time they reached the plateau, but the snow allowed her to see every building, and even the horses in the fields below.

She spread the blanket on the flat rock, sat, and

closed her eyes. Cleared her mind of the present, slipped back through the years to when she had Chase by her side and the world was theirs. She'd been young and ridiculously happy. Nothing could mess with the power they had. No one would ever...

She dug deep to remember the sound of his voice, the touch of his skin against hers. She tilted her head back and imagined him standing behind her, his hands strong on her shoulders, while they looked out over their land, celebrated yet another Christmas together. She turned her face to feel the roughness of his cheek against hers, and his mouth on her neck. His breath warm.

With her mind open to the places she only acknowledged once a year, she lay back and remembered pulling him down to her and teasing him with tequila-flavored lips, the shock of his response. Her heart had leaped into her throat, and she'd forgotten where she was. No man had ever done that to her before.

She reveled in the memories of Angel's race, and their celebration that night. Then there was the trip to Hawaii, filled with love, and his hands, his mouth, their hearts beating together in a primal rhythm so real not even air could get between them.

But what she'd thought was their honeymoon had been a long and passionate good-bye, and Chase had known all along. Had done what he believed was right for her, but he'd been dead wrong.

Brand new pain tore through her heart, forcing her mouth open in a silent cry while memories of his pale, thin face, and the terrible soul-deep sorrow in his eyes once, again ripped her open, and a keening wail decimated the pristine winter silence.

She welcomed the anguish like a long-lost friend. Embraced it, wallowed in it until she was reduced to sobbing like a lost child. She cried for what she had, what she lost, and what Chase had done to try and save them both. Wept tears of rejection and loneliness until the anger came, and then she screamed at the sky. At the gods for their uselessness. At her father and her mother for not loving her, and she begged to know why she'd been left alone. Shrieked at Chase for giving in and leaving her heart to die.

When she finally lay spent, empty, and exhausted on the cold, hard rock, she croaked sadly, "When? When will I ever stop loving you?"

Jake pushing on her shoulder with his nose brought her slowly back to reality, and she wrapped her arms around the old horse's neck. Buried her face in his mane, and with a voice still fragmented, thanked him for being her friend.

Once the tingling in her fingers and toes stopped, and she eventually felt lighter for the unloading of a year's worth of sorrow, she headed back down the trail and whistled for the dogs, who happily raced to greet her.

The guardian, having followed until she reached the fence line, turned back to his lair.

THIRTY-ONE

Sunrise Ranch, British Columbia,
December 2016

Hours spent crying and unable to sleep left Dusty feeling like she had a hangover the next morning. Even though she hadn't had any alcohol. Rarely drank anymore.

Walking into the kitchen, she squinted and groaned at the brilliance of sunlight on snow burning through the windows. She grabbed a pair of dark glasses and dove outdoors nearly two hours late to feed the hungry horses. About three steps across the porch she stopped dead in her tracks.

There were no horses hanging around the gate waiting for her. Even the dogs were nowhere to be seen. Dusty surveyed the area suspiciously, but could see nothing wrong. A round bale had been unrolled across the snow-covered field, and thirty-nine horses had apparently already filled their bellies, since most of them were down enjoying a nap. Houdini stood over Caesar while he slept on a bed of leftover hay.

Dusty's heart fluttered, and she spun around quickly at the sound of snow crunching under human feet. She could see nothing. The footsteps were fading. She jumped off the side of the porch and ran through knee-deep snow to the back of her house.

When she saw the figure covered head to toe in bulky winter gear, she yelled, "Hey there, wait."

He turned around, and she had to laugh, while relief and disappointment washed over her.

"What's wrong?" Billy asked.

"You're wearing a new coat," she said, stating the obvious. "How come you didn't bang on my door and get my lazy butt out of bed?"

He shrugged, looking serious. "I was early. Thought I'd let you sleep for once. Call it a Boxing Day present." Then his characteristic grin escaped. "I picked the stalls, too."

"Wow, thanks. Why were you so early?"

He kicked at the snow half-heartedly "My dad offered to drive me this morning, and he was up early. I didn't want to leave it too long, in case, you know?"

"You're learning."

"And anything's better than riding on the bunny bus."

"Don't call it that."

"Come on, even you have to admit…"

"I, don't have to admit anything. Mr. B did a great job of fixing that old bus up for the kids. And it sure saves me a bunch of time when he can drive the whole group around in one vehicle."

"Yeah, yeah."

"Well, seeing as you've taken care of the horses, I'll go dig out the driveway."

"Breakfast will be ready in about half an hour."

"Great. By the way, where are the dogs?"

"Last I saw they were headed that way," he said, pointing to the trail she'd been up twice the day before. "I think they must have spotted a rabbit."

Dusty shook her head. They would spend hours rabbit hunting, but she didn't have to worry about them hurting an innocent creature, because she'd seen what happened when they caught up with their prey. Ben and Flower would try to herd it while Justin got in between to protect it. And they were bound to show up once she started the tractor.

But she was wrong. The sound of the tractor didn't draw them out. And she was getting worried. Instead of taking an hour to clear the driveway, she drove up and down it a few times to simply pack the snow and make it passable.

She walked into the lodge kitchen, barely noticing the heavenly smell of bacon.

"You ready to eat?" asked Billy.

"Can I get mine to go?"

He grabbed a travel mug from the shelf over the coffee pot. "Where you off to?"

"The dogs haven't come back. I'll take a machine up a ways and see if I can find their tracks." She didn't like using a skidoo, hated the noise in such peaceful surroundings, but it was the best tool for the job.

Billy slid a loaded plate onto the table. "Eat this while I get a machine out and warmed up for you."

Dusty followed the tracks of the dogs up the hill, and well past where she'd been last night, before a flash of movement caught her eye. It was Justin, not too far ahead, but moving away from her.

She only took a second to call and whistle before giving up and following him into an area where nothing looked familiar. Deep into Crown land, the trail narrowed as it skirted the edge of a ravine, then widened again, snaking upward through the thinning trees.

Finally, she rounded a bend, and there was Justin, standing right in front of her. She stopped and called to him, but the most obedient, well-trained dog she'd ever known didn't move, except to look farther up the trail they were on.

She caught her breath when a man came into sight, limping ever so slightly. Ben walked calmly at his side, looking up at Flower, who was being carried under the man's coat.

Without a moment's thought, Dusty was off the machine and headed for them.

"What happened?" she asked the stranger, but only had eyes for the sad-looking dog staring out of the jacket at about mid-chest level. Her tail wagged feebly out the bottom of the coat.

"She got hung up in a deadfall." It was the strange, raspy voice of her wolf protector. Her eyes shot to his face, and she was instantly disappointed. The only part not covered by a ski mask was hidden under the brim of his fur-lined hat. "Her leg's broken."

He looked past her to the skidoo. "Get on and unbutton your coat."

Without question, Dusty climbed onto the machine, and the stranger gently set Flower against her—carefully cradling the leg wrapped in red tartan cloth—while Dusty buttoned her coat.

Then, without prompting, Ben slipped onto the machine in the spot he usually rode, between Dusty and the windshield. Her knees held him safely in place.

"Justin, you coming?"

He climbed reluctantly onto the seat behind her and sat with his butt against the back-guard installed to prevent the children from slipping off.

"Be careful," said the stranger.

She waved and yelled a thank-you to him as she set off down the mountain trail.

***

Dusty grimaced when she saw the crowd gathered at the gate. They'd heard the skidoo and come out to meet her. Thank goodness Mr. B spotted the dog inside her coat and quickly took control of the situation. He pointed to each of them and gave instructions. "Billy, go get her truck started and back it over here. Daryl, run to the house for the phone and Doc Taylor's number. Amber, get a blanket for the dog. Lucie, get Dusty's wallet and cell phone."

Molly started to cry.

"Molly, stop that right now. You go to the

fridge and get an apple for Dusty. She'll need fuel."

"Jonas and Jamie, you help Dusty climb off that machine, then use it and head down to open the main gate so she won't have to stop on the way out, and be sure to fasten it properly after."

The dispersal of children left her with Mr. B. and the dogs.

"What's wrong with her?" he asked.

"Broken leg."

Daryl ran up with the phone to his ear, then passed it to Dusty. "Hi, Doc, I've got a dog with a broken leg."

She listened for a minute then replied, "Yup, meet you there."

She handed the phone back to Daryl. "Doc's not at home. But he should get there about the same time as we do."

Daryl passed the phone to one of the girls and said, very matter-of-factly, "I'm coming with you. I can keep her calm while you drive."

Dusty glanced at him. "Good idea. Billy, could you and Mr. B get her from here into the truck?" Dusty undid her coat, and they carefully lifted the brave little dog, who never made so much as a whimper.

***

Doc Taylor was a very tall man, with a shiny bald head on one end and enormous black gum boots on the other. In between, there was kindness, gentle hands, and a smile that lit up his whole face. And apparently he was the one person on earth

Daryl was absolutely mesmerized by.

Doc, as he was called by everyone, gently removed the bandage from Flower's leg while Daryl stoked her head and told her she was a good girl. Dusty stepped back and became an observer instead of a participant. She had seen Daryl's response to the vet once before, at the ranch, and never given it a whole lot of thought. But it became clear there was something important going on.

Doc talked to the boy like an assistant, and together, in the space of an hour and a half, they gave Flower a shot of painkiller, a mild sedative, x-rayed her entire body, set her broken leg, and applied a waterproof cast. They carried her back out to the truck, placing her carefully on the backseat, and Doc thanked Daryl for his help. He held out his hand to the boy who, without hesitation, shook it.

"This young man has the makings of a good vet," Doc said to Dusty. "Keep him in school, and his future is very bright."

"Daryl is already an excellent student, especially in math and science."

"Those are the two that count the most." He chuckled then said, "But don't discount the rest. I had to repeat English to get a better mark for university entrance, so don't forget your other subjects. The only thing worse than English Lit is having to take it twice."

"Good advice, Doc." She winked at Daryl. "And when he's ready for a summer job, maybe you could give him a recommendation based on his work today."

"I'll go one better," He spoke directly to the

boy in a very serious tone. "When you turn sixteen, if your grades are good, you can work for me in the summer. Ride around to the ranches, and help me out like you did this morning."

Daryl's eyes widened, and Doc held up his hand. "One thing, though. It doesn't pay much money. So you'll still have to rely on good grades and scholarships to get you through vet school."

"My marks will be perfect, I promise."

"How old will you be next summer Daryl?"

"Fifteen."

"Okay then, a year from next June, you'll come to work for me. Deal?" He held out his hand again to the young man.

Daryl grabbed it and pumped. "Yes, sir!"

When they drove away, Dusty glanced in the rearview mirror at the boy in the backseat, watching over Flower. He was staring out the window, wearing a grin that looked like it might last right into next week.

A lump of happiness lodged in Dusty's throat. This was the kind of breakthrough that made the whole world seem brighter somehow.

***

Dusty bundled up and went out to sit on the porch. It had been one heck of a day, and now everyone was safely tucked into bed, she treated herself to hot chocolate and freezing air.

With the moon in the sky and snow on the ground, it was nearly daylight-bright. Justin and Ben lay beside her chair. Poor Ben had been heartbroken when they shut him out of Daryl's room, where Flower was spending the night.

Flower and Ben had been inseparable since she met them at a rescue center. They'd been dropped there after "failing" at life in the city, which she completely understood, because daily walks on a leash just weren't enough stimulation for the average border collie.

Dusty scratched Ben's head, and he looked up with solemn eyes. "I promise you can have your sweetheart back tomorrow, but she has to stay extra-quiet for tonight." Should she let him into the room? He'd likely be very careful with her, but still could innocently bump that leg.

Justin lifted his head at her voice, and she gave him a stern look. "I should be scolding both of you for running off this morning, but I suppose it's my own fault for sleeping in." She shook her head and murmured to herself, "Last night seems a very long time ago."

She leaned back in the chair and sipped hot chocolate, letting her thoughts drift back over the day's events. She was absolutely thrilled with what she saw between Doc and Daryl. The boy badly needed a dependable male role model.

And the man who had rescued Flower. When Doc commented on what a fine splinting job she had done on the dog's leg, Dusty simply said thank you, for some reason not wanting to tell anyone about the stranger.

Could it be Chase hiding behind a gait made awkward by a limp? Was the strangeness of the man's voice, in fact, a disguise?

But why would he bother? She gave her head a shake. She couldn't fathom Chase hiding out in the woods near her ranch. It didn't make any sense. Better to think of the guy as a wolf researcher.

Such interesting creatures, wolves. As a rancher, she sometimes hated them, because they preyed on the sickly and weak, and understanding the ways of the wild didn't mean she had to like the reality of it.

But with wolves, she was conflicted, because when it came to raising their young, they were incredibly efficient and smart. Unlike humans, who run around making babies left, right and center, then dumping them like trash, wolves carefully choose the alpha female as the only one to have offspring, and then the entire pack looked after them, with all the adults totally devoted to caring for the young.

The crunching of snow had Dusty's breath catching in her throat. She stayed very still, watching Justin's ears. He was following the sound, but wasn't worried in the least. The person came closer, and Justin's tail swished gently against the floor.

"What the heck are you doing out here? It's ten below, for crying out loud."

Dusty cocked her head at Billy. "What the heck are *you* doing outside?"

"Well, I was coming to talk to you, but had visions of sitting by the fireplace."

Dusty swung her legs over the side of her chair. "Okay, let's go in." She led the way, followed closely by the young man and both dogs.

Once comfortable by the fire, she studied his

serious face for a moment, and then asked, "What's up?"

"I, uh, wanted to talk." He stared at his hands for a moment.

"Then look at me and move your lips. Sound is likely to follow." Her smile was waiting for him when he glanced up.

"I have a girlfriend." Billy finally blurted. "Can I bring her here?"

"Yes."

He stared at her. "That's it? Yes? No questions?"

"You asked a question, I answered it."

"Yeah but..." He hesitated. "Wouldn't you like to know more about her?"

"I would." Dusty was beside herself with curiosity, but kept that detail to herself. "Let's start with her name."

"Tammy. We met at school. She's from Vancouver, and has never been outside of a city. I want to bring her here but...I'm not sure about things." His ears went bright pink.

Dusty took pity on him and decided to lead. "Things such as sleeping arrangements?"

His face reddened. "Yes."

This was something she'd contemplated happening, and was prepared.

"Here's the deal. *I* know you're an adult, but here, among the kids, you're one of them, too. Therefore, I would like for Tammy to stay in this house, not your cabin." He was about to say something, and she stopped him with a raised hand.

"These kids have already been exposed to

everything possible in life, but I'd still like to keep things simple, therefore, house rules stand as written. Boys and girls don't sleep together at night, unless they are on a campout and in separate sleeping bags." She pulled her braided hair over her shoulder and stared at it a minute, then gave him her sternest look, "For all I know, you and Tammy are already—" She didn't need to say the word lovers, because it was clear by the look on his face. She softened her voice and asked, "Do you love her, Billy?"

"I think maybe. I'm more alive when she's around, and she makes me feel important and smart and dumb all at the same time."

Dusty laughed. "I like her already. When do I get to meet her?"

"How about New Year's? Then we can go back to the coast together for the new semester."

"Sounds fine to me. But two things I'd like to add." She looked him square in the eye. "One, do I need to repeat the lecture about unwanted children being brought into this world by irresponsible adults?"

"Nope. We are very responsible." Again he reddened.

"Good. Then the second thing is this. The children have a nine o'clock curfew, but Tammy won't have to be in till midnight…if you get my drift."

***

Dusty stared into the fire for a long time after

Billy left. She knew what young love was like. She could still remember the tingling in her stomach and the breathlessness when Chase walked into the barn that first day so very many years ago. And the agony of waiting for him to notice her. Then, the day years later when she first saw him at Buck Hill, and her stomach had done an instant barrel roll. And later, those few glorious months…

Oh, Lord, I hope this is nothing that dramatic.

Dusty always checked on each child before she turned in, and tonight she left Daryl to last, and opened his door carefully. There, on the soft bed they made on the floor for Flower, lay both the boy and the dog, tucked under the quilt from his bed. The way his body was curved protectively around the sleeping patient had Dusty swallowing a lump in her throat.

That was two of her boys exhibiting growth and maturity, tonight. Both of which made her very happy, but a certain sadness crept in as well, because she knew there would come a time when they no longer needed her.

Crawling into her own bed, she was again niggled by images of the stranger in the woods, and she thought about the possibility of it really being Chase.

Imagined finally coming face-to-face with him and throwing herself in his arms.

His voice would be familiar but gruff as he declared his love for her, said he wanted to spend the rest of his life with her. And they would kiss, frantically excited at first, and then a deeper kiss, until she was on her toes pressing against him, while his beautiful, strong hands held her face, fingers threading into her hair. Her heart was pounding hard, rising up through her throat, and his hands slid down her back, then farther, holding her still against the hardness, making her back arch while a low moan slipped from her.

Dusty vaulted out of bed, scurried to the back door, stepped out onto the porch and leaned heavily against the closed door. She sucked in long, hard breaths of frigid air while her eyes darted around, searching for movement and finding none. She slid down, landing hard on the wooden porch, and dropped her head in her hands. But the feelings lingered, and her own fingertips moved slowly over her mouth, exploring the softness of her bottom lip, the dampness of the inside edge. A pained groan escaped her.

What the hell was she supposed to do with these crazy longings? They'd been put away safely for years, and now it was as though the lock had been broken, and they kept sneaking out when she wasn't looking. Hadn't she dealt with everything? Hadn't she made peace with Chase's decision to walk away from her? She had a new life, a good life, with purpose and direction. She didn't need complications. She didn't want...

***

For God's sake, the woman was wearing nothing but pajamas, and her feet were bare. Was she completely nuts? Watching from afar, he didn't like his choices. Let her freeze to death? Or let her know he was out there watching her? Surely she'd go back in the house.

He waited less patiently now, because his knee was beginning to ache, and he didn't know how much longer he could stay crouched in his hiding place.

And then she stood. Stretched her arms high above her head, then steadily downward until her hands touched the floor between her feet. She straightened slowly and, without even a glance around, opened the door and disappeared into the dark house.

It was as though she'd never been there. He watched for a while, and when he saw dim, flickering light appear in a small window near the back door, he slowly, painfully, got to his feet and hobbled away, around the other side of the house, and into the hills.

THIRTY-TWO

Annoyed with herself and her crazy imagination, Dusty marched into her office, determined to find answers, or at least eliminate a possibility. She woke up the computer and began to search, hoping she could find something to explain the presence of the man lurking in the corners of her mind.

She looked for current research projects on wolves, specifically in this province, but found nothing. She expanded her search to the country, the continent, and then continued on to broader areas, universities, grants, international studies, past, present, proposals for future. She tried everything, but came up with no one who seemed at all like her mystery man.

Giving up, she went a different direction. Scrolled through her favorite catalogue site for outdoor clothing, camping, hunting, and fishing supplies. She pondered for a while…then inspired by a tiny spark of hope, placed an order.

It was three in the morning when she went back to bed. This time she slept.

For the rest of the Christmas holidays, each and every day was crammed with fun, excitement, exercise, and fresh air.

Several mornings the entire group headed off into the hills on snowshoes, with a huge picnic lunch stowed among several backpacks. They built a bonfire from windfalls, and cut thin branches to make sticks for toasting hot dogs and marshmallows.

Other days were spent riding, cross-country skiing, tobogganing, building snow forts, and snowmen.

Evenings were filled with board games, scrabble tournaments, popcorn, fudge, and charades. Television was not an option, and neither were video games.

One afternoon Billy gave the kids cooking lessons, and helped them make the snacks and treats for their New Year's Eve party. They would be allowed to stay up until twelve-thirty, and the next morning Billy and Tammy would produce a New Year's Day feast.

Dusty was pleasantly impressed by the way Tammy took the kids in stride, and joined in the fun without shyness or hesitation. And the youngsters had great fun hiding around corners, trying to catch her and Billy kissing, then they'd run away, giggling, to tell Dusty, who would first scold them for spying, and then laugh at their earnest faces.

On the last morning of vacation, Lucie and

Dusty went for a morning ride together. Dusty made a point of spending time with each of the children one-on-one, and with Lucie it was always on horseback. Today Dusty rode Houdini, and Lucie was on Shylo, a big paint gelding, and Lucie's favorite mount.

Lucie grinned at Dusty, saying, "You are just like *Lozen*."

Dusty swallowed her surprise and asked, "How do you know about *Lozen*?"

"I read about her last night."

Dusty took great pride in the huge collection of books she'd collected about Native North American history.

"And what did you learn, Lucie?"

"Lozen was an Apache woman who helped to save her people. In the book it said she was a 'magnificent woman on a beautiful black horse.' Or maybe it was 'a beautiful woman on a magnificent black horse.'" She frowned. "I can't remember which way it goes, but that's what you look like riding Houdini bareback like that, with your buckskin and braids."

In the past, Lucie had shown a distinct lack of interest in her cultural studies, and tended to denounce her Native heritage, so it pleased Dusty no end that at the age of fifteen the light seemed to be coming on. "Did you know my mother was *Itsonna*? Which means Apache woman."

"Really?"

"Yup."

"Wow." Then her voice grew thoughtful, "I don't know what my mother was...I mean, what tribe or what..." She seemed to struggle for a word.

Dusty was tentative. "We can find out if you like. Then you could read about your own heritage."

"Were you born there? Where the Apaches are from?" Lucie apparently wasn't ready yet.

"My mother was born on an Apache reservation in New Mexico, but she gave birth to me in Kamloops. I never met her, but about ten years ago, I went to the reservation to meet her family."

"You never met your mother." She zipped past the enormity of that concept and said, "It must be exciting to be Apache."

"I'm not sure exciting is the word I'd use. But it *is* a heritage to be proud of. Did you know the Apache and Navaho, among others of the Southwestern states, actually have the same language base as the Shuswap people here in BC? According to some researchers, the shared Athapaskan language root probably means the people are, in fact, related, and they were quite possibly a single group that split and eventually traveled great distances over time. Hundreds of years ago, of course."

"We could be related? You and me?" Lucie's eyes were huge.

Dusty tipped her head to one side, then the other. "Who knows? But we're already family, with stronger bonds than many blood relations. And *family is everything*, Lucie."

"But we still might be related by blood."

Dusty laughed. "In a roundabout, somewhat convoluted way, yes."

"Wow. How do we find out where my mom

was from?"

"I'll do some checking through social services. But it will take quite a while. Maybe by Easter I'll have an answer for you."

Dusty was quite certain she'd know before then, but felt Lucie needed more time to get used to the idea of being solidly connected to something. She'd been a part of Dusty's family for six years, but before that, she'd lived in twenty-seven foster homes. Her mother was drug addicted, and always created trouble for the people trying to care for her daughter. Lucie was placed with the Butterwicks and Dusty shortly after her mother died of an overdose.

They rode in silence for a while.

Then Lucie asked, "Is Indian a really bad word?"

Dusty looked into the very serious young face, then up into the sky for a moment. This was one of those moments when she prayed for help. There was a need in this child, and it was important to address it properly. "That's up to you to decide for yourself. I, personally, am proud to be called Indian, if it is meant in a kind, respectful way. But there are people who use it as an insult."

"Then what do you do? Get mad? Tell them it's wrong? What do you say?"

Dusty leaned closer, and, in a conspiratorial voice, said, "My favorite response is to say 'thank you.'"

"That doesn't make sense. If they didn't mean it nicely, why would you thank them?"

"If you say thank you, with a smile, you

completely change the dynamics. By refusing to acknowledge an insult, you have the control, and the other person is suddenly powerless."

"So if a boy calls me an Indian slut, I smile and say thank you?"

Dusty's heart felt the blow, and she grimaced, but stayed firm. "Exactly. You take the power away from him by not being offended."

"And that's it? That's all it takes?"

She shook her head. "Sadly, no. He will probably try harder, and come up with an even worse name, but eventually, if you are no fun because you don't get upset, he'll give up and leave you alone."

A speculative glint sparked in Lucie's eye. Someone this week was going to meet a different girl when they went looking to cause trouble. Dusty hoped it went well for her. She made a mental note to call Mrs. Butterwick and give her a heads-up. Lucie might need extra support for a while.

Emerging from the shadowy mountain trail to the wide fields blanketed in sunshine, they urged the horses into an easy gallop, and with every stride, hooves shot glistening snow high into the air, and laughter gently tickled the sky.

THIRTY-THREE

The holidays had been such great fun, Dusty was left feeling very alone on Monday morning while she watched the taillights of the school bus disappear. She looked down at the dogs. "Well, now what do we do for entertainment?"

Justin stared back quietly while Ben and Flower whined.

"Okay, let's go home." she said, closed the gate and fastened the padlock before heading up the driveway. Justin walked solemnly at her side, while Ben loped on ahead and Flower, with only three useful legs and the awkward cast bumping along in the snow, scrambled to keep up with him.

After spending the morning feeding, cleaning, and puttering around with the horses, at noon, she sat on the porch with a cup of soup and gazed out over the fields. Her eyes moved of their own accord up to the hills, and she was almost positive she could see a wisp of smoke far beyond the outlook plateau.

Tiny fingers of anticipation curled in her belly, her breath quickened, and her heartbeat kicked up a notch while an idea whirled in her head.

Should she?

A glance at her watch confirmed there were almost four hours of daylight left, so why not?

Now she was in a hurry. She raced to the house, grabbed the package she'd picked up from the post office, and stuffed it—and her standard in-case-of-emergency-supplies—into a knapsack.

Equipped with shotgun, shells, and sat phone, she dragged on the big canvas coat, donned earmuffs and gloves, and headed out the door. Within minutes, the three dogs were watching pitifully from the gate while she zipped her snowmobile across the field and headed into the hills.

Dusty stopped the machine where she'd last seen him, where he carefully secured the injured dog under her coat. She hadn't expected to see tracks, or evidence he'd been this way again, but still she had to stomp hard on the rising disappointment and press on into unfamiliar territory.

Reaching a fork in the trail, she stopped, lifted her head like a horse, with nostrils flaring, trying to pick up the scent of smoke. Nothing. She surveyed the surrounding area. Not even a deer had been this way since last night's snowfall. She stared up both trails and waited, unsure, until a squirrel scurried boldly across the path to the right.

That was enough of a sign for her, and she

eased the machine that direction, barely hearing the very earnest squirrel's lengthy scold. For what seemed like miles, she wound on through the trees and into the shade on the north side of the mountain.

A shiver ran through her.

It wasn't exactly dark, but there was a strange feeling that came with the shadows, and from trees which had never in their lives been touched by the sun.

Dusty was glad when the trail led back into sunshine, and was startled to see an old cabin directly in front of her. Her breath caught in her throat. A tiny, bluish wisp of smoke was barely visible above the slightly lopsided chimney. This had to be the wolf-man's place.

She was finally going to meet him face-to-face, and she would know for sure. Driven by emotion, she marched through the deep snow to the door. Tapped on it. Nothing happened.

She frowned and knocked hard, but the sound cutting through the silence jarred Dusty enough to make her common sense sit up and take notice. She backed away.

He obviously wasn't there. Should she leave the package on the porch? Or try the door?

A queasy feeling of uncertainty slid into her belly, and she took a long, deep breath, let it out slowly. Then again.

She went back to the snowmobile and sat sideways on the seat, staring at the cabin. After a few minutes, she shrugged the knapsack from her shoulders and pulled out the package, slipping her fingers inside the paper to feel the softness of the new flannel shirts. The one he tore into strips to make bandages for Flower had been thin, old, and red. These were new, thick, and a rich mixture of deep blues and browns. Her mind was made up.

She approached the cabin slowly, and tapped only once before reaching for the wooden handle. The door swung open smoothly, silently, not even creaking as she'd expected, and daylight flooded the dark room. She hesitated.

"Hello?" she offered to the air. "Anyone home?"

Silence.

Tentatively, she stepped across the threshold, then stood very still, waiting for something, but she wasn't sure what.

"Hello?" Again she addressed the empty room, then muttered, "Stupid woman, the furniture isn't going to answer. There's obviously no one home, leave the darn shirts and get out."

But she hugged the package to her chest and began walking around the tiny space, missing nothing.

It was bigger inside than it appeared. Along one wall was a sort of built-in shelf about four feet wide and three feet off the floor. Most of it was covered by a thick piece of foam and a very expensive-looking green sleeping bag. The pillow tucked inside the top had a dark blue cover, and below the bed-shelf were cupboard doors which, for the life of her, she couldn't resist opening.

Amazing, she thought, gazing at rows of quart jars containing everything from tomatoes to peaches, and smoked meat. Closing the cupboard, Dusty turned her attention to the other side of the room. A small, rustic, handmade table and chair, a cast iron stove, a rocking chair, and a floor-to-ceiling bookshelf. She stepped closer to see the titles on the books, but heard a noise and swung around to stare at the back door.

Dusty frowned. A cabin with a back door? How odd for a one-room dwelling... She pushed it open slowly to find a bit of a lean-to stacked high with firewood, and a path worn in the snow leading to an outhouse about fifty feet away. Off to the right, at the edge of the trees, there was a large hump of snow with a stack of firewood beside it. A sweat lodge, she realized.

Suddenly feeling like an intruder, she jerked the door shut, set the package of shirts on the table, and left. She was on the snowmobile and far away very quickly…still trying to shake off an uneasy feeling.

***

From beneath the heavy tarps he watched her disappear into the wintery landscape, and once he was certain there was no one but him in the vicinity, he slipped back into the cabin. Stood in the middle of the room and looked around, wondering what exactly she'd seen. His eyes settled on the package, and with gentle fingers he traced her name and address printed on the front. Then he pulled out the two flannel shirts and chuckled.

She had tipped her hand. This was an offering destined for him, not a stranger. The fist gripping his heart loosened at last.

***

Dusty arrived back at the ranch well before dark—much to the delight of the dogs. They jumped and ran around like idiots, almost as though they'd been worried about her up on the same trail where Flower was hurt.

Oh, for heaven's sakes, woman, she scolded herself. *Get with reality. They were lonely. Get your head out of the clouds.*

Lord, but she needed a project, something to keep her hands and mind busy, or this was going to be one very long week.

Fencing wasn't possible with the ground frozen. She studied the rows of cabins. They'd already been cleaned and put away for the season. She could order fabric to make new curtains and bedcovers, but it wouldn't come for a week or two. Her attention swung again to the barns. Maybe she could redo the tack room.

She started by taking inventory. Thirty-two saddles, forty-one bridles, thirty-seven breast plates, sixty-three saddle pads, and thirty-eight halters. Odd numbers, but they made perfect sense, because the collection had grown over many years.

Because the tack room hadn't been upgraded since the place was built, there were only twenty saddle racks and doubling up really wasn't good for the tack.

First she went to the tool room to gather what she'd need, then to the lumber shed behind the barn, where she stored everything from replacement bed legs to fence rails. Dusty dug out several rails and began to cut them into two-foot pieces. After fastening V-hooks to them, she'd put new screw eyes into the wall to hang them on.

She kept at it for hours, sawing, measuring, pounding, and hanging. It had been dark for a couple of hours when she packed it in, and once the horses, dogs, and cats were fed, she warmed up the leftovers Billy left in her fridge.

Still not tired enough to go to bed, she sat by the fire and tried to read for a while, but her mind kept sneaking back to the cabin high in the mountains. Why was she uneasy all of a sudden? Was it a realization that it wasn't him after all? A shiver had run down her spine when she spotted the sweat lodge. Why? She'd been in one before, found it an incredibly peaceful and grounding experience.

She still couldn't put her finger on where the odd feeling had come from.

Dusty let her head fall back against the softness of the chair and closed her eyes. If it was him, wouldn't she have felt it? Wouldn't she have known in her heart?

THIRTY-FOUR

The next day, when she stopped the snowmobile in front of the cabin, she could feel the emptiness even before confirming there wasn't the faintest whisper of smoke coming from the chimney.

She still knocked before opening the door, but didn't bother to call out. The stove was cold, without even an ember to suggest there'd been a recent fire, yet his things—the books and the sleeping bag, at least—were still there.

Lifting the pillow to her face, she inhaled deeply, only to be disappointed when there was no instant recognition of his scent, just a niggle of familiar. Wood smoke, and perhaps witch hazel?

There was still a large supply of food in the cupboard, but nothing of a personal nature.

Dusty refused to be disheartened, and, being prepared for all contingencies, drew a pen, paper and envelope from the inside pocket of her coat, and sat at the table to write. She didn't fuss over words, made it short and to the point, *Call me*. Printed CHASE in large letters on the envelope, and left it on the pillow, and poking out from under the edge of the sleeping bag.

She returned on Thursday and Friday mornings, but the letter hadn't been touched. Nothing had changed.

She wasn't distracted on the weekend. Much to her own surprise, she was at peace. If she couldn't have Chase, if he wasn't the man in the cabin, then what she'd been feeling for weeks was the presence of his spirit.

With that in mind, every night before bed she sat out on her porch and talked to him, as though he was sitting in the chair alongside her. She'd tell him about her day, things the kids had said or done, stuff about the horses. She shared happy thoughts and sad ones.

Justin would park beside her chair, his head on his paws, listening to her one-sided conversation.

The following Wednesday, she returned to the cabin and found it empty. The letter, sleeping bag, pillow and books were gone. Whoever had been there wasn't coming back.

Hoping had allowed the hole in her heart to reopen over the last weeks, and tonight, believing Chase had either left, or never been there at all, she needed time to absorb the reality. Armed with hot chocolate and a "good to forty below" sleeping bag, she headed for the porch.

Laughed at Justin's pained expression, and said, "Go back in and snuggle with the other two."

Flower and Ben were dedicated workers, but they were also very serious about bedtime, and they were already curled up on their mats in the kitchen, with little concern about whether or not their mistress was tucked safely into her own bed. They would not even stick a nose through the doggy door unless they heard unusual movement from the livestock or, God forbid, needed to pee.

Justin, on the other hand, regarded Dusty as his responsibility, and after looking longingly at the door to warmth and comfort, stretched himself out on the rug beside her chair instead, and she dropped an afghan over him for extra warmth.

She snuggled deep in the sleeping bag, took tiny sips of scalding milk from the insulated mug, until after a while she drifted to sleep.

The dream began as always with her searching for something, someone.

It was a dark place full of doors she couldn't open. She found herself begging for help, pleading with the darkness, but nothing changed. She slowly moved from door to door, not knowing where she was going or why, but frantic to get there.

Someone was calling her. She turned and noticed the door behind her was open a crack, with a sliver of light shining through, and she dove for the handle, but missed, and it closed, leaving a hollow echo behind. Groping for the shallow seam where it fit into the wall, she dug and pried, with her fingers while she begged and pleaded to faceless gods, her voice sounding distant to her own ears, until all at once there was nothing. Nothing but grayness—no doors, no walls, only mist—and she simply floated for a while, forlorn and without purpose.

Her own name began to echo in her head, and she tried to push it away, wanted to cover her ears, until she heard the insistent howl of the wolf calling her, pulling at her, while Justin's wet nose pushed against her face, which was tucked low in the sleeping bag. She eased out her hand, stroked his head, her voice soft, sleepy, "Thanks pal. I musta been lost."

She pulled her hand back inside the warmth of the flannel, and he lay back down with a quiet thud. But she could still feel his warmth beside her leg, as though he'd been on the chair. And she felt him move.

He *was* on the chair. She reached way down inside the sleeping bag to shove at him, push him off, and he resisted. Finally opening her eyes, she propped herself up enough to scold him—

—and her heart slammed her ribs.

She must have made some kind of sound, because Justin scrambled to his feet when that raspy voice she'd heard only a few times said softly, "It's me, Dusty. Don't be afraid."

She fell back against the chair, barely able to breathe at the sight of him. Her voice came out a strained whisper, "Please, God, let this be real."

He touched her face, his fingers feathering over the skin, and her chest heaving as she sucked in the air her body screamed for. Snaked her hand out and grabbed him by the wrist. "Tell me you're real. Tell me this isn't a dream."

"We're both here, and this is real." He captured

her mouth hungrily, yet the kiss wasn't wild.

It was pure and deep and everything they needed to say.

It was the past and the future, it was about forgiveness and living. It was about breathing.

Chase slowly tasted and explored before moving down her throat, pushing aside the turtleneck to tease the golden skin stretched taut across her collarbone, and to the spot he knew would make her groan out loud. Then he whispered beside her ear, "If this is a dream, I am never waking up."

She pushed him far enough away to get a good look at his face, and then, as though he'd taken too long coming home from the store, demanded, "Where the hell have you been?"

He sat back and laughed out loud. "Have I mentioned lately how much I love you, Dusty Mathews?"

"Not getting around me that way, cowboy. Answer my question."

"I don't suppose, 'I've been around' will do?" When he brushed his knuckles across her bottom lip, and his thumb caressed the exposed edge, her teeth took him prisoner, and his breath lodged in his throat.

She drew him down to her mouth, and he found himself wanting to devour her in spite of his plan to be careful. Instead, he held her hard against his chest, and stood so he could feel the whole length of her against him.

A small sound, a presence, worked its way into their world. He lifted his head to look around, and she felt a low rumble in his chest before the deep chuckle escaped his throat, and he said, "I think they're concerned."

Dusty followed his look to see two sets of eyes peering at them from the dog door. Ben and Flower looked confused. Dusty waved at them. "It's okay you guys, go back to sleep." Justin's tail thumped on the floor beside the chair, and Dusty said, "I suppose they've got a point. It is a lot warmer inside."

"Plenty warm right here." He took her hands and held them against his mouth.

She smiled. "I find myself feeling like getting naked, and I think it would be better indoors."

"You? Bashful?"

"No, practical, you idiot. There are certain places I'd rather not have frostbite."

Grinning, he said, "I'll make sure nothing's exposed."

"But I like exposure. Come on." She slipped away from him, but her feet tangled in the damn sleeping bag. His arms shot out and saved her from a face-plant, and she muttered, "So much for graceful and athletic."

Once they were inside, he stopped. "Don't you have questions?"

Dusty threw back her head, and her laughter cascaded over him.

"What's so funny?"

"You."

"Why?"

"All I want to do is get naked with you right now, and you want to talk? Chase, I've been waiting for you to come home for almost fifteen years."

He shoved his hands into her hair, crushed her mouth with his, and didn't think about coming up for air until he found himself dragging her sweater over her head.

"Okay, two questions." The huskiness of her voice only added a layer to his need for her.

"Jesus, Dusty." He buried his face in her neck.

"Have you got any diseases I need to know about?" she asked, unbuttoning his shirt and shoving it off his shoulders.

"No." He slid her jeans to the floor.

"Do you love me?"

Laughing at her neck-to-ankle long johns, he swung her up in his arms. "I'm gonna show you how much right here where we stand, unless you point me to the bedroom."

"Floor's hard and cold. Soft bed that way." She pointed. "First left." She sank her teeth into his shoulder.

And that was the way they came together. Chase, trying to make it last, managed to gasp, "Dusty, wait."

"NO." And with great determination, she wrapped herself around him, and drove him until they'd both plunged over the edge into blinding heat.

THIRTY-FIVE

Nearly spent embers in the bedroom fireplace lent a reddish glow to their skin while Chase held her against his heart. He skimmed gentle hands down her back while her lips feathered across his throat.

"Chase?"

"Um?" He sounded drowsy.

"Why now? Why not the first night, when the wolf was after Caesar?"

"I had to be very sure I wasn't going to totally mess up your life and hurt you again."

"What makes you sure now?"

"Two flannel shirts and Linda."

She sat up to stare at him. "Please explain that."

He stuffed a second pillow under his head. "When you brought the shirts to the cabin—my size, my colors, my brand—I knew you had suspicions and didn't intend to back away from me."

"That I get. Where does Linda come in?"

"I went to Vancouver to talk to her, ask her if I was making a mistake."

"Was she shocked to see you?"

He closed his eyes and clenched his jaw for a second. "No." He took a deep breath and reached for her hands. "I stayed in their boathouse for a week in August, when I came back from Australia."

Dusty could almost see the blank, empty space in time suspended between them. Somewhere there must be a clock ticking off the seconds while she digested what he said. That her best friend had kept the truth from her, left her hung out to dry, wondering, waiting, when all she had to do was say something. But no, they conspired to keep her in the dark, made decisions for her.

She pushed away from him, from the bed, and went to the fireplace, crouched to stir the hot coals, added kindling, a small log... reached for the soft, woven blanket folded over the arm of the chair in the corner. She wrapped it around her nakedness, then sat on the floor and drew her knees to her chest, and rocked, staring into the flames.

Minutes passed, but she still couldn't focus, didn't want to be still, wanted to run, wanted to stay, wished he hadn't told her, but what was one more lie? The voice inside her head grew stronger. *John was the same. Didn't trust me to make my own decisions, tried to protect me from hurt. But it hurt anyway. Why can't anyone believe in me? Trust me? Why, for the love of God, can't things be simple?*

She jumped up and left the room. Dug a bottle

of brandy from the back of a cupboard. Tick, tick, tick, she upended the bottle, taking just enough to sear her tongue, burn a path of fire down her throat, and bring tears to her eyes. They spilled over and slid unchecked down her face. Once again she'd been betrayed by the people closest to her.

She sucked in a fiery breath and went to the sitting room, where the other fire had died earlier. She stared at the embers for a moment, knelt, and added paper and wood systematically until it came roaring to life.

Shivering, she sat back, sinking into the thick wool rug and swiping at her still-damp face, then tipped up the bottle, once more searing her insides. She hugged her updrawn knees and moaned softly while tears kept coming, and that inner voice continued taunting her, tearing at her heart and stripping away her confidence, until an angry yell awoke deep in her chest…but lost momentum in her throat.

Her mouth opened in a silent scream. Self-pity and anguish swamped her as she rocked, unaware of her surroundings, until an eerie, gut-wrenching sound permeated the walls.

Dusty focused on the soulful cries of a nearby wolf. Went to the window and opened it, allowing his beautiful, clean, sharp voice into the room. She searched the darkness. Couldn't see him, but didn't need to. He'd reminded her he was there, watching over her, as always, making sure she didn't slip backwards while she was being cared for and guided through complicated times. As the silence lengthened, she knew he wouldn't speak to her again now he'd yanked her back from the edge of darkness.

Dusty closed the window against the cold night air and hugged the blanket more tightly around her shoulders while she put a CD into the player.

She sat back down in front of the fire while a pounding, rhythmic chanting filled the room. Started slowly and built richness, layer after layer. The songs and prayers blended together as a base, before expanding skyward in celebration.

Chase, leaning in the doorway, had missed nothing, but felt too much an intruder to speak, to attempt to comfort her. Because *he* was once again the source of her pain.

Watching her anger and frustration fall away, he was spellbound by the growing peacefulness and serenity in her face as she sat cross-legged, with her back poker-straight and her eyes closed.

The blanket had slipped, exposing her shoulders, allowing the flames to glow golden on her skin. Four beautiful, jagged pieces of turquoise suspended on a fine silver chain lay brilliant and shining at the base of her throat when her head tipped back. Her hair hung between her shoulder blades as her voice joined the others, filling the air, creating an ethereal echo.

Although he didn't recognize the language, it was strangely familiar, not unlike his grandfather's chanting at a fire ceremony many years ago. When each new song began, she joined in, never missing a word, chanting, singing, as though directly from her soul.

After the music ended, he knelt behind her,

slipping his fingers under her hair, and slowly rubbing the last bits of tension from her neck and shoulders. His thumbs worked on the base of her skull, and first her head lolled forward, and then she finally leaned back into him and sighed.

"What were you singing?"

"Apache prayers from the Sunrise Ceremony."

"They transported you from furiously angry and hurt to relaxed and serene. An amazing transformation to witness."

"The Ceremony is for girls reaching womanhood. They chant and sing for four days, while making the transition, achieving goodness, confidence, sacredness, and embracing their own spirituality.

"When I was young, I used alcohol to get through the hard times, but now I pray to center myself. To achieve the serenity I need to deal with life as it is brought to me. I am powerful, yet pliable when I remember the discovery of my Self. It is then I am reminded I never walk alone. I am always in the company of great spirits, and their knowledge is there for my asking."

The incredible certainty of her spiritual strength left Chase speechless, as though he was sitting in the presence of an elder or a healer, while his own spiritual Self recognized how profoundly she had changed.

Life had sent them on separate roads, filled with twists and turns, yet somehow, while apart, they had met their challenges and grown in the same direction. They had been tested, and success was allowing them to finally travel together.

But then, right on the heels of such thoughts, Dusty said, "I let go of my past, of the emotional abuse, and everything else, but you and Linda stealing my right to make my own decisions sent me rocketing back into those memories."

Chase's fingers shook while he gently combed through the tangles in her hair. "Linda had no choice, because I didn't know if I could ever tell you." He took a deep breath. "She ranted and raved at my stupidity, explained how it wasn't fair to make your decisions for you. Said she trusted your instincts, and I had to let you make your own choices."

"Her mantra," she said. "It gave me back my life once."

"But I disagreed with her. I was afraid of intruding. How fair would it be? How could you trust me to love you if I just showed up and said, 'Hi, remember me? The guy who deserted you and broke your heart? I know I put you through hell back then, but now you've healed, and you've spent all these years having a good life without me, how about you shove everything aside and make room for me again?'" His voice lowered, "And I didn't have enough guts to face the possibility that you'd simply tell me to go fuck my hat."

Dusty managed a smile in spite of the huge lump in her throat, then asked, "What else did Linda tell you about me?"

"You had traveled a long road and become a very wise woman. You took the money from your father's estate and built this place for kids. I know you have about a hundred here in the summer months, and six year-round residents."

"It is so very much more than that."

"I know. I've watched and listened for months. You love those kids, and they know it." His fingers began to massage her scalp ever so gently. "And I have seen the sadness in you, watched your whole body sag when the bus pulls away from here on Monday mornings."

"That's nothing compared to when I've had to let a child go." When a guardian swore they'd take care of them this time, it tore pieces from her heart, and she bled for weeks. She stuffed the memories away. "Did she tell you about the letter? About my heritage?"

"Only that you stayed with your mother's family in New Mexico for a while."

Again, it was so much more than that. "And our father?" she prodded.

"I read Tyler's report a few months ago."

Her voice was quiet, "Are you okay with it?"

"It doesn't matter. He's dead and buried."

"It matters. To people like your mother, it mattered," she said.

"My mother is at peace. Her spirit has walked the sky since I was born. John cannot touch her there."

"You know he's not my father."

"Or mine anymore. Do *you* mind that I carry his DNA?"

She tipped her head back, and the chuckle bubbling up her throat made her sound free. "You can have the DNA of a billy goat for all I care."

"A billy goat, you say." He gently nibbled his

way from her ear to her throat.

"I love you, Chase. Always have, always will. Doesn't seem to matter how mad you make me, either."

He wrapped his arms around her and rested his rough cheek against her smooth one. "How mad are you?" He slipped a hand inside the blanket, his fingers setting off sparks beneath her skin.

"Hmmm. I don't remember." And she softened against him.

His mouth moved magically over the side of her face, tasting, tantalizing. She turned into him, her mouth seeking and finding his. She reached to cup his face, and the blanket fell away. She stroked his cheek. Smooth, then rough. She played with the unevenness until he said, "There was a fire."

She continued exploring, finding a collection of tiny scars barely visible in the firelight.

"The smoke made it black as night. The air was filled with burning embers, debris, whole branches."

"Is that why your voice is different?"

"For weeks I could barely breathe, couldn't speak, no sound came from my throat. Eventually I managed to achieve a voice, but it wasn't the one I'd lost, and it has no power. I can't yell or sing."

"You never could sing." She laughed softly.

"What do you mean by that?"

"You couldn't carry a tune in a bucket."

"Well." He leaned back to look at her, but she turned and followed, raining kisses down his chest, nipping her way across his belly until he was lying back on the thick rug, and her voice dropped an octave. "But you sure can dance."

He grinned and pulled her up to eye level. "If I promise I'm never leaving you again..." he rolled slowly over her and pushed the blanket from between them, locked his hands with hers, tucked them behind her head while his mouth tickled her ear. "Could we try a waltz this time?"

A smile lit her face and, her green eyes glowed in the firelight. "Want me to hum?"

He laughed out loud. "Oh, yeah." His mouth journeyed across her jawline before his lips teased hers. "You wanna lead, or shall I?"

Her tongue tangled with his, and she forgot to answer.

THIRTY-SIX

Hours later they were lying spent once again in her bed. Dusty's cheek rested on his damp chest, and she listened to his heart, still marveling at the reality of him, of them together. His fingers played over her skin, and wound into her hair, tugging gently until she looked up at him, her voice thick with emotion, "Do you have any idea how many hours I have spent in this bed in the past few months, imagining what it would be like to make love with you..." She hesitated, and then whispered, "…just one more time?"

His hands framed her face. "Probably as many hours as I've spent standing outside your window, imagining making love to you over and over again in the firelight, dreaming about waking up with your warmth beside me, and watching your eyes open and look into my soul."

"Outside my window?"

"Occasionally at first, but then I couldn't help

myself anymore. It became a habit."

"How long, Chase? How long have you been here?"

He knew it had to happen. The questions, the need for explanation. He never expected anything else. She was the strongest woman he'd ever known. The most loving, the most forgiving, yet at this moment, her openness and vulnerability were his responsibility. He wished this part could be over, wished he knew for certain the truth wouldn't hurt her, that she'd understand.

Although prepared to face it head-on, he couldn't help himself, and hedged a little. "I moved into the cabin about three weeks before Murray sent you the load of horses."

"Were you behind that?"

"Somewhat."

She had a flash of insight, a certainty, but asked anyway. "Houdini's yours, isn't she?" He nodded, and she went on. "Something happens to me the moment I slip onto her back. It's like I know her thoughts, and she knows mine."

"My heart stopped the first time I saw you riding her with nothing but a bit of denim between you. You looked like something out of one of my dreams. I'm still amazed you never heard me gasp."

"I was afraid a saddle would press on the scar, and after I'd ridden her bareback once, I was hooked."

"I watched you a couple of days after New Year's, when you rode with one of your girls. She was on a big paint horse. You were both bareback, and looked like a couple of free spirits galloping through the snow, laughing as it flew up around you. I was certain I could see your eyes flashing with excitement. God, what I would have done for a camera. Made me wish I could paint, capture every detail."

Dusty's eyes turned distant. "It was a wonderful day. We were connected. It was as though a glistening, silken web encased us, insulated us from everything but the moment, while my Lucie perched, excited, on the brink of discovering her spirit."

Silence hung, not uncomfortable, but waiting, softly expecting. She slipped her hand into his and said quietly, "Its time."

He tensed, but she squeezed his hand and said, "I'm ready to hear it all, Chase. From the beginning. I need to know before I can put it away forever." Her voice faded to a whisper. "Why did you leave me? And why did you stay away for so long?"

He didn't hesitate. "Even though John forced the actual moment, I was leaving anyway." He heard the sharp, shallow breath she sucked in, and veered slightly, leaving the painful alone and sticking to facts. "He arranged for the job in Australia in order to keep an eye on me, and promised he would have me delivered to you in pieces if I didn't go."

She interrupted with a statement, confirmation of what he assumed she'd already figured out. "While we were in Hawaii, you already knew you were going to leave me."

"When I met with Mr. Sanderson, he told me he'd been pressured into offering me the job in

Australia. He believed John was crazy, and would make good on his threats. He offered to hide us together, but I was afraid it would only incense John, and endanger you in the end. My leaving at least kept you safe."

She shook her head. "After I found out John wasn't my father, I tried to find you, but Mr. Sanderson said he had no idea where you were. Said you'd disappeared."

"That was true. I only worked at his ranch for a few weeks before I drove into the vastness of the outback and vanished."

"Why?"

He sighed. "It seemed like the right thing to do at the time."

"Was it?"

"Probably."

"Why?"

Chase lay back against the pillows and stared up at the ceiling for a few minutes. His thumb idly stroked the back of her hand while she waited patiently for him to put his thoughts together.

"The man who raised me was actually my *great*-grandfather. He was the chief of our band until I was born. He gave it up to look after me, and taught me from birth that I was to respect my elders. I respected him, loved him, honored him as the most important person on earth. And then he got very sick.

"From his deathbed, when I was only twelve, he told me I was a good boy, and I should follow my strength. He said animals trusted me, therefore it was my responsibility to keep that trust. I would be a protector. And he promised me if I always gave others the respect I had shown him, my life would be good, and each sunrise would bring me closer to my own spiritual fulfillment."

He turned to look at her. "But I forgot that lesson, Dusty. I disrespected your father. I crossed the line with you, even though he repeatedly told me not to. And I lost something of my Self."

"But—"

He put a finger on her lips, "I know John was an evil person, and what he did was wrong, but when he produced the DNA results, it rocked me to the core of my soul, as though Grandfather was speaking to me from the grave." He shook his head, "And I couldn't overcome it, no matter how hard I tried. And I knew I had to walk away from you. John's threats only deepened my conviction, and justified what I was doing." He sighed again.

"Without John's interference, I probably would have told you what was wrong with me, and spent a few months with my elders, regaining my spirituality and confidence. There would have been long hours in the sweat lodge, and many days alone on the mountain, but in the end, I could have returned to you a whole man. Instead, I sank slowly into a deep hole, and sacrificed both of us in order to keep you safe from the hell I knew he was capable of dishing out."

His hand was restless on the covers, so she took it between hers and held on.

"Once I was in Australia, in the Outback, I spent six years as Dan Smith, a drifter, working for cash and keep, then I bought a small place of my own and started working with thoroughbreds again. I knew your father had long since passed, but I kept my new name anyway, because Chase Mathews still eluded me.

"The only connection to my old life was the Christmas card I sent to Linda and Rick every year. I was careful to mail it from a town far away, so there was no chance I could be tracked down. I had a nice, simple existence, and people regarded me as reclusive and a bit odd, but damn good with a rough colt or a skittish filly. I built a clientele and led a decent life. Until the fire."

He was quiet for a bit.

"What happened?" she finally asked.

"Bush fires aren't anything new. Each year there were tense times, and somebody would need stock moved fast. Everyone in the area pitched in, and I could squeeze eight into my trailer, so I was always there to help.

"That morning, because my farm was safe, I went to move horses for someone else. But the wind shifted. At noon the fire changed direction, and I got word my place was in danger. I barreled home, parked the trailer, dropped the ramp, and then for a horrible moment stood frozen by indecision. I had twenty horses on the property. Which twelve would I choose to leave behind? I couldn't do it. My grandfather's voice rattled around in my head. I had to keep their trust. It was up to me to save them all."

Knowing he was there again, she stayed very still.

"I didn't want to use halters and shanks, or anything that wouldn't fall away quickly if the fire touched it. I grabbed baling twine and quickly made figure eight-style halters with long leads hanging from them and put them on four fillies. I made one more, and looped the lead back to make a rough set of reins. I put that one on my black filly."

"I opened the gate where the colts were and chased them out of their pen, swung up on the black, opened another gate, grabbed the lead strings of the fillies and led the way out. We went down the dry creek bed at a dead run, heading straight into the flames. The horses I pulled along were scared but willing, and the black—the black was as fast and brave as I expected her to be while fifteen colts thundered right along on our heels." He rubbed a hand over his chest.

"The band of fire we had to get through was about a quarter mile wide, but it felt like ten miles. When we reached the other side of it, we were burned, and the smoke had taken a horrible toll. Apparently."

"Apparently?"

"I was found unconscious, and miles away, by a family group of Aboriginal people. They nursed me using bush remedies for ages before I could even talk. Concoctions of mint and eucalyptus were heated over open fires to create healing vapors I spent hours inhaling, and they plastered my burns with cool mud dug from deep water holes. Later they smeared crushed insects onto my healing flesh.

"I was with them for thirteen months. They painted me, danced around me, and they sang while they worked diligently to heal my whole Self. I learned about their family, their land, and their spiritual ancestors of the Dreamtime. Then after months of being with them, one morning the powerful one said to me, 'Your flesh is healed, but you have also suffered a loss of your soul. You cannot be well until that, too, is taken care of. Your spirit is sad. You must go home to where your heart is. You are ready to be where you belong.'"

"I knew that meant I should be with you. But I was afraid. Afraid to ruin what your life might have become. When I left there, I searched for my horses. Most had died of smoke inhalation, but a few made it. Four colts and two fillies had been rescued, rehabilitated, and placed in new homes when I wasn't found, but the black filly…"

Chase shook his head. "She was something else. She had ended her flight in an old man's yard. He found her in his vegetable garden one morning, barely able to stand, shaking uncontrollably, with fluid dripping from her burned nostrils and mouth. He called a local vet to look at her, and was immediately told she should be euthanized."

His expression went from bleak to amused. "The old man threw the vet off of his property, and called a friend who had lots of Aboriginal connections. Together the old man, his friend, and a group of healers helped her fight for her life. They used the same kind of old bush remedies for her burns and her damaged lungs as I had received—but they relied on modern drugs for her pain."

"How long?"

"Apparently it took nearly a year to heal the burn on her shoulder." He took Dusty's hand and slid her fingers down his scar, from high on his inner thigh right down to his knee. "There was a burning branch trapped between us. But she never faltered. Kept on running for our lives."

Dusty gently caressed the smooth, thickened skin. "The first time I touched Houdini's scars, I experienced a flash of memory, as though I was on her back when she raced through the flames. I rode as you had, felt your pain, and then everything went black." She traced the outer edges with a fingertip. "She carries your memories with her. That's why you brought her here."

"I hadn't intended to. Told the old man she could stay with him, and I would pay for her care, but he refused. He said he could tell we belonged together. And when I explained I had nowhere to keep her, he got an odd expression on his face, and said, 'She needs to go home with you. The long journey won't hurt her.' I was about to ask him what he meant when I saw the look on his face. He knew. Somehow, like the wise ones of the tribe who had rescued me, he knew. And then, I did too. It *was* time to go home. I was ready to finish becoming whole again."

Tears dripped unchecked off Dusty's chin, and she fought to speak past the lump in her throat. "You sent her to me."

"We made the trip together, flew to Vancouver in the belly of a cargo jet, then vanned to Murray's place. It was his job to get her to you."

"What if I'd sold her like the rest of them?"

There was a cocky look on his face and a twinkle in his eye. "I knew you wouldn't."

"What made you sure?"

"I know you."

"Used to know me."

His hand slid behind her neck, and his mouth lowered to her throat and lingered briefly before he lifted away, his mouth hovering over hers. And when she sighed he said, "You see? I know you."

"You still play dirty." She shoved him away, fighting for control over the hunger for him.

"And you know me."

"Something about Houdini seemed incredibly familiar. I actually fantasized that she was related to Angel."

"She is."

Startled, she stared at him. "Really?"

"Remember Angel had a brother who was a champion in Australia? He's the black filly's sire."

"What's her name?"

"She's registered as 'CN Dark Magic'."

A shiver ran through her. "Could it be more fitting?"

"What about me?" He was suddenly very serious. "Do I fit, Dusty?"

She stared at him. "What do you mean?"

"Your world? Will I fit?"

She gave him a wobbly smile. "Like a glove. Like a single, well-worn, favorite, full-of-holes glove. The kind I always keep, just because."

He touched the tears on her cheeks.

"I've learned about spirit, Chase. I know what it means to be broken as well as I understand becoming whole."

"Can you forgive me for ruining our lives, tossing our future to the wind, changing everything we were sure of?"

She stayed quiet for far too long, and his heart started to pound.

"Dusty?"

She stared at him. Wondering how he could ask. How he could say such a thing. He really didn't know. Time did matter, after all.

She shook free of her own thoughts and saw the fear on his face. She climbed off the bed. "There's something you need to see." She tugged on his hand, drawing him up from the bed and behind her to the sitting room. She pointed at a big armchair and said, "Sit."

Then, going to the shelves completely lining one wall, she gathered an armful of photo albums and dumped them in his lap. "They're in chronological order. See if you can find the answer to your question in there." Then she stoked the embers in the fireplace into a roaring blaze and left him alone.

THIRTY-SEVEN

In the kitchen, she dug around in the freezer until she found bacon. It was hours from daylight still, but she wanted to smell bacon and him together. She needed to go back just once more, even though she'd given him the tools to leave the past behind.

Chase turned the pages slowly. Taking in the faces, the transformations. They were the kids who came to her summer camp, and there were two pictures of each child with Dusty. One when they arrived, and one when they were leaving. And each page told the same story. They arrived suspicious, uncertain, and closed. And when they left, there was new life in them. Happiness and trust shone on their faces. And in every picture, he saw Dusty change, too. Through the photos he watched her grow, saw the knowledge and the peace in her eyes.

"You learning anything, cowboy?"

He looked up at the glittering green eyes watching him from the doorway. She went to another shelf, one up high, and lifted down a set of journals, handed them to him. "Now get a smidge closer," she said softly, and walked away.

He marveled at how confident she was, walking around naked. God, she was something to look at.

He opened the first book and found a child's photo, then the journal entries. They were the personal stories of each of her fosters. He thumbed through, reading entries here and there, looking at pictures. There were breakthroughs, setbacks, growth and notes of hope. There were heart-wrenching descriptions of loss. Dusty walked into the room and saw his tears when he looked up.

"Kevin?" Not that she needed to ask.

He nodded. And her own tears threatened. She curled herself into his lap. "He was one of the few I've lost. But he was happy while he was here. At least I gave him that."

"His own mother killed him?"

"Drug-induced psychosis. She'd fallen through the cracks, should have been under care…but the system, well, it failed both of them. She loved him. He was only six."

Chase pushed the hair away from her face. "How do you live with that pain and not let it cripple to you?"

"Oh, it cripples me. It peels the skin from my bones, rips away every ounce of my confidence, and leaves me bleeding. But eventually, because the other kids need me, I claw my way back. In the end it makes the next child walking through my door even more important. Makes me work that much harder."

"How many have you lost?"

"Too many. Kevin and four summer campers. Micky was killed in a car accident, Sonja died of leukemia, Nancy had a rare heart defect, and Sheldon hung himself on his sixteenth birthday."

"Jesus, Dusty. Doesn't it make you want to harden your heart? Avoid the pain?"

"Nope. Opens it wider for the next one."

He stared at her. "You're amazing."

"Always was."

"Not."

"Okay. So, I was a lost soul myself for a very long time." She traced his lips with a fingertip, "Now do you understand what losing you did for me? How it forced me to grow up and face what I was, or wasn't? Only by hitting rock bottom did I discover that my Self, my spirit, was missing. I had thrown everything I had into *us*, lock, stock, and barrel, without actually knowing *me*."

A tiny frown on his face made her smile gently. "I loved you with every bone in my body. Of that I have never had any doubt. And I'm sure if you hadn't left me I still would have discovered my spirituality, the core of what makes me who I am, and I'd have been happy forever." She held his face in her hands and stared directly into his eyes. "But what happened instead is still a gift. It was meant to be this way, Chase. Everything in life happens for a reason, and I am at peace with that."

He locked his arms behind her.

"I understand what you're saying, Dusty. But I

saw something else that has stayed with me, makes my heart ache when I think about it." She frowned at him. And his voice was gentle, "Talk to me about Christmas night. Up on the mountain. You were in such pain."

She focused on his beautiful, strong face. His golden skin, and gray eyes that could see right into her soul. "It's over now."

"Not until you tell me. I need to understand what I saw, what I heard."

She started to move away, but his arms tightened. "Please, Dusty? You know, besides me, you scared the shit out of a lonely wolf that night. I'm not sure what he was thinking, but I was beginning to worry you'd throw yourself off that cliff at any moment."

"The wolf knew I wouldn't do that."

"The wolf knew?"

"It seems I have a guardian spirit in the form of a wolf, and he's watched over me for many years, both here and elsewhere." She looked down at her hands. "Did Linda tell you about my, ah, brush with hypothermia at the watering hole?"

Chase grimaced and nodded.

"Well, that's when it began. The doctors were amazed none of my fingers were frostbitten, even though I wore no gloves that night." She shrugged. "I never told them it was because a wolf kept me warm. I figured I was close enough to being put in a rubber room without saying something like that out loud. But years since, I came to understand he was, *is*, my spirit wolf, my guide and protector. I still have dreams about that night, and can feel his warmth, coarse coat, pounding heart, and curious scent."

Chase had an odd expression on his face. "Would he be the same wolf who brought you outside that first night when I was sneaking down to check on Houdini?"

"I believe so, because you said he looked lame and hungry, but when he got a distance away, I saw him stop limping. I know he created the situation that brought us together again. I felt him look right through those lenses and into my heart that night."

"But you were going to shoot him."

"No, I wasn't. I've never shot at an animal. But I'd have blasted the air to scare a wolf away from Caesar if his life was in danger." Dusty smiled. "My spirit wolf looks out for me, Chase. He watches from a distance, and only steps in when he has to, but even tonight he was there."

Chase's eyes showed the realization even before he spoke. "I heard the howling just before..."

"Before I focused. He made me reach for the recordings, for the songs, the sounds that soothe my soul."

His lips gently grazed hers, "Enough diversion. Tell me about Christmas night."

She shrugged. "It's a simple ritual."

"Dusty."

She laid her head against his shoulder. "Years ago, I promised myself that if I stored away all the old hurt and sadness of losing you, didn't let it interfere with my day-to-day life, I could bring it out once a year and wallow in it. And I do. Every Christmas. I go up there to my rock, lie back, and allow myself to feel everything."

"You scream like that every year?"

She shook her head. "No, it's usually just a bit of a pity party. I wish, I imagine, and then the sadness comes. I cry, feel sorry for myself, and then tramp back down the mountain."

"And that's it for a whole year?"

"Well I usually finish up with a bubble bath, chocolate-covered macadamia nuts, a piña colada, and a steamy romance novel."

"Hmmm." He rubbed his jaw against the top of her head. "A bubble bath, you say."

"Easy, cowboy."

"But this year was different."

She sighed. "I guess, subconsciously or instinctively, I was reacting to your presence. It ignited something in me. Something that burned away the years, and I felt incredibly alone. Desperately missing you. I was ripped open as raw as that first Christmas, and it terrified me. I had to get the feelings out in order for the healing to begin again."

"Did it work?"

"Yes and no. When I got home that night, I skipped the bubble bath and Hawaiian treats. Instead I took a boiling hot shower, stood there until the water ran cold, then crawled under the covers and cried myself to sleep."

"I should have given in."

"Meaning?"

"It took every ounce of willpower I had to not step out of the shadows to try and rescue you from your demons that night. In the end it was Jake.

When he saw me, I stopped for an instant, to think about what *you* would want, and that's when the wolf stepped into my path. We stared at each other silently until he turned his back on me and sat down to watch you."

"He was telling you it was the wrong time."

"I got that as clearly as if he had spoken."

Dusty smiled.

"Why was it the wrong time?"

"I guess I still needed to come to terms with my own feelings. I'd been blindsided by the desperation. Up until that night, I was certain my life was exactly as I wanted it. Then I had to acknowledge that, although the kids fill me with joy, I still have other needs and desires." She smiled. "My spirit would rather not sleep alone.

"If you marry me, you'll never have to sleep alone again."

Her smile widened. "I can't. I'm still married to the man I fell in love with about a hundred years ago."

"Really?"

"Really. When I received the divorce papers, I tossed them in the fireplace." She placed her fingers on his lips just as he was about to speak. "I learned much later the papers were sent by John, and your signatures were forged. But the important fact remains, I burned them even before I knew."

"If we don't have a wedding, how will you explain to the kids about the man in your bedroom?"

"We tell them the truth. That we've been married forever."

"And my absence for the last fifteen years?"

"You were kidnaped by aliens."

"Be serious, Dusty."

She rose up on her knees and looked down at him. "My dear dense, sometimes pig-headed, husband, I learned long ago that being serious is not all it's cracked up to be." She straddled him, leaned over, and used her silky black hair to tickle his chest, then his face. The chain around her neck was hanging in front of his eyes when she said, "Do you see that?"

"What?"

"On the chain."

His eyes widened as he studied it. There, among the four beautiful pieces of turquoise, hung her wedding band. The white gold was nestled between the stones, and he hadn't noticed it earlier. He looked into her eyes and found them twinkling at him.

"I've only taken it off once, and that was to put it on this chain. Once I was able, I went on with my life, Chase. I have lived with purpose and direction. I have been the rock, the arms, the heart the children needed like breath. And they have filled me with unbelievable love. But I never gave up the dream that one day you'd come home." She kissed him gently.

"Dusty."

"Hmm?"

"You are such a contradiction."

"In what way?"

"Incredibly strong and resilient, yet you've stayed soft and loving too." His mouth grazed her throat just above the necklace. "And I have never, for one godforsaken moment, stopped loving you."

He threaded his fingers through her hair. "I thought it would be enough to see you but..." His mouth gently brushed against hers. "But then I became obsessed with a driving need to touch you again."

His lips moved over her face, "And when I listened to you up there on the mountain, first telling that boy how you lost the man you loved, and then later, screaming at the gods—my heart bled for you, for both of us. But I had to wait. Wait until I was sure I wouldn't complicate things even further by stepping into your tidy world. I couldn't jeopardize what you found with those kids. I would have walked away if Linda had told me to."

She stiffened, took his face in her hands, and pinned him with bright green eyes. "Cowboy," her voice was deep, raspy and deadly serious. "Don't you ever do that again."

"What?"

"Don't you *ever* take choice away from me, put my life in somebody else's hands. It makes me powerless, and that scares the hell out of me. I may have made some bad choices in the past, but none have been as devastating as a couple that were made *for* me."

Chase looked at her with sad eyes. "I am sorry, baby. Sorry for everything. And I promise I will never again try to decide what's best for you. I will simply ask you."

She kissed him softly. "I don't mind you wanting to be my knight in shining armor. And I will always love knowing you've got my back."

Chase chuckled. "Knight in shining armor?"

"Okay, brave, painted warrior."

"That's much better." He hesitated. "Before we drop this subject altogether, the one about choices, I need you to understand something."

"I'm all ears, cowboy."

"Oh, you're a lot more than ears, baby." His voice was low. "But I need you to know I wasn't trying to manipulate you as John did. I was simply afraid to ruin the happiness you had."

She tipped her head sideways in question before he continued.

"Did you know the sound of your laughter carries way up to the lookout rock? And aside from that one night at Christmas, you always seemed very happy, and I doubted whether I should disturb your life."

"I do have a good life, Chase, and I *am* happy here. I love my kids, and I'd walk through fire for them. But they are *not* a substitute for what I had with you. That hole in my heart has never been filled until now, tonight. Just like I need my kids, I need you. My life will not be complete without you."

Chase smiled into her serious face. "And bacon."

"Oh, shit." Her eyes widened, and she jumped off his lap, running toward the kitchen. She had completely forgotten about the bacon.

He came up behind her at the stove and checked out the shriveled black strips. "Looks way beyond hope to me."

KATHRYN JANE

She put a lid on the pan and shoved it to a back burner. "I wasn't really hungry. Mostly wanted to smell it."

Chase raised an eyebrow and she laughed.

"I have very fond memories of you whenever I smell bacon. Memories of those first few mornings I woke up at your place."

"Ah, yes." He turned her around. "The morning after I came home, when you threatened to make love to me before Murray came back. First time I ever saw someone scramble an egg by crushing the whole thing in their hand, shell and all."

"You saw?"

He grinned. "I was stunned you could kiss me like that and then be so cool. After I turned on the shower, I came back to get you and drag you in there with me."

"You caveman, you."

"But you were leaning against the stove with egg dripping from your clenched fist, and I had a feeling I should leave well enough alone."

"God, how I wanted you."

He pushed her back against the counter, and let his hands slide down until they rested gently on her hips. "What about now, baby?"

"Now, cowboy? Now I'm old and wise and know better than to turn down a good offer." She slid her arms around his neck, and he kissed her deeply, lovingly, and with all the passion she could ever have imagined, then carried her to the soft, thick rug in front of the sitting room fire.

He caressed every inch of her with his mouth and his hands, teased and tantalized, taking her to the precipice over and over again before finally giving in to her pleas.

In one smooth, possessive move he pushed her over and then waited. Waited while she swam back to the surface, whispering his name. And when those green eyes focused on his once again, in the faint light of dawn, she rose with him, and their souls spiraled into the sunrise together.

DEAR READER

I sincerely hope you enjoyed reading INTO THE SUNRISE, as much as I loved writing it way back in 2006. At that time, publishing was a distant dream, and Dusty's story was tucked away in a bottom drawer. I never thought it would see the light of day because it was so early in my career.

But Dusty's story began whispering to me, years later, so I dug out the manuscript, read it through in one sitting and knew. This story needed to be told, and I worked on revisions for many months until I was satisfied Dusty's story was ready to share. She's an amazing woman, complete with flaws, and a gutsy personality I adore.

My next Women's fiction is about an equally flawed woman, who was also once a jockey, but her life has taken many twists and turns of a much different type than Dusty's.

If you want to stay in the loop, so you know when new releases are coming out (they're usually on sale for the first day or so which makes it a good idea to stay in the loop), pop over to my website and sign up for the newsletter.

Cheers!
Kat.

PS. *For anyone who has ever taken the time to write a review for one of my books, even just a single sentence, I thank you a thousand times over!*

ACKNOWLEDGEMENTS

As always, I need to thank my wonderful team, because I couldn't publish these books without their help. Whether it be catching typos, spending weeks on full blown edits, or taking me out to lunch when I need to get away from my characters for an hour or two, each and every one of my "people" plays an important role in my life. (Yes, the four-legged ones too because who doesn't need a cat walking on the keyboard now and then, or a dog passing gas for comic relief.)

Many thanks to: Demon For Details for your fantastic editing; author L. j. Charles for your wonderful critiquing skills and advice; Judicious Revisions LLC and Barb for the sharp-eyed proof-reading; The Killion Group Inc. for the fabulous cover; Brenè Brown for Daring Greatly—an inspiration; Nora Costigan and Anne Bailey, you are the eternally-brilliant smiles in the back of my mind—I'll never forget you; Al, my own charming prince, for taking care of us while I was immersed in this story; Barb and Judy—how do I put it into words? You are the constants in my journey. You've egged me on and believed in me always. I love you both

ABOUT THE AUTHOR

Award winning author Kathryn Jane writes about the kind of women she'd like to hang out with—smart, self-reliant, think on their feet ladies just as happy eating a loaded hot dog at a ballgame as sipping champagne in the back of a limo. Women who laugh as hard as they cry, appreciate good sweaty sex, and know how to keep a secret.

Kat lives on the west coast of Canada with her very own prince, a sweet dog, and an obnoxious cat. Among her favorite things are the smell of the ocean, crisp sunny days, cats with a sense of humor, faithful mutts, the warm breath of a horse, music, sunflowers, orange gerbera daisies, beach glass and rocks, and kind people. She loves to start each day with a walk alongside the Pacific Ocean with her two favorite people.

For more information about Kathryn and her other books, check out her website and sign up for the newsletter at kathrynjane.com.

www.ingramcontent.com/pod-product-compliance
Lightning Source LLC
Chambersburg PA
CBHW051942240626
47153CB00005B/1592